Between Heaven and Hell: Pride

Between Heaven and Hell, Volume 1

Dr.Matthew Lewis

Published by Dr.Matthew Lewis, 2026.

This is a work of fiction. Similarities to real people, places, or events are entirely coincidental.

BETWEEN HEAVEN AND HELL: PRIDE

First edition. May 14, 2026.

ISBN: 979-8995706601

Written by Dr.Matthew Lewis.

Table of Contents

Between Heaven and Hell: Pride 1
Chapter 1 3
Chapter 2 15
Chapter Thirteen. 23
Chapter 3 25
Chapter 4 35
Chapter 5 45
Chapter 6 55
Chapter 7 67
Chapter 8 77
Chapter 9 87
Chapter 10 97
Chapter 11 107
Chapter 12 119
Chapter 13 129
Chapter 14 139
Chapter 15 149
Chapter 16 159
Chapter 17 167
Chapter 18 177
Chapter 19 187
Chapter 20 197
Chapter 21 207
Chapter 22 219
Chapter 23 229
Chapter 24 239
Chapter 25 249
Chapter 26 259
Chapter 27 271
Chapter 28 283
Chapter 29 291

Chapter 30 301

Pride

Book One of Between Heaven and Hell

Dr. Matthew Lewis

2026

BETWEEN HEAVEN AND HELL Book One: Pride Rome Dr. Matthew Lewis

---

LEWIS PUBLISHING HOUSE lewis-publishing-house.com

ISBN (eBook): 979-8-9957066-2-5 ISBN (Paperback): 979-8-9957066-0-1

First edition: 2026

CONTACT THE PUBLISHER

General · dr.lewis@lewis-publishing-house.com Rights & translation · rights@lewis-publishing-house.com Press & review copies · press@lewis-publishing-house.com Web · lewis-publishing-house.com

Join the Advance Reader Copy program at lewis-publishing-house.com — receive each new release four to six weeks before public launch in exchange for an honest review on launch day.

For the readers who know the difference between the institution and the thing it was built for, and who keep choosing the thing anyway.

Superbia est appetitus excellentiae inordinatus.
— Thomas Aquinas, Summa Theologica II—II, Q162
Pride is the disordered desire for one's own excellence.

Chapter 1

The Eternal City Does Not Hurry

"It was pride that changed angels into devils; it is humility that makes men as angels." — Augustine of Hippo, City of God

Rome does not apologize for its darkness.

Other cities light themselves against the night — anxious, performative, afraid of what the dark might reveal about the stones beneath their streets. Rome lets the dark come. Rome has always let the dark come. It has stood in this darkness since before the name for darkness existed, and it has found the dark unimpressive, and it has endured. Two thousand years of confession and corruption and faith and violence and the slow patient erasure of every certainty — and still Rome endures. Still Rome waits. Still the stones hold their secrets in the specific silence of things that have seen too much to be surprised by anything the living might bring them.

4:47am. Via Pinciana.

The Borghese Gallery sat at the end of its long approach like something that had been waiting since the seventeenth century for this particular morning to arrive. Like it had known. Like the marble and the light and the bodies inside it had all been arranged for this specific hour and this specific pair of eyes and the twenty seconds of stillness that preceded them.

Sonya stood at the outer gate and let her eyes adjust.

Twenty seconds. Always twenty seconds before entering any scene. The officers who worked with her had learned not to interrupt those twenty seconds. The ones who hadn't learned that were no longer working with her.

The gallery's security director met her at the gate with a flashlight he kept pointed at the ground and the specific expression of a man who had not yet decided what he had seen.

His name was Ferretti. Sixty-one years old. Nineteen years at the Borghese. His hands were not shaking. This told her something useful: either he had seen worse, or he had not yet understood what he had seen tonight. She would know which within the hour.

"Ho many people have been inside since the body was discovered?" She asked in Italian. Functional Italian, deliberately imperfect at the edges — people underestimated a woman who spoke their language badly more usefully than they underestimated a woman who spoke it perfectly.

"Myself. The overnight guard who found him. Two of my staff I called immediately. That is all." He paused. A hesitation with weight in it. "And the priest."

Sonya looked at him. "Which priest."

"He was already inside when I arrived. He had —" Ferretti stopped. Started again. "He had a press credential. Vatican Press Office. He said he received a call from someone inside."

"From whom inside."

"I did not ask."

She filed this. A journalist already inside a restricted scene. Vatican Press Office credential, which meant Church access, which meant the Vatican already knew about a dead man in the Borghese Gallery before Interpol's Rome liaison had finished his first coffee. The institutional machinery was already moving. She had less time than she'd thought.

"Show me the room."

The gallery at this hour was a different building than the one that opened its doors to the living in daylight.

The marble absorbed the beam of Ferretti's flashlight and gave back almost nothing. The sculptures emerged from the dark one at a time as they moved through the ground floor — figures caught mid-motion, eternally suspended in white stone, their faces arranged in expressions of yearning and terror and grief that had been perfectly accurate for four hundred years and would be perfectly accurate for four hundred more. The dead were like that. The dead held their expressions.

Sonya did not look at the sculptures. She looked at the floor. The floor always told you more than the walls. The floor was where things fell, where people stood, where the evidence of presence accumulated without intention.

The floor here was immaculate. This was the first thing she noted.

The main room. Ferretti stopped at the threshold and did not go in.

She went in alone.

The room was a theology.

She understood this before she understood anything else about it — before she had processed the victim's identity, before she had catalogued the evidence, before she had begun the procedural inventory that twelve years of this work had made as automatic as breathing. She understood, standing in the entrance to the primary gallery of the Borghese at 4:53 in the morning, that whoever had made this had not been making a crime scene. They had been making an argument. A complete, considered, formally structured argument, composed with the patience of a person who was entirely certain they were right.

Cardinal Emilio Voss, sixty-three, Papal Nuncio to the Holy See's Secretariat of State, thirty years of Vatican diplomacy, four languages, a reputation for discretion so complete it had become its own form of power — Cardinal Voss was arranged before Bernini's Apollo and Daphne.

Arranged. Not fallen. Not dropped. Not positioned by panic or haste. Arranged with the careful attention of someone who had spent considerable time thinking about exactly this.

He was in full ceremonial robes. The red of them was very dark in the emergency lighting and she took a moment to confirm that the darkness was the fabric itself and not blood. There was no blood. She noted this. She noted the position of the hands — extended, slightly raised, palms forward, fingers open. She noted the angle of the head — back, upward, the line of the gaze directed with specific intention toward the sculpture above him. She noted the eyes.

Open.

And directed not randomly upward but at a precise point: the marble hands of the Daphne figure, the moment of transformation rendered in stone, fingers becoming laurel branches mid-reach, the god's hand eternally, permanently, exquisitely short of its destination. Apollo always reaching. Always falling just short. The reaching hand that would never hold what it was reaching for.

Someone had placed a dead Cardinal in the attitude of a god who could not stop wanting something he could not have.

Sonya stood in the room for a long time.

She photographed the full room first. Then the body at distance. Then the approach to the body in measured segments. Then the body itself in sections — hands, face, robes, feet, the specific disposition of every element. She did this in silence. Ferretti, in the doorway, said nothing. The gallery said nothing. Rome outside said nothing. The Bernini above said nothing, which was its nature. It had always been about to speak. It never did.

Then she saw it.

On the floor beside the Cardinal's right hand. A square of material approximately fifteen centimeters by fifteen centimeters, the color of old teeth, slightly irregular at the edges in the manner of something cut by hand rather than machine. She crouched beside it without touching it. She brought her flashlight to bear. She photographed it three times from three angles before she read it.

The handwriting was small and deliberate. The ink had a quality that the flat black of a modern pen did not have — depth to it, texture, the specific darkness of something made rather than manufactured. A single word in Latin in the center of the square, surrounded by so much empty vellum it looked almost modest. Almost humble.

Superbia. She had not studied Latin formally. Twelve years of European cases had given her enough to navigate a menu and understand a liturgy. She crouched beside the parchment in the dark of the Borghese Gallery with the Cardinal above her and the Bernini above him, and the word was not difficult.

Pride.

She stood. She turned in a slow circle — body outward, reading the room from the evidence of staging outward to the walls, the exits, the windows, the sight-lines. She was looking for what was wrong.

There was always something wrong. The missed detail, the thing that didn't fit, the element that revealed the edge of the frame where the person who made the scene had run out of patience or time or precision.

She found nothing wrong.

The room was complete. Every element in service of the same argument. No haste, no error, no seam where the staging ended and the reality began. Whoever had placed Cardinal Voss before the Bernini had not been in a hurry. Had not been afraid. Had stood in this room in this darkness and worked with the unhurried precision of someone for whom this was not the first time and not the last.

The absence of error was, in twelve years of reading crime scenes, the most alarming thing she had ever encountered in one.

She called it in at 5:03am. Interpol's Rome liaison arrived with a forensics team at 5:47am. Commander Hale called from Brussels at 6:12am.

She took the call outside, standing on the Via Pinciana in the grey pre-dawn, her breath visible in the October air, watching the technical team file through the gallery entrance with their cases and their lights.

"Cardinal Voss," Hale said. He said it the way people said the names of the powerful dead — carefully, as if the authority of the name outlasted the man who had carried it.

"Cardinal Voss," she confirmed.

"The Vatican has already —"

"I know."

"Sonya." His voice carried the specific weight of a man who was about to say something institutional. She had been listening to that weight for six years. She knew its shape before it arrived.

"I know, Commander." She watched a forensics officer emerge from the entrance and speak into a radio. "I need sixty hours before this becomes a diplomatic conversation. I need the scene intact and I need jurisdiction while it's still useful."

A pause. The pause of a man doing political mathematics. "You have forty-eight."

"Sixty."

"Fifty. And I need something substantive by end of day that tells me what I'm managing here."

This was the negotiation they always had. She asked for more than she needed. He offered less than he could give. They met somewhere in the middle and both of them knew the middle was what she'd wanted from the beginning. Six years of this and he still ran the same play.

"I'll tell you what it is when I know what it is."

"Sonya."

"Commander."

She ended the call. The sun was beginning to suggest itself above the Pincian Hill — not rising yet, simply indicating its intention to eventually do so. Rome receiving this information without particular urgency. The eternal city did not hurry for the sun any more than it hurried for anything else.

Fifty hours. She had learned to work with less.

The forensics team was working the main room when she went back inside. She found Ferretti in the entrance hall and asked him where the priest was.

He pointed at the secondary gallery. The Caravaggio room. East wing. Not where the body was, not where the evidence was, not where any legitimate observer would position themselves. Which meant he was either hiding or he understood that the main room was not where the interesting thinking happened.

She went there alone.

He was standing in front of "David with the Head of Goliath."

The leather satchel was across his left shoulder — brown, worn soft from years of daily use, the monogram H.M. on the flap so faded it was barely legible. A press credential hung around his neck on a lanyard that had been to too many scenes in too many cities and showed it. He was wearing a dark jacket over a grey shirt and he had not shaved that morning, and none of this read as careless. It read as a man who had been somewhere more important than a mirror when he got dressed.

He did not turn when she entered. He knew she was there. She could tell by the quality of his stillness that he knew — not the stillness of someone pretending not to notice, but the stillness of someone who had already decided how this conversation was going to begin and was letting her begin it.

"This is a restricted scene."

"I know." His Italian was excellent. Not native — seminary Italian, she would later learn, learned young and in a context where imprecision was not tolerated. He turned.

Dark wavy hair, longer than his credential photograph suggested it should be, falling slightly across his forehead. A mustache. The kind of face that had taken its time arriving at itself — strong jaw, a mouth that defaulted to stillness rather than expression, dark eyes that were warm in a way his face otherwise wasn't. He met her assessment of him without flinching from it, which told her he was used to being assessed and had decided not to find it uncomfortable.

He looked like a man who had been somewhere difficult and come back without bitterness. That specific quality — the absence of bitterness in someone who had earned the right to it — was the first thing she noticed about him. She did not yet know why it was the first thing she noticed. She would understand it later, in Paris, in a room that was not a gallery, and she would not find the understanding comfortable.

"You've been in the main room," she said.

"Briefly." He reached into his jacket with the ease of someone who did this often — the press credential produced, extended, identification completed before she could ask for it. She took it. Mateo. Vatican Press Office. The photograph showed him in better light than this and without the stubble and with the jacket buttoned. He looked more official in the photograph. He looked more interesting in the room.

"The parchment," he said, as she was still reading the credential. "It's a quotation. Augustine's City of God. Book Fourteen. Chapter Thirteen."

She looked up from the credential.

"You read it."

"I recognized it. There's a difference." He said this without apology, which she noted. Not defensive. Not performing modesty. Simply accurate. "The full quote is: It was pride that changed angels into devils; it is humility that makes men as angels. Augustine's argument was that pride is not simply one sin among others. It's the originating condition. The root. Every other sin grows from it the way a tree grows from a single damaged seed."

He said "Book Fourteen, Chapter Thirteen" the way people said their own phone number — without recalling it, simply knowing it. She had been in rooms with a great many people who knew a great many things. She had rarely been in a room with someone who knew something the way this man knew Augustine.

She looked at him for a moment. The Caravaggio behind him. David's face — that particular expression, exhausted compassion, the mercy that costs something — framing a man who had walked into a restricted crime scene at five in the morning on a Vatican Press credential and was now quoting the Church Fathers at her without being asked.

"This is a restricted scene," she said again. "You will stay in this room until my team takes a formal statement. You will not return to the primary gallery."

"Of course." He turned back to the Caravaggio. Then, almost as an afterthought, without turning: "The positioning of the body. The sightline of the eyes."

She stopped.

"Apollo's reaching hand," he said. "The one that never arrives. That's not incidental. That's the argument." He paused. "Augustine's definition of pride is the refusal to be known truly. By others. By God. By yourself. The Cardinal spent thirty years constructing a version of himself that no one — not his colleagues, not his enemies, not the institution that made him — could see past. Whoever staged this understood that. They're not just quoting Augustine. They're illustrating him."

She stood in the doorway a moment longer than she needed to.

Then she went back to the main room where the Cardinal was waiting in his eternal posture of reaching, and she put Mateo's press credential in her evidence bag, and she thought about the words "Book Fourteen, Chapter Thirteen" said without a moment of recollection, and she thought about the phrase "They're not just quoting Augustine. They're illustrating him."

She did not call Hale to tell him about the man in the Caravaggio room.

She worked the main room for another four hours. At 9:17am she crouched beside the parchment one final time, now catalogued and bagged, and looked at the single word through the evidence plastic.

Superbia. Pride. The root. The originating condition. The damaged seed.

Outside, Rome was fully awake, moving through its ancient business with the specific indifference of a city that has absorbed two thousand years of human drama and found all of it, ultimately, insufficient to disturb its stones. Emperors. Saints. Cardinals. One more body in the Borghese Gallery. The city received this information and continued.

Sonya stood up.

She had fifty hours.

She went back to the Caravaggio room to find the man who knew Augustine the way most people knew their own names — not because she had decided to trust him, and not because she had decided to use him, and not because she had any professional justification for what she was about to do.

She went back because he was right. And because in twelve years of walking into rooms where something terrible had been done with great care and intelligence, she had never once stood in a room that felt like this one. Like a question asked in a language she almost spoke. Like something that was waiting to be understood rather than simply solved.

And because whatever had made that room — whoever had stood in the dark of the Borghese with a dead Cardinal and a square of vellum and the patience of a person who was entirely certain they were right — was still out there.

And she was going to need better Latin.

She stood in the gallery courtyard for a moment before going back in.

The Borghese in the October dawn. The specific quality of Roman morning light — not the aggressive warmth of the midday city but the tentative arrival of illumination over terracotta and stone, the light of a city that had been waking up in this specific way for two thousand years and had developed a relationship to morning that was neither urgent nor indifferent but simply practiced.

She had been in this city for six hours. She had a dead Cardinal, a Bernini, a parchment, and the specific feeling she associated with the beginning of a case that was going to require everything she had.

She went back in. She had work to do.

Chapter 2

What Sonya Carries

She had been awake since 3am.

This was not unusual. The hours between three and five belonged to her in a way no other hours did — before the day made its demands, before the case reasserted itself, before the institutional machinery started turning and required her to be a specific kind of person inside it. She used these hours the way other people used sleep: to become herself again after the performance of the day before.

She made coffee in the small kitchen of the temporary apartment Interpol kept on the Via Margutta for visiting consultants. Good building. Bad beds. Adequate coffee maker. She had learned to evaluate temporary apartments by these criteria alone. The bed was where she stopped thinking. The kitchen was where she started again. The coffee maker determined the quality of the transition.

This one was adequate.

She took the cup to the window. The Via Margutta below was completely empty — cobblestones and silence and the specific Roman darkness that was different from other cities' darkness, heavier somehow, as if the weight of centuries had settled into the air itself and was only slowly being lifted by the approaching day. A cat crossed the street. Nothing else moved.

She stood at the window and drank her coffee and did not think about the Borghese Gallery.

She did not think about the Cardinal's eyes directed upward at a precise angle. She did not think about the specific quality of the staging — the patience it required, the knowledge, the thing she did not have a procedural word for. She did not think about the absence of error, which was still the most alarming thing she had encountered in twelve years of crime scenes.

She thought about Brussels instead. The apartment on the Rue du Commerce that was her real life — the one she returned to between postings, the one that contained her actual possessions and her actual routines and the specific quiet of a person who had arranged their life with some care to contain exactly as much as they wanted it to contain and nothing more.

The Brussels apartment had a better kitchen. A worse view. The coffee maker was excellent.

She had left it three days ago with a carry-on bag and the Voss file and the particular focused emptiness she had learned to carry into a new case — the deliberate absence of expectation, the clearing of space. You could not see a new crime scene properly if you arrived at it carrying the residue of the last one. This was the first thing the training had taught her and it was the only thing the training had taught her that she still considered entirely correct.

She finished the coffee. She rinsed the cup. She put on her jacket.

Rome at six in the morning belonged to the delivery drivers and the priests and the very old men who had nowhere to be and had decided this was precisely where they would be anyway. She walked from the Via Margutta toward the temporary Interpol offices on the Via della Conciliazione because the briefing was at seven-thirty and she did not take taxis in cities she was learning.

This was a rule she had made for herself at twenty-six, after a posting in a city she had taken taxis in and left not knowing. She needed to feel a city's layout in her feet before she could understand it. The case required the city. You could not separate them.

Rome in the early morning required her to slow down. Not because the streets were difficult to navigate but because the streets were eight hundred years old and demanded a certain acknowledgment of that fact. The buildings were not backdrop. They were participants. The church on the corner of the Via del Babuino had been there since the fifteenth century and it knew things about the particular darkness she was investigating that no forensics report was going to tell her. She did not believe in mysticism. She believed in accumulated history. In this city they were the same thing.

She passed a café that was just opening its shutters. The smell of coffee and something baking. A man in an apron who nodded at her without curiosity. She did not stop. She had already had coffee. But she noted the café the way she noted everything — its position, its sight lines, its proximity to the Borghese approach route, the fact that it had been here long enough that its awning had faded to a color that had no name left.

She noted things. She had always noted things. It was the first gift and also, in certain circumstances, the most exhausting one.

Her wallet was in her jacket pocket. She stopped at a tabacchi to buy a bottle of water and when she paid she saw it: the edge of the photograph, visible above the notes.

She was aware of it the way she was always aware of it — not looking at it, simply knowing it was there. A photograph in a wallet was not unusual. People carried photographs. It was a normal thing to carry.

She had been carrying this one for four years and had never shown it to anyone and had been asked about it once, by a colleague in Lisbon who had seen it by accident and asked who it was, and she had said no one and had not been asked again because she had used the tone that meant the question was finished.

She put the water in her bag. She zipped the pocket closed.

The man in the photograph was not relevant to the case. He was not relevant to Rome or the Cardinal or the parchment or the single Latin word that she had been carrying in a different part of her mind since 4:53am yesterday. He was not relevant to anything that was happening in this city in this week. He was simply there. He had been simply there for four years. She had learned to stop examining why she had not removed him.

She walked on. Rome received her without comment. This was what she appreciated about very old cities: they did not require explanation.

The temporary Interpol offices occupied the third floor of a building that had, in previous centuries, been a palazzo and before that something she hadn't looked up. The elevator was slow. She took the stairs.

She was the first to arrive. This was also not unusual.

She arranged the morning's evidence reports on the table in the order she would address them: forensics, timeline, background on the Cardinal, the conference registry cross-reference, the Vatican liaison's initial communication, which she had read twice and found remarkable primarily for the density of its meaninglessness. Twenty-three years of diplomatic training in four paragraphs that communicated nothing except the Vatican's strong preference that whatever had happened had not happened in the way that it had.

She made a second coffee from the office machine, which was worse than the apartment and considerably worse than Brussels, and she stood at the window while the city completed its transition from night to day below her.

She thought about the staging. She could not stop thinking about the staging.

Not the evidence of it — she had catalogued that completely, nothing left to process. The intention of it. The specific quality of the intention. She had stood in rooms where terrible things had been done with great care before. She had investigated crimes that required intelligence and patience and a particular kind of conviction. She had never stood in a room that felt like this one.

Like a question asked in a language she almost spoke.

Like something that had been waiting to be understood rather than simply solved.

The distinction between those two things was not procedural. She was aware of this. She filed it.

The team arrived by seven-fifteen. Four Interpol officers, the forensics lead, the Vatican liaison — a thin man named Rossi who wore his discomfort like a second jacket and who she had already identified as the person most likely to obstruct and least likely to do so directly — and the theological consultant she had requested: Father Giovanni Albani, S.J., seventy-three years old, a specialist in patristic literature at the Gregorian University who had been recommended by the liaison with the specific enthusiasm of an institution offering a resource it did not expect to be useful.

The room adjusted when she entered it. She was aware of this without attending to it. She had been aware of it since her first posting at twenty-four — the specific recalibration of a room when she walked into it, the subtle redistribution of attention, the people who straightened slightly and the people who made themselves slightly smaller and the people who did neither and were therefore the most useful. She had learned early to identify the useful ones quickly and direct everything else.

She ran the briefing efficiently. The forensics report: the parchment was aged vellum, genuine, the ink iron gall, the handwriting consistent with someone trained in formal calligraphy, the single word written with a steel-nibbed pen. The timeline: the Cardinal had been placed in the gallery between nine and eleven the previous evening. The gallery's overnight security had been compromised through means still under investigation. The false window in the alibi: the conference registry at the Gregorian University, which she did not yet discuss openly because she did not yet discuss things she had not fully verified.

Then she turned to Father Albani.

"Tell me about the word," she said. "Augustine. What he meant by it specifically."

Father Albani was the kind of old man who had spent seventy-three years in the company of large ideas and had developed a specific relationship to questions — not impatient with them, not performing patience with them, simply present with them, as if a question were a guest that deserved to be properly received before being answered. He took a moment. Then he spoke.

"Augustine's conception of superbia is not what the popular understanding assumes," he said. "Most people think of pride as arrogance. Self-importance. Too high an opinion of oneself. Augustine means something more specific and more disturbing. He means the refusal to be known truly. By others. By God. By oneself.

It is not an excess of self-regard. It is the construction of a false self so complete that the true self becomes inaccessible. Even to the person who built the false one."

The room was quiet. The Vatican liaison shifted slightly in his chair.

Father Albani continued. "In the City of God, Augustine argues that pride is not one sin among others. It is the originating condition. The root. Every other sin is pride in disguise — pride expressing itself through different appetites. To understand any of the other sins, one must first understand superbia. It is always where you begin."

Sonya wrote this down. She was not certain why she was writing it down. She had a forensics report and a conference registry and a Vatican liaison with twenty-three years of diplomatic training and none of it told her what she needed to know and this old Jesuit in his black shirt was telling her something that felt adjacent to what she needed to know, if not exactly it.

She wrote: The refusal to be known truly. Even to the person who built the false one.

She looked at what she had written.

She put the pen down.

The briefing ended at nine-fifteen. She sent the team to their assignments. She told Rossi she would be in touch with the Vatican liaison office by end of day and she said this in a tone that meant she would contact them when it was useful to her and not before. He understood. He left.

She sat alone in the briefing room with the evidence reports and her notes and the second coffee she had not finished and the specific quiet of a room from which everyone has recently departed.

She reviewed her notes from the beginning.

The Cardinal's biography. The gallery's security. The parchment's composition. The conference registry. Father Albani on Augustine. The refusal to be known truly. The originating condition.

And at the bottom of the page, in her own handwriting, in the margin of the note she had made during the forensics report, two words she had written without fully deciding to write them:

Book Fourteen.

Chapter Thirteen.

She looked at these words for a moment. She had written them at some point during the briefing — she could not have said exactly when. She had been thinking about the forensics report and about Father Albani and about the parchment and somewhere in the middle of that thinking she had written these words in her own handwriting as if she had decided they were important enough to record.

She had not decided this. She was not certain who had.

She capped her pen. She closed the notebook. She gathered the evidence reports into a precise stack and put them into her bag in the order she would need them and she stood up and she put on her jacket and she did not think about the specific quality of how the words had been said — without pause, without effort, without the moment of recollection that would have told her he had looked it up. She did not think about this.

She was working. She had fifty hours and a conference registry and a Vatican liaison who knew more than he was saying and a theological consultant who had just told her that pride was the refusal to be known truly.

She picked up her bag.

She left the room.

The walk back to the gallery took twenty-two minutes. Rome was fully awake now, the morning traffic moving through the ancient streets with the particular Roman philosophy that rules existed primarily as suggestions, and she walked through it thinking about conference registries and iron gall ink and the gap in the alibi she hadn't mentioned in the briefing because she didn't yet have enough to protect it.

She was not thinking about the way he had already been in the Caravaggio room when she found him. She was not thinking about the stillness of a man who had decided how a conversation would begin before it started. She was not thinking about dark eyes that were warm in a way the rest of his face was not. She was not thinking about "Book Fourteen, Chapter Thirteen" said the way people said their own name.

She was working.

She walked faster.

She sat with the crime scene for three more minutes after the forensics team moved to the secondary room.

Not reviewing — she had reviewed everything three times and the evidence was catalogued and she had her initial read of the room and it was solid. She sat with it the way you sat with a piece of music you had just heard for the first time and were deciding whether it was what it appeared to be or whether something in the architecture was waiting to be understood.

The room was not what it appeared to be.

That was the thing she would have difficulty explaining to Hale in the morning briefing — not the evidence, which was photographed and bagged and documented, but the quality of the staging. The specific deliberateness of it. She had been in many staged scenes. This was different in the way that the difference between a decoration and an argument was different: one was placed for visual effect, the other was placed because it meant something.

She looked at the Bernini one more time. Apollo reaching. Daphne transforming. The marble certainty of a moment that had been captured at the instant before everything changed.

She thought: whoever did this is very patient. Whoever did this has been waiting for the right room.

She left the gallery. She had a briefing in four hours. She had more to understand before then.

Chapter 3

Pride Is a Theology, Not a Feeling

Cardinal Emilio Voss had spent thirty years becoming a man no one could see past.

Sonya read his file the way she read all files — once quickly for the shape of a life, once slowly for the gaps in it. The shape was impressive: born in Verona in 1961, ordained at twenty-six, assigned to the Vatican Secretariat of State at thirty-one through the specific combination of intellectual gifts and social fluency that the Church identified early and cultivated carefully. Twelve diplomatic postings across four continents. Fluent in Italian, Latin, French, and

English. Working knowledge of German and Spanish. A reputation for discretion so consistent and so documented that it had become, over three decades, less a personal quality than an institutional asset.

The gaps were more interesting than the shape.

There were no close friends documented. No relationships outside professional contexts. No record of personal correspondence beyond what his role required. People who knew Cardinal Voss described him in terms of function: he was reliable, he was precise, he was effective. Nobody described him in terms of character. Nobody said he was kind or difficult or passionate or cold. They said he was effective. Thirty years of effectiveness and not one person in his life who could tell her what he had wanted when he was not being effective.

She put the file down. She picked up the forensics report.

The parchment. This was where the morning's first significant fact lived.

The vellum was genuine — aged, consistent with material produced in the sixteenth century, available from specialist suppliers who served bookbinders, archivists, and academic institutions with an interest in historical authenticity. The ink was iron gall — the same formulation used in medieval manuscripts, made from oak galls and ferrous sulfate, available to anyone with the knowledge to make it and the patience to do so. Both the vellum and the ink were consistent with material that could be sourced legitimately by a scholar with institutional access.

The ink was fresh.

The forensics chemist had been precise about this: the iron gall ink on the parchment was between eighteen and thirty-six hours old at the time of collection. The Cardinal had been dead for approximately fourteen hours when the body was discovered. The parchment had been prepared before the murder. Possibly the day before. Possibly two days before.

Someone had made this. Deliberately, in advance, knowing exactly where it was going to be placed.

This was not opportunistic. This was not a crime of circumstance or passion or proximity. This was a crime someone had scheduled.

She wrote this in her notebook and underlined it once. Not twice. Once was enough.

The formal briefing began at ten. By then the room contained: four Interpol analysts, the forensics lead, the Rome liaison from the Vatican Press Office — a different man from the one the night before, younger, more carefully managed in his expressions — Father Albani from the Gregorian University, and Commander Hale's deputy from Brussels, who had flown in overnight and whose presence communicated, without anyone saying so directly, the institutional anxiety that accompanied the death of a Vatican Cardinal in a gallery owned by the Borghese family.

And Mateo. Who was in the corridor outside the briefing room because Sonya had not yet decided what to do with him and had therefore told him to stay there.

She could see him through the glass panel in the door. He was sitting with his back against the wall and his notebook open across one knee and the H.M. satchel on the floor beside him, reading something. He had accepted the instruction to wait in the corridor with the equanimity of a man who had been told to wait in corridors before and had learned that waiting productively was more useful than objecting. She noted this and returned her attention to the room.

"Cardinal Voss," she said, "was not a random selection."

She walked them through it in the order that would land most effectively: the biography first, the gaps in it, the thirty years of documented effectiveness and undocumented interior life. Then the forensics: the parchment prepared in advance, the ink fresh, the staging requiring knowledge of both the gallery's layout and Bernini's specific sculpture. Then the implication.

"This person knew the Cardinal. Not socially, perhaps. But professionally. They knew his public architecture well enough to understand what it was constructed around. And they had access to the Borghese Gallery's security vulnerabilities, which means either prior familiarity with the building or significant advance preparation." She paused. "Neither of those things is consistent with a spontaneous crime."

The Vatican liaison shifted in his chair. The specific shift of a man who understood what she was saying and preferred that she not say it.

She continued.

"The word on the parchment — Superbia — is not decorative. It is diagnostic. Whoever placed it there understood something specific about the Cardinal's psychology and chose the most precise available term for it. Father Albani." She turned to the Jesuit. "Tell them what you told me this morning."

Father Albani told them. He was better the second time, she noticed — the long practice of a man who had taught the same material to many rooms and had learned which version of it each room needed. This room needed it precise and brief. He gave them precise and brief.

The refusal to be known truly. The originating condition. The root from which every other sin grows.

The room was quiet when he finished. The Hale deputy was writing something. The Vatican liaison was very still in the way of a man processing an implication he would prefer to process alone.

"So the killer understood Augustine," the forensics lead said. He was a practical man who used theology the way he used all unfamiliar material: as evidence to be catalogued rather than ideas to be considered.

"The killer," Sonya said, "understands Augustine well enough to use him as a diagnosis. That is a specific kind of knowledge. It belongs to a specific kind of person."

The briefing concluded at eleven-forty. She gave the team their assignments, fielded three questions from the Hale deputy that were really one question about institutional liability asked three different ways, and waited for the room to empty.

Father Albani was the last to leave. He paused at the door.

"Commissioner," he said — the Italian title, which was not quite accurate but which she had stopped correcting after the first day because it communicated something useful about how he saw her. "May I ask what you will do with the theological analysis? Practically speaking."

"I don't know yet," she said. This was true and also the most useful answer.

He nodded slowly. The nod of a man who had spent seventy-three years in the company of questions and had made his peace with the ones that didn't resolve quickly. "The difficulty with Augustine on pride," he said, "is that the people who most perfectly embody his definition of it are also the people least capable of recognizing it in themselves. The Cardinal, if what I understand of his profile is accurate, would not have called what he built a false self. He would have called it a necessary self. A self appropriate to his responsibilities."

He paused.

"Whoever chose him understood that. They understood not just the sin but the specific way the Cardinal experienced the sin as a virtue. That is a very intimate understanding of a person."

He left. She looked at the door for a moment after it closed.

A very intimate understanding of a person. She wrote this in her notebook beneath the line she had underlined once.

Then she went to the door and opened it.

Mateo was still in the corridor. He had finished whatever he'd been reading and was writing now, the notebook balanced on one knee, the pen moving with the ease of someone for whom writing was less a skill than a reflex. He looked up when she opened the door. He did not appear surprised.

"The ink was fresh," he said. Not a question.

She looked at him. "How did you know that was what I was briefing?"

"I didn't. But it's the most important thing in the forensics report and you were in there for ninety minutes, so." He closed the notebook. "The parchment was made for the Cardinal specifically. Which means whoever made it chose him before the night of the murder."

"How long before?"

He stood up. This took slightly longer than she expected, not from any physical difficulty but from the specific deliberateness of a man who stood up when he had decided to stand up and not before. The satchel went over his shoulder in one practiced movement. "That depends on what it means to choose someone for this." He considered the question as if it were interesting rather than rhetorical, which it was. "Augustine's diagnosis of superbia requires observation. You can't identify the refusal to be known truly without first attempting to know the person and being refused. That takes time. That takes access. That takes the kind of sustained attention most people never pay to anyone."

He paused.

"Months at minimum," he said. "More likely years."

Sonya looked at him.

Years.

She had written: not opportunistic. She had underlined it once. She had not yet understood how far that conclusion extended.

If the selection of Cardinal Voss had required years of observation — if the Augustinian diagnosis of his specific sin had required sustained, intimate, professional access to a man who gave intimate access to no one — then whoever had made the parchment and carried it to the Borghese Gallery and arranged a dead man before a Bernini sculpture with the patience and precision of a person making an argument they were entirely certain of had been making that argument for a very long time before that night.

This was not a first.

She did not say this aloud. She filed it in the place where she kept things that were not yet verified, which was a different place from the evidence file but no less organized.

"You need a coffee," Mateo said.

She looked at him. He had the expression of a man who had said a practical thing and was waiting to see whether it was received as a practical thing or as something else.

"I need you to tell me what the Greek annotation means," she said.

"Archē," he said. "Origin. Root. First principle. It's Aquinas's term for the originating cause. The thing from which all subsequent things proceed." He looked at her steadily. "Someone annotated the parchment with the word for root. Which means they were not simply illustrating Augustine. They were footnoting him. Adding a scholarly apparatus to a crime scene."

"You saw the annotation."

"I recognized it. There's a difference." The same phrase he had used the previous morning in the Caravaggio room. The same precision about the distinction. "The annotation was in a different hand from the main text. Finer. Smaller. The kind of marginalia a reader adds to someone else's argument. Which means either there were two people involved, or—"

"Or the same person annotated their own work," Sonya said. "For an audience."

Mateo looked at her with the expression she was beginning to recognize as the one he had when someone had arrived at the correct conclusion ahead of his explanation. It was not quite surprise. It was closer to the recalibration of an expectation.

"For a specific audience," he said. "The annotation is in a citation style that went out of use in academic theology approximately forty years ago. Nobody writing today would footnote that way unless they learned it from a text produced before the style changed. Which means either the person who made the annotation is very old or was trained by someone very old in methods that have since been superseded."

She processed this. It was a small detail. Small details were where the cases lived.

"You need a coffee," he said again. "And so do I. And I think better when I'm not standing in a corridor."

She looked at him for a moment longer than the professional situation required. He waited, with the patience she was accumulating evidence of, for her to decide.

"One hour," she said. "You tell me everything you know about the citation style and the conference registry and then we establish the formal terms of your access to this investigation or lack thereof."

"Of course," he said. The same two words he had used in the Caravaggio room. The same complete absence of triumph in them.

She picked up her bag. She walked toward the stairs. He fell into step beside her at a distance that was professionally appropriate and personally aware in ways she did not examine.

The corridor was long and the building was old and Rome outside the windows was doing what it always did — continuing, indifferent, ancient, entirely unbothered by the speed at which the living moved through it.

She was thinking about years.

She was thinking about a person who had watched the Cardinal for years — who had studied his specific form of pride with the sustained attention of a scholar, who had prepared a parchment in advance and annotated it for an audience, who had left a Greek word in a citation style that had not been taught for four decades.

She was thinking that whoever this was, they were not finished.

She was thinking that the Cardinal was not the point.

The lesson was the point.

And lessons, by definition, had more than one.

She walked from the crime scene to the Interpol temporary office and spent the afternoon building the preliminary case map.

Not the suspect map — she didn't have enough for that. The case map: what was documented, what was consistent, what was inconsistent, and what the inconsistencies suggested. She did this for every investigation. She did it early, before the case had accumulated enough mass to feel like it had direction, because the early map was the most honest one. It showed the shape of what you actually had before your own intelligence started imposing a shape on it.

What she had: a body arranged with academic precision. A parchment with authentic Latin in an authentic historical hand. A staging that required scholarly knowledge the victim's social circle didn't have. A method of entry that suggested either stolen access credentials or a legitimate contact inside the gallery.

What she had that was inconsistent: the body hadn't been moved. The parchment had been placed, not left — the specific care of its positioning beside the right hand was deliberate. The gallery entry had been during a window when the security rotation created a seventeen-minute gap that you would need specific knowledge of the building to identify.

This was not a random act. This was not an opportunistic act. This was a prepared act executed by someone who had been in this building before, who had studied the security routine, who had chosen this specific night and this specific sculpture and this specific body position with the care of someone who was making something.

She added to the inconsistency column: *The staging is too precise. This is not someone acting out a fantasy. This is someone executing a plan.*

She looked at the column. She looked at the window. She looked back at the column.

She thought: I have not seen this before. Not in twelve years. I have seen rage and greed and jealousy and desperation, all the ordinary engines of murder. I have not seen this: a crime staged as an argument.

She added: *Find who the argument is for.*

She looked at this for a long time.

Then she started on the evidence review.

Chapter 4

A Man Who Reads Crime Scenes

The café was on a side street three minutes from the Interpol building, small and specific in the way of Roman establishments that had decided what they were and had not revisited the decision in forty years. Four tables inside. One outside that was too cold this morning to be useful. A counter with a machine that produced the kind of coffee that reminded her, involuntarily, of the Brussels apartment and the routine she had left there three days ago.

She ordered in Italian. He ordered in Italian that was better than hers and she noted this without commenting on it.

They sat across from each other at the table nearest the window. The H.M. satchel went on the floor beside him. He opened his notebook to a page that was already dense with writing she could read upside down: names, dates, a diagram she couldn't fully interpret, three questions marked with stars. He had been working in the corridor. Of course he had.

"The citation style," she said.

"The citation style." He turned the notebook so she could see it. The diagram resolved into a schematic of the Borghese gallery's main room, sketched from memory with the specific accuracy of someone who had been in the room and paid attention to it. Around the edges: notations in a handwriting that was small, dense, and completely legible — the handwriting of a person who had trained themselves to write fast without sacrificing precision. "The style in the annotation is what's called the Leonine apparatus. Standardized in 1884 for the first critical edition of Aquinas's complete works. By the 1980s it had been replaced in most academic institutions. Nobody teaches it now. The people who still use it learned it from someone trained before the transition."

"Which means?"

"Which means your suspect was formed in theological scholarship before 1980 at the latest. Someone who has been working in this field for at least forty years." He picked up his coffee. "Consistent with the depth of the staging. You don't quote Augustine and Aquinas from memory with that precision without decades of engagement with the material."

"You did," she said. "This morning. Book Fourteen, Chapter Thirteen. Without looking it up."

He looked at her over the rim of his cup. Something crossed his face — not quite surprise. Something closer to a person being seen more clearly than they expected.

"I did," he said. "But I was ordained at twenty-eight. Fifteen years of formation before I left. And I'm not your suspect."

"I know you're not my suspect."

She did know this. She had known it from the Caravaggio room. The specific quality of his presence in the gallery had been that of a person who belonged in rooms with difficult things — not the presence of a person who had made the difficult thing. She had learned to distinguish these qualities in twelve years and she trusted the distinction.

She said: "Tell me what the room is saying."

They went back to the Borghese at half past noon.

The forensics team had completed their initial sweep. The gallery was technically restricted but operationally quiet — the evidence catalogued and removed, the room returned to something approaching its ordinary state except for the small numbered markers on the floor indicating where the body had been, where the parchment had been, where each element of the staging had been positioned.

Mateo stood in the entrance to the main room for a long moment without moving into it. He looked at it the way she had learned, in twelve years, to look at her own crime scenes — taking the whole of it before taking the parts, letting the room communicate before beginning the inventory. She had not expected this from a journalist. She filed the expectation and its failure.

Then he walked in. Slowly. Not toward the markers. Toward the Bernini.

He stood before Apollo and Daphne and looked at it for a long time. She stood beside him and let him look.

The sculpture was extraordinary in the afternoon light. She had processed this the night before as an aesthetic fact and moved past it because aesthetic facts were not evidence. Standing beside Mateo now she found herself processing it differently — not as beauty but as argument. The god reaching. The woman transforming. The moment of forever-almost, the reaching hand that would always be this close and never arrive. Bernini had spent four years on this. Four years on the moment before the end of the story. The capture that never happened. The love that turned into laurel at the very instant of its own completion.

She did not know why she was thinking about this.

"The sightline," Mateo said, still looking at the sculpture. "The Cardinal's eyes were directed at the hands."

"At the moment of transformation," she said.

"Apollo's reaching hand. Bernini rendered the instant before the grasp. The god still believes he is about to hold her. He doesn't yet know that the moment of contact will be the moment of losing her entirely." He paused. "Augustine wrote that pride always reaches and never holds. Whatever it grasps it transforms into something it cannot keep. The Cardinal built a self so complete, so carefully maintained, that no one could reach it. Not to harm it. Not to love it. Not to know it. He reached for influence and accumulated a version of himself that was entirely unreachable."

He turned from the sculpture and looked at the floor markers.

"Whoever staged this understood that completely. They're not illustrating Augustine's definition of pride. They're illustrating the Cardinal's specific experience of it. Which is a much more intimate act."

A very intimate understanding of a person. Father Albani's words. The same conclusion from a different direction.

She wrote it in her notebook and this time she did not underline it at all because underlining had started to feel insufficient.

They moved through the room systematically, which was not how he moved naturally but which he adapted to without being asked.

She described each element of the staging and he translated. Not literally — there was nothing in the staging requiring literal translation. He translated the intention behind each choice.

The positioning of the hands: not simply extended but in the attitude of the orante, the ancient prayer posture of early Christianity — arms raised, palms forward, the posture of a person presenting themselves openly to God. The Cardinal's hands had been arranged in the posture of radical openness. The willingness to be known.

"The irony is exact," Mateo said. "Augustine's definition of pride is the refusal to be known. The staging places the Cardinal in the posture of the person who refuses nothing. It's the accusation made physical."

The angle of the head: the specific angle of contemplation in medieval sacred art — the upward gaze indicating the soul in communication with the divine. The Cardinal had been posed in the attitude of a man in prayer. A man whose soul was, in this moment, entirely visible.

"He's being shown what he never permitted himself to be," Sonya said.

Mateo looked at her. The recalibration she was beginning to recognize.

"Yes," he said. Simply. As if she had translated something correctly and the only appropriate response was confirmation.

She did not examine the specific quality of how he said it.

The placement of the parchment: beside the right hand, not beneath it, not above it. The position of something laid down by a person who has finished with it. An object placed with the specific care of a final gesture.

"It's not a calling card," she said.

"No."

"It's a grade."

He went very still. The stillness of a person in the presence of an idea arriving at its correct formulation.

"A grade," he said slowly. "Left by a teacher. At the end of a lesson."

The room held this between them for a moment.

Rome outside continued. The Bernini above continued. Apollo reaching for what was already gone.

They were in the room for two hours.

At the end of it she had six pages of notes and a clearer picture of the staging than any forensics report could have given her and a specific professional problem she had been deferring for thirty-six hours.

She addressed it directly.

"You cannot have official access to this investigation," she said. They were standing at the gallery entrance, the afternoon light doing something specific to the stone of the Via Pinciana. "You are press. Whatever access you've had has been irregular and I have not yet explained it to Commander Hale."

"I understand," he said.

"What I can offer is a source relationship. You do not publish anything I share without my approval of the timing. In exchange I will tell you what I can when I can and I will not ask you to leave rooms that are useful to both of us."

He considered this for a moment. Not performing consideration — actually considering it, with the specific seriousness of a man who took the terms of agreements seriously because he had learned what it cost to be casual about them. The iron ring on his right hand caught the light briefly.

"What do you need from me right now?" he said.

"The conference registry from the Gregorian University. The week of the murder. Anyone attending whose published work specifically engages Aquinas's taxonomy of the seven sins and who uses the Leonine citation apparatus."

He nodded once. He did not ask how she knew about the conference or why she hadn't run this through official channels. He understood, she thought, that certain queries were more efficiently conducted by a person with academic credentials than by Interpol. He understood because he was the kind of person who had always found ways around the official channels without ever quite breaking them.

"How long?" she said.

"This evening." He picked up the satchel from where he'd set it against the gallery wall. "I have a contact at the Gregorian who owes me a conversation." He paused. "One condition."

She waited.

"When you know what it is — when you have enough to understand what you're actually looking at — you tell me before you tell Hale."

She looked at him. The request was professionally unreasonable and personally the kind of thing she had told herself she would not agree to.

"If it doesn't compromise the case," she said.

"Of course," he said. The two words he always said when he had gotten what he came for.

He walked toward the Via Pinciana. She watched him go for a moment — the olive jacket, the satchel, the specific ease of a man who had just negotiated terms he found acceptable and was already thinking about the next thing. At the corner he paused without turning.

"The lesson," he said. Still not turning. "It's the point. Not the Cardinal."

She did not say she had already arrived at this conclusion. She said nothing.

He turned the corner. He was gone.

She stood for a moment in front of the gallery where a Cardinal had been arranged with the patience and precision of a person making an argument they were entirely certain of. The Bernini was inside. The markers were inside. Six pages of notes were in her bag.

Lessons, she thought. By definition.

Had more than one.

She had known what kind of man she was looking at since the first photograph in the file. Not from the photograph itself — a professional headshot, the particular composure of an academic who had spent decades occupying institutional spaces and had learned how to present himself inside them. She had known from the absence in the photograph. There was nothing in it. No tension, no performance, no the specific managed quality of a person who was aware of being photographed and was adjusting accordingly. He was simply looking at the camera with the neutrality of a man who had decided the world beyond his intellectual work was of limited relevance.

She had met men like this before. In academic settings, in institutional investigations, twice in criminal proceedings. The intelligence was extraordinary and the ordinary human engagement was correspondingly narrow. Not psychopathy — psychopathy had a quality to it she could read at distance, a specific flatness in social interaction that was detectable. This was different. This was the specific withdrawal of a man who had found the interior life so much more interesting than the exterior one that the exterior had ceased to constitute a full reality for him.

A man like this did not commit crimes of passion. He did not commit crimes of opportunity. He committed, if he committed, the crimes of someone who had thought very carefully about what a crime could mean and had decided it could mean something worth the specific investment of care and patience it required.

She looked at the Borghese Gallery entrance.

The investigation was six hours old. She had one name in her notebook and no evidence and the specific feeling she had learned, across twelve years, to trust: the feeling of a room that was going to take time to understand but that was going to be understandable. Not all rooms were. Some rooms were simply violence, simply chaos, simply the human capacity for destruction expressed without architecture. This room had architecture. This room had been made by someone who thought the making mattered.

She went back inside. She had more to see.

She saw what she had needed to see.

The gallery in the morning light — not the dawn quality of the crime scene, which had been pre-dawn, the specific suspended quality of a world that hadn't committed to being a world yet, but the proper morning of a museum being prepared for public access. Staff moving with the efficiency of people who had been doing this same preparation for years. The forensics team completing their final documentation. The marble floors and the plaster ceilings and the Bernini still in its alcove, still white, still absolutely itself regardless of what had been done in its proximity.

She did a second pass of the room.

Not looking for new evidence — the forensics team had done three passes and she trusted their documentation. She was looking at the room the way you looked at a room after you had read a text, when you returned to the text and saw things you had not seen on the first reading. She was returning to the room knowing something she had not known on the first reading: that the staging was an argument, that the argument had an intended reader, that the intended reader was not Commander Hale or the Italian prosecutor or any institutional body with the authority to process an arrest.

The intended reader was an investigator.

She thought about this. A crime scene staged as an argument addressed to the investigation — not as a taunt, not as a provocation, but as a text. A first chapter. An opening of a conversation that the perpetrator believed would continue.

She looked at the Bernini one more time.

She thought: he chose this. He stood here and looked at this and decided that this was exactly right for what he wanted to say about this particular man. The Cardinal arranged before Apollo and Daphne — before the sculpture of pride reaching for what it cannot hold and in the reaching destroying what it was reaching for.

He had read the Cardinal the way she read rooms. He had read him from the inside, from the architecture of the man's institutional position and the specific quality of his pride, and had found the right image for what he saw.

She thought: he and I are doing the same thing.

She filed this. She was going to return to it later, when she had more of the evidence assembled and could look at it properly.

She went back inside. She had more to see.

Chapter 5

Superbia: The Root and the Flower

The conference registry arrived at 7:43pm.

Mateo sent it without preamble — a scanned document, four hundred and eleven names across eleven pages, attendees of the Symposium on Thomistic Moral Philosophy held at the Gregorian University the week preceding the Cardinal's death. Below it, a single line of text: Narrowed to seven. Call me.

She called him.

He answered before the second ring. She could hear Rome behind him — the specific evening Rome of a city that had been at this for two millennia and had developed its night sounds accordingly. A café. People. The particular acoustics of a narrow street.

"Seven," she said.

"Seven who attended the conference, whose published work engages specifically with Aquinas's taxonomy of the seven sins, and whose citation style in published papers is consistent with the Leonine apparatus." A pause. "Of those seven, two are women, which the staging doesn't exclude but statistically narrows. Two are American institutions and didn't arrive in Rome until the day of the conference, which the forensics timeline narrows further. That leaves three."

"Send me the three."

"Sending."

The three names arrived while she was still on the call. She read them. Two she did not recognize. The third she did.

Dr. Heinrich Paulus. Visiting lecturer in patristic theology, Gregorian University. German. Sixty-one years old. Eleven peer-reviewed publications. Two monographs. A bibliography that read like the academic biography of a man who had spent his entire career in intimate conversation with Augustine, Aquinas, and the Desert Fathers.

She had met him this morning. In the briefing room. He had been sitting three chairs from Father Albani, and he had said nothing, and she had not found this remarkable because there were always people in briefings who said nothing.

She found it remarkable now.

"Mateo," she said.

"I know," he said.

She pulled his file from the conference registry supplementary materials, which included brief academic biographies of all registered attendees.

Dr. Heinrich Paulus. Born Munich, 1964. Formation in classical languages and theology at the University of Tübingen, where he had completed his doctorate in 1991 under the supervision of a scholar whose name she recognized from Mateo's explanation of the Leonine apparatus — a man who had himself been trained in the pre-1980 system and had carried it forward into his students. Paulus had published consistently since 1993. His specialization: the phenomenology of sin in Thomistic and Augustinian moral theology. The taxonomy of the seven capital sins as a diagnostic framework for understanding human psychology.

The taxonomy of the seven capital sins.

She read this line twice. Then she read his most recent publication title: "The Staging of Moral Argument in Medieval Sacred Art: Bernini, Caravaggio, and the Embodied Theology of the Roman Baroque."

Published eight months ago. In a peer-reviewed journal of theological aesthetics.

She set the file down on the hotel room desk. She picked it up again. She put it down.

The Bernini. The Caravaggio. The staging of moral argument in art. Eight months before a Cardinal was arranged before a Bernini sculpture with a parchment beside his hand and a Latin word that was the precise theological diagnosis of his life's defining sin.

She called Mateo back. He answered on the first ring again.

"He published a paper," she said.

"I read it this afternoon," Mateo said. "It's very good."

She did not ask him when he had found the time. He was Mateo. He had found the time the way he found everything — by deciding it was necessary and making it so.

"The paper," she said. "Tell me what it argues."

She heard him settle somewhere. A chair. The ambient café noise slightly reduced.

"That Bernini and Caravaggio were not primarily creating art," he said. "That they were staging theological arguments in three-dimensional space. That the viewer standing before a Bernini is being placed inside an argument the sculptor has already constructed — positioned to experience the theology through the body rather than the intellect. The paper's central claim is that this is more effective as moral instruction than any text, because the viewer cannot remain objective. They are inside the argument. They cannot choose not to feel it."

She was quiet for a moment.

"He didn't stage a crime scene," she said.

"No," Mateo said.

"He staged a lecture."

"And chose the Bernini because his own published work identifies it as the most effective theological staging in Rome." A pause. "He used his own academic methodology. At the scene of a murder. And then submitted it to a peer-reviewed journal eight months before anyone was killed."

She sat with this for a moment. The hotel room was very quiet. Rome outside her window was doing its late-evening things — the specific diminuendo of a city that had been performing itself all day and was now becoming something more genuine in the dark.

"He was in the briefing room," she said. "This morning."

"I know," Mateo said. His voice had a quality she hadn't heard in it before. Not fear exactly. Something more considered. The voice of a man processing what it meant to have been in the same room as a particular kind of intelligence and to have taken forty-eight hours to understand what he was standing next to.

"He said nothing," she said.

"He didn't need to," Mateo said. "He was there to observe. Not to participate."

She spent the next two hours verifying.

The paper was real. The journal was legitimate. The eight-month publication timeline was confirmed by the journal's editorial records, which were publicly accessible online. Dr. Heinrich Paulus had submitted the paper fourteen months ago, which meant he had written it at least a year before the Cardinal's death.

This did not constitute evidence of anything except academic publication. A scholar who wrote about the theology of staged art and who attended a conference on Thomistic moral philosophy and who had been present at an Interpol briefing was, by himself, not a suspect. The Vatican liaison would tell her this. Commander Hale would tell her this. Every procedural instinct she had developed in twelve years would tell her this.

She was not listening to any of them.

She was listening to the thing that had been present in the Borghese Gallery at 4:53 in the morning and that she had not yet found a procedural word for. The thing she had filed as "the quality of the intention." The room that felt like a question asked in a language she almost spoke. The grade left by a teacher at the end of a lesson.

She was listening to that, and she was reading Dr. Paulus's bibliography, and she was thinking about a man who had spent thirty years developing an intimate understanding of how sin expressed itself in human psychology and in sacred art — and who had, eight months ago, published the methodology of the crime that had not yet been committed.

She opened a new document on her laptop. She wrote his name at the top. She wrote three words beneath it: the originating condition.

She stared at what she had written.

Then she picked up her phone and called Mateo again.

"He's in the registry as a visiting lecturer," she said. "Is he still at the Gregorian?"

"My contact says he's scheduled through the end of the week. He's been teaching a seminar on Thomistic moral philosophy every Tuesday and Thursday morning." Another pause. "The seminar is open to graduate students. My contact attended last Thursday."

"What did he say? In the seminar."

"My contact said he spent ninety minutes on Augustine's definition of pride. Specifically on the refusal to be known truly. He called it the most misunderstood sin in the tradition because it masquerades as virtue."

Pride masquerading as virtue. The Cardinal's thirty years of documented effectiveness. The self so carefully constructed that not one person could see past it.

"Mateo."

"Yes."

"Do not approach him. Do not contact your source at the Gregorian again tonight. Do not publish anything."

A beat. "Understood."

"Good." She paused. "Thank you for the registry."

She ended the call. She looked at her laptop screen. Dr. Heinrich Paulus. The originating condition.

She had forty-one hours of her fifty remaining.

She had a name.

She did not yet have anything she could put in front of Commander Hale without watching him hand it to the Vatican liaison and listening to twenty-three years of diplomatic training explain why a visiting academic who attended a conference and sat quietly in a briefing room was not the kind of thing Interpol built cases around.

She needed something procedural. Something that left no room for diplomatic training.

She looked at the name on her screen for a long time.

Then she opened the conference registry and began, methodically, to find the procedural thing.

The procedural thing, in this case, was a cross-reference she had not run yet.

Conference attendees against the Gregorian visiting faculty roll for the same week. Not the same list — the conference registry Mateo had sent was external attendees. The Gregorian's internal records would include the visiting and adjunct faculty who had been on campus that week, who would have had access to the building at hours the conference registration did not cover.

She requested it through the Rome liaison at 8:04pm. The liaison would request it from the Gregorian's administrative office. The administrative office would respond in the morning because it was now after hours and the Gregorian, like all Roman institutions of a certain age and self-assurance, operated at the pace it had always operated at.

She called Mateo.

"The visiting faculty list," she said. "The Gregorian's internal roll for the conference week. Not the external registry — the people who were already there."

"I can get it faster than the liaison." He said it without emphasis, which was how he said things he was confident about. "I have a contact in the administration office. An old source."

"A source who owes you a story you didn't publish."

"A different story. A better one." She heard paper moving. "Give me an hour."

She gave him thirty minutes because the hour was late and they had the morning approaching and she did not have the patience for the hour. She worked through what she had. The Paulus file was thin in the way that academic files were always thin — a curriculum vitae that communicated everything about professional accomplishment and nothing about the man. Eleven publications. Two monographs.

A university affiliation in Cologne that she cross-referenced against the Gregorian's visiting lecturer program for the past eight years and found three previous residencies, the most recent two years ago.

He had been here before. He knew the building. He knew the gallery access points.

She wrote this down.

Mateo sent the internal faculty list at forty-two minutes past eight. She cross-referenced it against the external registry in eleven minutes. There were seven names that appeared on both. Of those seven, one had a publication record that overlapped with the crime scene's theological architecture. Of those one, the name was already in her file.

Dr. Heinrich Paulus. Visiting lecturer. Conference attendee. Former Gregorian resident. A man who had been in this city three times in eight years, who knew the gallery access protocols, who had published forty-three years of scholarship that read like the intellectual biography of the crime scene she had walked into at 4:53am.

She sat with this for a long time.

She was not yet certain. Certain required evidence she could stand behind in a briefing room with Commander Hale and the Vatican liaison and the Italian prosecutor's deputy all looking at her with the specific institutional skepticism of men who needed to be satisfied before they would authorize the next step. What she had was pattern. What she had was the specific feeling, in her body and her professional instinct simultaneously, of a pattern that was not random.

She had learned to trust this feeling. She had also learned to verify it before she named it to anyone who would use it as a reason to act prematurely.

She needed one more thing. One piece of evidence that connected Paulus not just to the location and the methodology but to the specific victim. A man who kills with academic precision does not choose his subject arbitrarily. The Cardinal had been chosen for a reason. The reason was in the theology of the staging — Superbia, pride, the Bernini, the specific arrangement of a man whose private certainty had been his defining characteristic.

Paulus had known that. Paulus had read it in the Cardinal and had chosen him for it.

She needed to know when Paulus had read it. And how.

She sent Mateo one more message before midnight: *Cardinal Voss — academic publications, correspondence, conference appearances last three years. Anything that puts him in Paulus's orbit.*

His response came at twelve-forty: *Already looking. Sleep. I'll have it by morning.*

She did not sleep immediately. She lay in the temporary apartment with the lights off and the file in her mind — not reviewing it, simply holding it, the way you hold something fragile you have not yet found the right container for — and thought about a man who had spent forty-three years building an intellectual architecture and had decided, at some point she could not yet identify, to test it against a life.

She thought about what kind of mind made that decision.

She fell asleep thinking about Mateo's voice at midnight saying *sleep* and the specific quality of a man who had been awake as long as she had and was telling her to rest anyway.

She did not examine this. She slept.

She worked until 2am.

The conference registry, the file, the cross-reference against the Gregorian faculty roll, the three names that emerged from the intersection of academic specialization and institutional access. She worked through each name with the systematic care she applied to everything that mattered, building the evidentiary record from the outside in.

The third name was the right one. She had known it when she read his file the first time and had filed the knowledge under things that required verification before they were admissible. She had been verifying for six hours. The verification was holding.

She sent Mateo the cross-reference documentation at 2:04am with a single line: *The third name. Verify the Tübingen connection.*

His response arrived at 2:09am: *Already looking.*

She sat for a moment with the phone in her hand and the case building correctly around her and the specific knowledge that the next twenty-four hours were going to determine everything. Then she put the phone down and went back to the registry.

She was working. She was very good at this.

Chapter 6

The Cardinal's Enemies Are a Long List

The Vatican operated on its own time.

This was not a figure of speech. The Vatican State had its own legal jurisdiction, its own judicial system, its own calendar of institutional priorities that bore no particular relationship to the urgency of an Interpol investigation into the murder of one of its senior diplomats. It would cooperate. It was cooperating. The cooperation would proceed at the pace the cooperation would proceed at, and any attempt to accelerate that pace would be received with the specific courtesy of an institution that had outlasted every empire that had ever tried to pressure it and had found the experience educational.

Sonya had been in enough rooms with enough institutions to recognize this posture. She adjusted her timeline accordingly and scheduled the Vatican interviews for eight in the morning, which was two hours earlier than anyone in the relevant offices would have preferred.

They were there when she arrived. Of course they were. The Vatican did not give Interpol the satisfaction of being visibly inconvenienced.

The interviews were conducted in a conference room on the second floor of the Apostolic Palace that had been built in the sixteenth century and furnished in the twentieth with the specific tasteful neutrality of an institution that understood it was being watched. High ceilings. A long table. Chairs arranged with the precision of a seating chart that communicated hierarchy without naming it.

She interviewed eleven people over four hours.

The first was Monsignor Ferraro, sixty-seven, who had worked alongside Cardinal Voss for nineteen years and who described him as a dedicated servant of the Church with an extraordinary gift for the delicate work of international diplomacy. When she asked what the Cardinal had been like privately, Monsignor Ferraro explained that a man of the Cardinal's responsibilities necessarily maintained a careful distinction between his public duties and his personal life. She asked what his personal life had contained. The Monsignor explained that the Cardinal had been deeply devoted to his spiritual practice. She asked if he had friends. The Monsignor explained that the Cardinal had maintained many meaningful professional relationships.

The second was Sister Agnese, fifty-two, who had served as the Cardinal's administrative assistant for eleven years. She described him as exacting, fair, and possessed of a memory for institutional detail that she had found both impressive and occasionally exhausting. She volunteered this last observation and then appeared to reconsider it. Sonya did not pursue it. She filed it.

The third through the eleventh were variations on a theme.

He was respected. He was effective. He was discreet. He had no documented enemies. He had no personal relationships that anyone was prepared to characterize as close. He had spent thirty years in service to the Church and the Church, by all available testimony, had received his service gratefully and knew him not at all.

The refusal to be known truly.

Father Albani's words in the briefing room. Mateo's translations in the gallery. She was beginning to understand that the staging had not been the killer's interpretation of the Cardinal. It had been the killer's documentation of him. The crime scene was an accurate portrait. Whoever had made it had done the work.

She closed her notebook after the eleventh interview. She thanked the Vatican liaison, whose name was Rossi and who had been present for all eleven conversations with the specific alert passivity of a man ensuring nothing useful was accidentally disclosed. She told him she might have further questions. He told her the appropriate offices would be happy to facilitate any additional cooperation that fell within the scope of the existing agreement. She thanked him again.

She walked toward the exit.

The corridor outside the conference room was long and high-ceilinged and lined with the accumulated portraiture of men who had wielded institutional authority across five centuries. Sonya walked through them without attending to them. She was thinking about Sister Agnese's almost-observation — exacting, fair, and occasionally exhausting — and what it might have contained if the sister had not reconsidered it.

At the end of the corridor, near the staircase, a young woman was waiting.

She was perhaps twenty-five. Dark hair, a Vatican archival pass around her neck, a tablet under one arm, and the expression of a person who had been standing in this specific location for long enough to be certain they were there for a reason. She met Sonya's eyes directly. Then she looked away. Then she looked back.

Sonya slowed slightly without appearing to.

As she passed, the young woman moved toward the staircase in the same direction. Their paths converged naturally at the top of the stairs. Sonya felt something pressed into her palm — quickly, efficiently, with the specific practiced ease of someone who had thought about how to do this and had decided that the doing of it was going to happen regardless of the thinking about it.

A folded piece of paper. Small. Tight.

The young woman was already moving down the stairs ahead of her. She did not look back.

Sonya descended the stairs at her ordinary pace, through the courtyard, through the gate, out onto the Via della Conciliazione where Rome received her with its customary indifference. She walked half a block. She turned into a side street. She unfolded the paper.

Two words. A name and an address.

The name was Voss.

The address was in Trastevere.

She called Mateo from the side street.

"Voss," she said when he answered.

"Common name. Context?"

"The Cardinal's. And an address in Trastevere. Passed to me by a Vatican archivist on the way out of eleven interviews that collectively produced nothing a press release couldn't have told me."

A beat. She heard him writing.

"Trastevere address suggests a private residence rather than an institutional connection," he said. "The Cardinal had family?"

"A nephew. Documented in the biographical file. Marco Voss, thirty-one. Removed from seminary eight years ago. The reason for removal is not in the file."

"Reason for removal from seminary is almost never in the file," Mateo said. His voice had a quality she had not heard in it before — something flat, something that came from a specific and personal knowledge of how institutions documented the people they discarded. "I can find out."

"Do that." She paused. "The archivist who passed me the note. Young woman, twenty-five, Vatican archival pass, dark hair. She took a risk."

"Which means she thought the risk was worth taking."

"Which means she knows something she can't say inside that building."

"Which means when you find her again you'll need to find her somewhere else."

"Yes."

She folded the paper and put it in her jacket pocket. She looked at the side street — old stone, washing lines between windows, a cat on a windowsill performing the specific feline indifference to human urgency that Roman cats had been performing since the Republic. The city was very quiet here. Very old. Very aware of nothing she was doing.

"Mateo."

"Still here."

"The Paulus question. I need something procedural before I take his name to Hale. The bibliography and the paper aren't enough."

"I know." Another pause. The sound of him thinking, which she was learning to recognize — a particular quality of silence that was not the silence of a man with nothing to say but the silence of a man assembling something. "There's one more thing I didn't mention last night. About the parchment."

She waited.

"The ink."

"We know the ink. Iron gall, eighteen to thirty-six hours old, consistent with —"

"Not the composition. The source. Iron gall ink isn't commercially available in the formulation on that parchment. It has to be made. The specific ratio of oak gall to ferrous sulfate in that sample is consistent with a formulation documented in one place: a 1962 treatise on the restoration of medieval manuscripts published by a press at the University of Tübingen."

Tübingen. Where Paulus had completed his doctorate. Where he had studied under the scholar who taught the Leonine apparatus. Where he had spent eight years in intimate proximity to the literature of medieval theological scholarship.

"How do you know this?" she said.

"I called a conservator at the Vatican Library this morning. It took four phone calls to reach someone who knew the formulation. She was very interested in the question."

"Don't let her be interested in the question."

"She won't talk. She owes me a significant professional favor from 2019 that I would prefer not to describe in detail."

Sonya filed this. The life of a journalist who had been operating in Rome for a decade was composed, apparently, of professional favors owed in both directions, contacts in institutions that should not have contacts, and a specific talent for finding the four phone calls that reached the person who knew the thing nobody else knew.

It was, she reflected, not entirely unlike the life of a detective.

"The Tübingen connection," she said. "It's still circumstantial."

"It's consistent. Which is different from proof but in the same neighborhood."

"I need more than the neighborhood."

"I know," he said. "Trastevere first. Then Paulus."

He was right. She did not say so.

"Thirty hours," she said.

"I'll be ready."

She ended the call. She looked at the folded note in her hand. The name Voss and a Trastevere address. A nephew removed from seminary for reasons not in the file.

She had thirty hours remaining.

She had a nephew who didn't have an alibi yet.

She had a visiting lecturer who had published the methodology of a murder eight months before the murder happened.

She had an ink formulation from a 1962 treatise at a German university.

And she had an archivist who had pressed a name into her hand and walked away without looking back.

She put the note in her pocket. She walked back toward the Via della Conciliazione. Rome continued around her, indifferent, ancient, keeping its own counsel as it always had.

One of these threads was going to break open the case.

One of them was going to break open the case in the wrong direction entirely.

She did not yet know which was which.

Monsignor Ferraro, she decided, was the one she did not need to return to.

Not because he was uninformative — he had given her three hours of careful testimony about a man he had worked alongside for nineteen years and had, in that time, developed the specific talent of the long-serving subordinate: the ability to describe his superior in complete sentences that communicated nothing useful about him at all. Nineteen years of careful proximity. Nineteen years of learning exactly which observations were appropriate to share with an Interpol investigator and which were institutional property.

She moved to the second interview.

Father Benedikt Schäfer, German, sixty-two, head of the Cardinal's diplomatic secretariat for the past eleven years. He entered the conference room with the bearing of a man who was not accustomed to being on the receiving end of questions and had decided, this morning, to be cooperative in a way that did not require him to be vulnerable. He sat straight. He arranged his hands. He looked at her with the specific attention of a man who was also, simultaneously, assessing her.

She let him assess.

"The Cardinal's enemies," she said. "Not his professional opponents — every diplomat has those. His actual enemies."

Father Schäfer's hands did not move. "The Cardinal served the Church with absolute dedication. He was respected across—"

"Father." She said it quietly. "I am investigating his murder. Not his memorial service."

A pause. She watched him recalibrate.

"There were disagreements," he said. "The Tübingen affair, from five years ago. An academic dispute over archival access — the Cardinal had blocked a German research consortium from accessing certain fifteenth-century documents. He felt the documentation was too sensitive for secular academic review. The consortium felt otherwise."

She wrote down: *Tübingen. Five years ago.*

"What was the nature of the sensitive documentation?"

"Theological correspondence relating to a disputed council decision. The specifics were above my clearance at the time." He paused again. The calibrated pause. "One of the consortium's affiliated scholars became particularly... persistent. There were letters. The Cardinal found them inappropriate."

"The scholar's name."

"I would need to consult records."

"You remember it."

He looked at her steadily for a moment. She held the look. He said: "The name on the correspondence was Paulus. A German academic. I cannot recall the institution."

She wrote it down without change of expression.

"Was the dispute resolved?"

"The Cardinal's position was upheld. The consortium's request was denied. That was the end of it, as far as I know."

As far as he knew. She noted the qualifier. The qualifier meant there was more.

She spent another forty minutes with Father Schäfer, taking him through the Cardinal's final week with the precision of a woman who needed every hour accounted for. She got the conference attendance — yes, the Cardinal had been present at the Gregorian symposium for the opening session. He had spoken briefly to several of the visiting scholars. Father Schäfer had not attended. He did not know which scholars, specifically.

At the end of the interview she thanked him, collected her notes, and walked to the window that overlooked the Vatican gardens. Below her, groundskeepers moved with the unhurried efficiency of men who had been doing this particular work in this particular garden for a long time.

The Tübingen affair. A blocked research consortium. Persistent correspondence that the Cardinal had found inappropriate. And now, five years later, a murder staged with the intellectual precision of a scholar who had spent his career in intimate correspondence with the exact theological tradition the Cardinal had used to deny that access.

Not random. Not a crime of opportunity or institutional politics. A specific, patient, constructed response. The curriculum of a man who had decided that the best argument was the one that could not be refuted.

She had three more interviews and six hours remaining in the Vatican.

She did not think she would learn more than she already knew.

She was right. The remaining three — a Vatican archivist, the Cardinal's personal secretary, and a senior figure in the diplomatic corps who had clearly been briefed to say nothing that could be quoted — gave her background and texture and nothing she could use in a briefing room.

She left the Vatican at 1pm. The sun was high and Rome was loud and she walked across the Piazza San Pietro with the case file building itself in her mind, connection by connection, until she reached the edge of the piazza and stopped and looked back at the Basilica.

He had stood somewhere like this. He had looked at something like this — the institution, the weight of it, the specific pride of an organization that had maintained its architecture across centuries — and had found his subject inside it.

She understood the selection now. Not completely. But the shape of it.

She called Mateo.

"The Tübingen affair," she said. "Five years ago. The Cardinal blocked an archival consortium. I need everything."

"Give me two hours," he said.

She was already walking.

She left the Vatican at one o'clock with eleven interviews behind her and the specific feeling of a building that had been constructed to reveal nothing and had succeeded.

But the Tübingen name had surfaced. Schäfer had said it carefully, with the specific care of a man who was sharing what he had been told to share, and had said nothing more. She had written it down and had not reacted and had moved to the next question and had spent the remaining twenty minutes of the Schäfer interview thinking about what it meant that the Vatican's institutional memory contained the name of the man she was already looking at.

It meant the Cardinal had known Paulus. Not personally — probably. But institutionally. The Tübingen consortium request, the blocked access, the correspondence Schäfer had described as inappropriate: the Cardinal had encountered Paulus as a professional opponent and had dismissed him with the specific confidence of a man who had the institutional authority to make dismissals permanent.

She walked across the Piazza San Pietro and thought: the selection was not random. The selection was the specific response of a man who had been dismissed by this specific institution in this specific way.

She thought: he selected the man who embodied the reason the institution dismissed him.

This was the most precise version of the motive she had arrived at. She wrote it down in the piazza and kept walking.

Chapter 7

The Nephew in Trastevere

Trastevere at midday was a different Rome than the one she had been working in.

This was the Rome that belonged to its residents rather than its history — narrow streets, laundry overhead, the smell of olive oil and stone and the particular urban intimacy of a neighborhood that had been continuously inhabited since before the Caesars and had developed, over those centuries, a specific indifference to being found interesting by outsiders. Tourists came here for the atmosphere. The atmosphere ignored them with the practiced ease of long experience.

Marco Voss lived in a third-floor apartment on the Via della Lungara. The building was old and the staircase was narrow and the door at the top had a lock that had been replaced recently — she could see where the original fitting had been removed, the wood around the new lock lighter than the surrounding door. Someone had changed their locks in the past few months. She noted this without deciding what it meant.

She knocked.

He answered after the third knock. Thirty-one years old. Dark-haired like the Cardinal but without the Cardinal's precision — the same bone structure worn differently, less maintained, the face of a man who had stopped attending to his appearance at some point and had not resumed. He was wearing clothes that had been slept in. His eyes were clear, which told her the dishevelment was grief or anxiety or both rather than alcohol. He looked at her identification for a long time.

"You're Interpol," he said. His Italian was Roman, native, with the specific flatness of the city center.

"I am."

"He's really dead."

She watched him process this. It was not a question. It was a man arriving at a fact he had been told and had not yet made real. She had watched this happen in many doorways. She let it happen.

"May I come in?" she said.

The apartment was small and specific.

Two rooms visible from the entrance: a main space that served as living room, study, and kitchen, and a bedroom whose door was open onto a bed that had been slept in and not made. The main space contained: a desk with a laptop, a chair, a small table with two chairs, a shelf of books that covered one full wall from floor to ceiling, and the accumulated paper of a person who worked with texts — stacked, annotated, cross-referenced, the organized chaos of a specific kind of scholarly mind.

She noted the books. Theology, primarily. Patristics. Church history. Medieval philosophy. The bibliography of a person who had been trained in these subjects and had not stopped engaging with them after the training ended.

She noted the laptop. She noted the specific placement of it on the desk — open, screen dark, positioned facing the window.

She noted that Marco Voss had sat down at the kitchen table without being asked and was looking at his own hands in the manner of a person who needed to look at something that was not her face.

"When did you last see your uncle?" she said. She sat across from him without asking. The kitchen chairs were mismatched. Hers was older.

"Six months ago. We had a conversation about the inheritance." He said the word inheritance with a flatness that contained a great deal of history. "It wasn't a good conversation."

"Who initiated it?"

"I did. My grandmother left money. The Cardinal —" He stopped. Started again. "My uncle managed the estate. He decided the distribution differently than the will specified. I asked him to explain the discrepancy."

"What did he say?"

"He said the estate had been managed in accordance with the family's best interests. He said this twice. The second time he said it, I understood that the conversation was finished."

She wrote this down. Financial motive. Documented. She had found it in the file and she was finding it again in his face — not grief exactly, more the specific exhaustion of a person who has been angry for a long time and has just been told that the object of their anger is no longer available.

"The night of the murder," she said. "Where were you?"

He looked up. She saw the calculation in it — not guilt, something more complicated. The calculation of a person who knows that what they are about to say is true and inadequate simultaneously.

"Here," he said. "Alone. Working."

"Is there anyone who can confirm that?"

"No."

She wrote this down. She looked at the shelf of theological texts. She looked at the laptop.

"May I?" She gestured toward the shelf.

He nodded. He was watching her the way people watched detectives move through their spaces — the specific vigilance of a person whose private life was being read by a professional.

She looked at the spines. Augustine. Aquinas. Dante. The Desert Fathers. Kierkegaard on despair. A worn paperback copy of Bernini's complete works in Italian. She stopped at the Bernini.

"You're interested in Bernini," she said.

"I studied art history before the seminary. The Baroque period." He said this without defensiveness. "Bernini is the Baroque."

She put the book back exactly where she had found it.

She thanked him. She told him she might have further questions. She told him not to leave Rome. He said he had nowhere to go. She believed him. She left.

She sent Mateo the summary from the staircase.

Theological library consistent with seminary formation. Bernini text. Laptop present. No alibi for the night of the murder. Financial dispute with victim documented and recent. Will forward digital forensics request for the laptop search history.

His response came back in four minutes.

Two words.

"Too perfect."

She stood on the Via della Lungara and read those two words three times. She thought about the lock on the door — new, recently replaced. She thought about the Bernini book, present on the shelf of a man who had studied art history before the seminary. She thought about the inheritance dispute and the financial desperation and the no alibi and the laptop.

She thought about a person who had spent years studying a victim before choosing them.

She thought about a crime scene that had contained no errors.

A frame this complete had been assembled by someone. The question was whether Marco Voss had assembled it himself or whether it had been assembled around him by a person who had been paying sufficient attention to know exactly what a frame for Marco Voss would need to contain.

She sent Mateo one word back.

"Explain."

His response: "I went back to the gallery. Meet me."

She walked.

Trastevere to the Borghese was forty minutes at the pace she kept when she was working through something, which was faster than a tourist and slower than urgency — the pace of a person covering ground while their mind covered something else entirely. She went along the Tiber first, north toward the Ponte Regina Margherita, then east and up through the Villa Borghese park, which was green and quiet in the midday heat and full of families who had no interest in her.

She thought about Marco Voss.

He was not the killer. She had known this before she walked through his door and the interview had confirmed it eight different ways, the most important of which was not the alibi documentation but the quality of his relationship to his uncle's death: a man who had spent eight years constructing a careful distance from a powerful man who had embarrassed and diminished him, and who was now, in the specific aftermath of that man's murder, grieving in the way you grieve for something you had already partially lost. The grief was real. The alibi was real. The books were real.

Marco Voss had been chosen because he was convenient. Because his history with the Cardinal was documented and readable. Because an institution under pressure to close a case quickly would see what had been arranged for it to see.

Which meant someone who understood how institutions read evidence had arranged it.

She was still thinking about this when she reached the café near the Borghese entrance and saw Mateo at a corner table with two coffees and his notebook open and the specific look of a man who had been waiting with the patience of someone accustomed to his own company.

"You walked," he said.

"I needed to." She sat. She did not look at the coffee immediately. "Tell me the three things."

He told her.

The impression in the dust was the first — she absorbed it with the full professional attention it required, asked three clarifying questions about measurement and consistency and the forensics team's documentation of the floor surface, and filed it under *Observer: confirmed.*

The second was the thread.

It had been in the forensics photographs, which she had reviewed four times. Mateo had looked at the same photographs and seen something she had not: a thread — single, dark, wool — caught in the decorative ironwork of the rope barrier near the sculpture. Not the same barrier section that the forensics team had catalogued. A different section, further back, closer to the observer's position.

"A thread from what?" she said.

"A coat. Wool, dark weight — the kind of thing you wear in October if you're walking between air-conditioned institutions and still-warm streets. The forensics team photographed it and tagged it as potentially pre-existing contamination. They're not wrong — it could have been there for days. But combined with the impression in the dust—"

"Someone stood there. In a dark wool coat." She thought of the academic figure she had been building in her mind for four days. Of a man who would have dressed appropriately for a Roman October. Of a professor who moved between institutions. "The third thing."

The third thing was the card.

It was in the gallery's visitor records rather than the crime scene itself — Mateo had requested the visitor log for the seventy-two hours preceding the murder from his contact in the administration. Among the names logged for an after-hours scholarly access: *Dr. H. Paulus, visiting lecturer, Gregorian University. Authorized by gallery director. Duration: 2 hours 17 minutes. Purpose: research access, Bernini collection.*

Four days before the murder. He had been in this gallery, alone with the Bernini, for two hours and seventeen minutes. He had studied the space. He had studied the sight-lines. He had stood, very likely, in exactly the position marked by the impression in the dust.

She sat with this for a long time.

"This is not enough," she said.

"I know."

"It places him here. It does not place him here on the morning of the murder. It does not connect him to the parchment, to the knot, to the Franciscan binding technique."

"I know." He closed his notebook. "But it tells us where to look next."

"The bibliography."

"The bibliography," he agreed. "Eleven publications and two monographs. If he developed the knot technique for his own academic binding work, there will be a reference. Scholars document their methods. It's the specific vanity of the academy — they want credit for everything, including how they tie their books."

She looked at him across the table. This was the third time she had looked at him and noticed the specific quality of his intelligence — not the journalist's facility for narrative, which she had clocked on day one, but something underneath it, the thing that the narrative facility was built on. He thought architecturally. He understood how things connected before he could name the connections.

"The Leonine apparatus," she said. "In his published footnotes."

"If it's there—"

"It places him in the specific Tübingen tradition he denied being part of." She stood. She picked up the coffee she had not touched and drank half of it standing. "I need the full bibliography. All eleven papers. Tonight."

"Tonight," he said. He was already reaching for his phone.

She left him at the table. She walked back out into the Roman afternoon with the thread count and the visitor log and the two-hour-seventeen-minute gap and thought about a man who had stood in a gallery with a Bernini and had stood there long enough to understand exactly what he intended to make of it.

She thought: he was not rushing. He has never rushed. This has been a very long time in preparation.

She walked faster.

She walked faster. She had three things from the gallery — the impression, the thread, the visitor log — and a journalist she had authorized to operate at the edges of a restricted scene and who had found what her own team had missed. Both of these things were true. She was holding them simultaneously.

She was also aware that the holding was getting easier. The specific friction of working with someone outside the institutional framework — the adjustment of professional habits built around clear jurisdictional lines — was diminishing with each day. She was not certain this was entirely professional.

She filed this under things she was not reading. She walked to the café.

The café was on a side street between the Piazza della Rovere and the Borghese entrance, which was not on any tourist map and which Mateo had found by the specific method he found everything — by moving through the city with the attentiveness of someone who was always looking for the next useful thing. She sat across from him and drank the coffee he had ordered without asking and thought about Marco Voss.

She had not yet told Mateo what she had found in the Trastevere apartment. Not because the information was restricted — he had earned more than enough institutional trust at this point — but because she had been working through it on the forty-minute walk and had not yet arrived at the complete interpretation.

She arrived at it now.

"Marco Voss is not the killer," she said.

"I know." He said it the way he said things he had known for some time but had been waiting for the right moment to confirm. "His psychological profile doesn't fit the staging. The staging requires someone who has spent decades developing a methodology. Voss is thirty-one. Whatever his relationship to the Cardinal was, it wasn't the engine of something this patient."

"He's a convenience," she said. "Someone with a documented grievance and a plausible motive and enough proximity to the victim to be readable as a suspect."

"The framing was prepared."

"Before the murder. The accommodation arrangement, the conference positioning — whoever staged Rome also staged the misdirection. The same deliberateness."

He looked at her steadily. "You've been thinking about this since Trastevere."

"Since the apartment. The theological texts." She had not said this to anyone. She said it now because Mateo was the person in this investigation who would understand what she was saying. "He reads theology. Not for faith — for scholarship. He has the Augustine bibliography, the Aquinas, the Gregory the Great. He's been reading the same tradition the crime scene is citing."

"He understands the argument."

"He grew up inside a version of it." She looked at her coffee. "And he was chosen because of that. His history with the Cardinal made him the perfect false subject. Someone who could be framed using institutional logic that the investigation would recognize and accept."

"But the framing was too neat."

"The framing was too precise," she said. "A man who stages a murder as a theological argument doesn't choose a suspect arbitrarily. He chooses a suspect who fits the narrative exactly, which requires studying the available candidates and selecting the one whose history is most readable as motive."

"He knew about Voss's history with the Cardinal."

"He researched it." She stood. She picked up the coffee. "Which means he had access to institutional records, or he had someone who did." She looked toward the Borghese entrance. "Tell me the three things."

She filed this under things she was not reading. She walked to the café.

Chapter 8

What Mateo Found in the Gallery

She found him at the café near the Borghese entrance. He had ordered for both of them without consulting her and there was a coffee and a small plate of something she wasn't going to eat waiting at the chair across from his. She sat. She looked at the plate. She looked at him.

"You went back to the gallery," she said.

"I did."

"Without authorization."

"I have a contact at the Borghese administration."

"A contact who let you into a restricted crime scene."

"A contact who owed me a conversation from an article I didn't publish in 2021." He opened the satchel and produced his notebook. "I found three things. None of them are in the forensics report."

She looked at him steadily. The professional calculus of the moment was straightforward: he had violated a restricted scene and found things her team had missed. Both of these facts were true simultaneously and she was going to have to hold them simultaneously without letting her response to the first contaminate her use of the second.

"Tell me," she said.

The first thing was the impression.

A faint compression in the marble floor approximately four meters from the primary crime scene marker, consistent with a standing figure — weight distributed as someone who had been still for an extended period. Not the forensics team's footprints, which were documented and excluded. Not the security team's. A separate standing point. Someone had been in that position long enough to leave an impression in the dust that had accumulated on the marble between cleaning rotations.

"Whoever staged the scene stayed to observe it," Mateo said.

"How long?"

"Long enough to leave that impression. Half an hour minimum. Possibly longer." He turned a page in his notebook. "The position is interesting. It's not a vantage point for the body. It's a vantage point for the Bernini."

She processed this. The killer had arranged the scene and then stood for half an hour looking not at what they had made but at the sculpture above it. Looking at the argument. Standing inside it the way Paulus's paper described — positioned to experience the theology through the body rather than the intellect.

"The second thing," she said.

The second thing was the knot.

The Cardinal's ceremonial robes had been arranged with a specific fastening at the left shoulder — documented in the forensics photography as "robe closure consistent with ceremonial dress." Mateo had looked at the photograph for eleven minutes before identifying it as something else entirely.

"It's a Franciscan knot," he said. "A specific liturgical knot used in the binding of sacred texts in the Franciscan tradition. It's not decorative and it's not standard ceremonial dress fastening. It's a knot with a specific meaning — it's used when a text is considered complete. When a document has been sealed. Finished."

She looked at him.

"The lesson was sealed," she said.

"The grade was given and the document was closed." He held her eyes. "The knot isn't taught in general seminary formation. It's specific to a monastic tradition within the Franciscan order. A very small number of institutions still practice it. Primarily in Germany and Austria."

Germany.

Tübingen was in Germany. Paulus had trained in Tübingen. The ink formulation was from a 1962 Tübingen treatise.

The accumulation of German connections was no longer coincidence. It was evidence. Still circumstantial. Still not enough for Hale. But building toward something with the specific momentum of a case that was beginning to understand itself.

"The third thing," she said.

The third thing was the most important.

Mateo had, with the contact's permission and a macro lens he carried in the satchel for exactly this kind of purpose, photographed the parchment evidence bag from directly above at maximum magnification. The photograph revealed what the standard forensics photography had not captured at normal resolution: along the lower right edge of the vellum, in a hand smaller and finer than the hand that had written the central word, a single annotation.

Not Greek this time.

Latin. Two words. In a script so small they were barely legible even at maximum magnification.

"Prima lectio," Mateo said.

She looked at him.

"First lesson," he said.

The room went very quiet in the way rooms went quiet when something that had been a theory became a fact. She had known, since the gallery, since the conversation about lessons having more than one. She had known since Mateo translated the grade left by a teacher. She had carried the knowledge as a professional inference, carefully, without committing to it until she had enough to commit.

Prima lectio. First lesson.

He had labelled it himself.

"Nobody found this," she said. It was not a question.

"It's two millimeters of text on the edge of a vellum square that was photographed at standard forensics resolution. Nobody was looking for a second inscription." He paused. "Because nobody was looking for a curriculum."

She sat with this for a moment. The café around them was entirely ordinary — the noise of an afternoon in Rome, the smell of coffee, the specific indifferent Roman light that fell through the windows and illuminated everything with equal impartiality. She was aware of the ordinariness and aware of what it contained: a man across a table from her who had gone back to a crime scene without authorization and had found the thing that changed the nature of the crime.

She was furious with him.

She was also aware that without him she would be building a case against a nephew with a Bernini book and no alibi and that the case would close badly and the person who had written "prima lectio" in two millimeters of Latin on the edge of a square of vellum would be on a train to the next city.

She did not let him see the second part.

"You will not," she said, "go back to that gallery again."

"Understood."

"You will send me every photograph you took today through a secure channel I will provide. You will not retain copies."

A beat. "Understood."

"The knot. I need documentation of the specific institutions that still practice it."

"I'll have it tonight."

"Good." She stood. She picked up the coffee. She drank it because she needed it and because standing and leaving immediately would have communicated something she was not prepared to communicate. She set the cup down. "Mateo."

"Yes."

"Prima lectio means there is a second lesson."

He looked at her steadily. "I know."

"Which means we have —" she checked her watch — "twenty-two hours before my jurisdiction in this city becomes a diplomatic discussion and we are significantly behind whatever schedule he is keeping."

"What do you need?"

"The institutions. Tonight. And the nephew's seminary record — the real reason he was removed, not the official one."

"Also tonight," he said.

She left without thanking him. She thanked him in her mind, precisely and completely, where it produced no professional complications. She walked back toward the Interpol offices through an afternoon Rome that was moving through its ordinary rhythms She looked at the notebook. At the three items Mateo had found.

At the annotation he had made in the margin beside the visitor log entry: *He came back to see what he had made.*

She had seen this in other crime scenes — perpetrators returning. It was not unusual. What was unusual was the motive. Most returned from compulsion, from the need to revisit the thing they had done. This was different. He had returned while the gallery was still accessible, before the security regime changed, specifically to observe the space from the position he had planned for and to confirm that it would read the way he intended.

He had come to review his own work. He had found it satisfactory.

She looked at the impression in the dust. At the specific standing position of a man who had been there and had looked not at the body but at the Bernini and had evaluated what he had made against what he had intended to make.

He had found it satisfactory.

She stood outside the gallery in the Roman afternoon and thought about what kind of person checked his own work like this. The answer arrived without difficulty: the same kind who spent forty years building a methodology in private before applying it.

A careful person. A patient one.

She had her work cut out for her.

entirely unaware that a man somewhere in this city had labelled his own first lesson and was already preparing the second.

She walked with this for the length of the Via Pinciana.

Three things from the gallery: the impression, the thread, the visitor log. Three things that individually could be dismissed and together constituted the beginning of something she could not yet name to Commander Hale but could feel in the specific professional register she had learned to trust — the certainty that arrived before the language for it.

The visitor log was the most important.

Not because it placed Paulus in the gallery — the gallery was a public institution and his presence before the murder was not evidence of involvement in the murder. It was important because of what it told her about the time. Two hours and seventeen minutes with the Bernini collection. Not the collection generally. The record specified *Bernini collection* as the access purpose. He had stood in front of that sculpture for a significant portion of that time. He had studied it the way a person studies something they intend to use.

She had seen crime scenes that were accidental and crime scenes that were planned and crime scenes that were both. She had never seen a crime scene that was also an argument. This was the first.

He was making an argument in marble and silk and parchment. He had chosen the location because it was exactly right for the argument — a sculpture about the moment when pride reaches for the thing it cannot hold and in the reaching destroys both itself and the object of its desire. He had placed the Cardinal before it with the precision of a man who wanted the message to be read. He had left the parchment as a citation.

He was treating the crime scene as a published text.

She stopped walking. She was in the middle of the Villa Borghese park, which was green and indifferent around her, and she stopped because something had just become clear that had not been clear before.

He expected someone to read it.

Not the forensics team. Not Commander Hale. A specific reader — someone who could understand the theological argument being made, who had the scholarly apparatus to recognize the citation, who would know what the Leonine footnote system meant and why it mattered. He had written this for an audience. A specific one.

She called Mateo.

"The bibliography," she said. "I need it now. Not tonight. Now."

"I'm working on it." She could hear him moving. "What changed?"

"He left this for a reader. He made it readable. The Leonine apparatus — if it's there, it's not just evidence of Tübingen training. It's a signature. He signed it." She paused. Organized. Continued. "Who would be able to read it? Who in the conference pool would have the Tübingen background, the theological paleography knowledge, the familiarity with the Leonine footnote system?"

"The same pool of seven we already narrowed to Paulus."

"Narrower. Who would Paulus expect to find his signature? Someone who knows him. Someone who knows his work. Someone with access to his unpublished—" She stopped.

"Unpublished," Mateo said. The specific quality of his voice when something arrived.

"He has a monograph," she said. "Two, actually. Published. But a man who has been developing a methodology for forty years — there will be private work. Notes. A framework he hasn't published because it's not finished or not meant for publication."

"Or not meant for that kind of publication."

She understood what he meant. Not a peer-reviewed paper. Something addressed to a specific reader. A reader who was, or would be, capable of understanding what the published papers circled without landing.

"Find me the monographs," she said. "And find me any unpublished correspondence that ended up in institutional archives — university libraries, research centers. Paulus is sixty-one and has been publishing since 1982. Forty years of academic correspondence with other scholars will have left a record somewhere."

"I know a theologian at the Lateran with archival access. Old contact. Owes me a conversation I've been saving."

"Use it."

"Sonya." His voice had a quality she was still calibrating — the specific register he used when he was about to say something careful. "This is going to take longer than tonight."

"Then start now." She looked at her watch. 4:17pm. "And Mateo. The visitor log. He was in the gallery two hours and seventeen minutes. I want to know if there are any other records of Paulus accessing restricted research spaces in Rome in the past three years. University libraries, Vatican archives, private collections. Anywhere he would have needed a scholarly credential."

"I'll look."

"Tonight."

"Tonight," he agreed.

She ended the call. She stood in the park for another moment, the afternoon light gold through the trees, Rome doing its Rome things in every direction, and thought about a man who had spent forty-three years building the precise intellectual apparatus required to make this argument, and had then made it.

She thought: he has been patient. The patience of a man who was not yet finished.

She walked back toward the Interpol office. She had a briefing to prepare for Hale in the morning, a Vatican interview to review, a bibliography to read the moment Mateo sent it, and the specific knowledge, sitting in her chest like something waiting to become language, that the man she was looking for was not gone from Rome because the first lesson was over.

He was gone because the second lesson was ready to begin.

Chapter 9

Four Hundred Names and One Pattern

The Franciscan knot documentation arrived at eleven-seventeen that night.

She was at the desk in the Interpol temporary office, which was empty at this hour except for her and the accumulated paper of three days of investigation and two cups of coffee that had been adequate and one that had been excellent and was now finished. The Rome liaison had gone home at nine. Commander Hale's deputy had gone home at eight-thirty with the specific expression of a man who was professionally required to be here and personally required to be somewhere else. She had been alone in the office since eight-forty-two.

This was when she worked best. She knew this about herself the way she knew which hotels had good coffee makers and which Vatican officials were lying — through accumulated experience, without sentimentality.

Mateo's documentation was thorough. Five institutions in Germany and Austria that still practiced the Franciscan binding knot as part of active liturgical and archival training. Four of them were monasteries with closed communities — no external scholars, no visiting lectureships, no connection to the academic conference world in which Dr. Heinrich Paulus operated. The fifth was a graduate program in theological paleography at the University of Tübingen.

Tübingen. Again.

She added this to the document she had titled Paulus, H. — Consistencies and wrote Tübingen (3) beside the new entry. The ink formulation. The Leonine citation apparatus. The Franciscan knot. Three separate pieces of evidence pointing at the same German university. None of them individually sufficient. All of them together beginning to constitute something she could defend in a briefing room.

She was reaching for her phone when it rang.

Mateo.

"The seminary record," he said. He sounded like a person who had been on the phone for several hours and had found what they were looking for at the end of them. "Marco Voss was removed from seminary eight years ago for a formal complaint filed by a senior faculty member."

"What kind of complaint?"

"Theft." A pause. "He removed two manuscripts from the seminary library without authorization. He claimed he was borrowing them for research. The faculty member claimed the manuscripts were returned damaged. The seminary's determination was that Marco had exercised insufficient care with materials entrusted to him."

"That's the official record."

"The unofficial record is that the faculty member who filed the complaint was a personal friend of Cardinal Voss. And that the manuscripts Marco had borrowed were, by every independent account, returned in the same condition he had taken them. And that the real reason for the complaint was a theological paper Marco had written criticizing the Cardinal's position on a specific matter of Church doctrine." Another pause. "The Cardinal had his nephew removed from seminary for writing a paper that disagreed with him."

She sat with this for a moment.

The refusal to be known truly. The self constructed so completely that disagreement from a nephew could not be tolerated. Pride that could not permit a family member to hold a different theological position in print. Augustine's diagnosis, lived in intimate miniature within a family.

"Marco knew," she said. "About his uncle's specific psychology. Better than anyone."

"He'd been living inside it his entire life," Mateo said. "Which makes him a more plausible suspect for understanding the sin well enough to stage it. And a more plausible victim of a frame built by someone who researched the Cardinal's biography and found the nephew waiting there, perfectly positioned."

"Both things are true," she said.

"Both things are true," he agreed.

She worked through the night.

Not because the case required it — she had twelve hours remaining before the diplomatic clock ran out and she needed sleep before she could use twelve hours effectively. She worked through the night because the case was in that specific state of near-resolution where stopping felt like a form of abandonment.

She built two parallel documents. The first: the case against Marco Voss. Motive documented. No alibi. Theological knowledge consistent with the staging. Presence in Rome confirmed. The Bernini text. The laptop search history, which digital forensics had returned that evening and which showed seven searches for the Borghese Gallery across the preceding week, five of them for the Bernini room specifically.

Seven searches. Five for the Bernini room.

She looked at this for a long time.

A person planning a murder did research their location. But a person who had already been to the Borghese Gallery — who had stood in the Bernini room and knew it precisely — did not need to search it five times in a week. You searched what you didn't know. You searched what required verification. Five searches for a room you'd already been in suggested you were learning something about the room for the first time.

Or it suggested that someone who knew you had not been to the Borghese had searched from your laptop to ensure you would appear to have been.

She opened the second document. The case against Paulus, H. She wrote: access to laptop? and underlined it.

A person who had studied Cardinal Voss for years — who knew his family, his history, his nephew's seminary dismissal — would know what a frame for Marco Voss needed to contain. Seven gallery searches on a laptop. Theological texts on a shelf. A Bernini book. All of these were acquirable. All of them were the work of a person who understood what evidence looked like rather than a person who had committed a crime and left evidence accidentally.

Evidence left accidentally was always imperfect. It was always incomplete. It always contained the gaps of a mind that had been focused on something other than how it would appear.

The evidence against Marco Voss was complete. It was coherent. It contained no gaps.

It was the evidence of a person who had thought carefully about what evidence needed to be there.

She wrote this in the second document and looked at it and then looked at the first document and then looked at the clock. 2:47am. Rome outside the window was doing its deep-night things, the sounds reduced to the occasional vehicle and the specific silence of a very old city that had learned to be quiet in the dark.

She needed something that connected Paulus to the apartment in Trastevere. Something that placed him in proximity to Marco Voss. Something procedural enough to protect from a Vatican liaison with twenty-three years of diplomatic training.

She picked up her phone. She did not call Mateo because it was 2:47am and because she had already asked him for enough tonight and because she did not want to examine what it meant that calling him at 2:47am was the thing she was stopping herself from doing.

She put the phone down.

She looked at the conference registry. Four hundred and eleven names. Eleven pages. She had been through it three times.

She went through it a fourth time. Not looking for Paulus. Looking for anyone who appeared on the registry who also had a documented connection to Trastevere.

On the ninth page, in the section listing institutional affiliations, she found it.

Not Paulus. Someone else.

A graduate student from the Tübingen theological paleography program — the program that taught the Franciscan knot — who had attended the conference as a junior delegate and who had listed, in the participant information form, a Rome accommodation address.

Via della Lungara. Trastevere.

She checked the address number. She checked it again.

It was four doors from Marco Voss's building.

She sat very still for a moment. Then she wrote two things. A name: the graduate student's. And a question: who referred him to that address?

She looked at the question for a long time.

Then she picked up her phone.

It was 2:47am and she had eleven hours remaining and she was calling Mateo and she was not examining why this felt like the correct decision.

He answered before the second ring.

"I found a connection," she said.

"I know," he said. She could hear in his voice that he had not been asleep. "I found the same one fifteen minutes ago. I was deciding whether to call you."

She looked at the clock. 2:47am.

"And?" she said.

A pause. Brief. The pause of a man who had made a decision and was implementing it.

"And I called you," he said.

She stayed on the line.

She did not often stay on the line after a professional exchange had concluded. She ended calls when they were finished. This was not finished.

"You called me," she said. "At midnight. From the seminary record."

"I did." His voice was quiet. Rome behind him still — she could hear it through whatever window he had open, the city continuing its nocturnal arrangements. "You were working."

"I'm always working."

"I know." A pause. Not the pause of someone choosing words. The pause of someone choosing whether to say what they had been thinking. "What were you working on?"

She looked at her desk. The four hundred names. The three confirmations. The Tübingen thread she had pulled until it was a rope. "The pattern," she said. "I was sitting with the pattern."

"And?"

"It holds." She turned her chair slightly toward the window. The Roman night outside was doing what Roman nights did — continuing. "He's precise. He's deliberate. Every element of the staging is functional — nothing decorative for its own sake, nothing theatrical beyond what the argument requires. The Bernini wasn't chosen for drama. It was chosen because it is the exact right image for what he was saying about the Cardinal."

"The reaching hand," Mateo said.

"He was saying: this man reached for what he could not hold and in the reaching destroyed what he thought he was holding." She paused. This was more than she usually said on a working call. She noted this. She did not examine it. "He made a theological argument in marble and silk and one Latin word."

"He made it for a reader."

"Yes."

"Do you think—" He stopped. Started again. "Do you think he expected someone who could read it, or someone who would be capable of reading it after being given the tools?"

She considered this. The distinction was precise. A reader who already had the apparatus versus a reader who could acquire it. The difference between a message left for a colleague and a message left for someone you were — educating.

"The second," she said. "He left the tools. The parchment, the Leonine citation, the Franciscan knot — each one points to the tradition. He expected someone who could follow the pointing."

"A good student."

"Or the right one." She looked at the window. "He's not finished. This is a first lesson."

"I know." Something in Mateo's voice. Not quite tiredness. The specific quality of a man who had been thinking about this for the same number of hours she had and had arrived at the same place from a different direction. "The Avaritia sketch in the curriculum notes. He's already prepared the next argument."

"Venice."

"Venice." A breath. "Sonya."

She waited. The quality of the silence before her name was different from the professional silence. She had been cataloguing these differences for five days without deciding what to do with the catalogue.

"Yes," she said.

"Get some sleep." He said it simply. Without the inflection that would have made it something other than what it was. "The bibliography will be there in the morning. The seminary records will be there. Heer's travel documentation will be there. All of it will still be there."

"I know."

"You've been at this for—"

"Eleven days since the murder. Nine since I arrived in Rome." She looked at the case file. "I know how long."

"Then you know you can stop for six hours without losing anything."

She did not answer immediately. This was also a catalogued thing — the specific experience of being told to stop by someone whose opinion of stopping she had come to weight more than she had expected to.

"Good night, Mateo," she said.

"Good night." A pause. "Good work tonight. The Tübingen connection — that was yours."

She ended the call. She sat for another four minutes at the desk, not working, which was unusual. Then she packed the case file into the carry-on and stood and turned off the desk lamp and walked to the temporary apartment.

She thought about the registry. She thought about the seminary connection and the Franciscan knot and Tobias Heer on a plane to Germany the morning after a murder he was not scheduled to leave for.

She thought, briefly, about the quality of Mateo's voice at midnight saying *good work*.

She did not stay with this thought.

She went to bed. She lay in the dark and thought about patterns and readers and the specific patience of a man who had built an intellectual architecture and was, she was now certain, taking considerable pleasure in watching someone navigate it.

She thought: he underestimated me. Or he estimated me correctly and is counting on it.

She did not know yet which.

She slept.

She held the phone for a moment after ending the call.

The Rome liaison had gone home. The Interpol office was quiet. Outside the window Rome was doing its late things — the specific low-volume city sounds of a place that had been conducting its nighttime arrangements since before most civilizations had invented the concept of nighttime.

She had been awake for nineteen hours. This was not unusual. She had a threshold of approximately twenty-two hours before the quality of her investigative thinking began to degrade in ways she could detect, and she was within the threshold, and the Franciscan knot documentation and the Tübingen third connection were sufficiently important to justify the remaining three hours.

She also knew she was not going to sleep immediately even when she lay down, because the case was at that specific point in its architecture where the next connection was visible in outline — she could feel the shape of it, the way you felt the outline of a word you knew but couldn't immediately retrieve. The shape was: Heer was not accidental. Heer's accommodation adjacency to Voss was not a coincidence processed by a defective conference housing algorithm.

She wrote: *Investigate accommodation booking mechanism — who entered what data and when.*

She looked at the note. She added: *Check if Heer's academic record shows any prior connection to Paulus's published work or conference appearances.*

She put the notebook down. She made the fourth coffee of the evening. She sat in the quiet of the temporary office and held the shape of the almost-word and waited for it to arrive.

She was working.

Chapter 10

The Arche of Everything

The graduate student's name was Tobias Heer.

Twenty-six years old. Enrolled in the theological paleography program at the University of Tübingen since the previous autumn. His supervisor: a full professor in the department of medieval theological studies whose name appeared, when she looked it up, in the acknowledgments section of three of Paulus's eleven published papers.

She wrote this down. The connection between Paulus and Tübingen was no longer circumstantial. It was direct, documented, and navigable. Paulus had been in active professional contact with this university for at least the duration of those three papers. His former supervisor was now supervising a graduate student who had been staying four doors from the Cardinal's nephew at the time of the murder.

She called Mateo at 3:14am. He answered on the first ring again and she noted this without examining it.

"Tobias Heer," she said.

"I found him twenty minutes ago," Mateo said. "He flew back to Germany the morning after the murder. His conference registration shows he was scheduled to stay three more days."

She processed this. A graduate student who left Rome the morning after a murder he was not scheduled to leave for three more days.

"He ran," she said.

"Or he was told to leave." Mateo's voice had the quality it had when he was assembling something in real time. "Heer isn't the killer. He's too young, too junior. But if Paulus sent him to Rome for a specific purpose —"

"To be near the nephew," she said. "To access the apartment."

"Four doors away in a city of three million people is not coincidence."

"No." She looked at the clock. 3:16am. "I need to reach Heer before Tübingen knows we're looking."

"I have a contact at the university's theology faculty. Not Paulus's circle. Someone who has reason to be cautious about Paulus."

"What kind of reason?"

A pause. The specific pause of a man deciding how much of a private conversation to translate into professional information. "The kind that involves a stolen methodology and a publication that should have had a different author."

She was very still.

A stolen methodology. Paulus had written, in his developmental arc bible she was only now beginning to read correctly, about the wrong done to him by a peer who stole his work. She had read this as professional injury. She was reading it differently now.

"This contact," she said carefully. "They know Paulus personally."

"Very well. From before the work was stolen." Mateo's voice was flat in the way it was flat when he was speaking about something that carried personal weight. "He's been cautious about sharing this. He has a career and Paulus has connections. But if I tell him what we're looking at—"

"Don't tell him what we're looking at. Not yet. Find out if Heer was placed in that Trastevere apartment by someone connected to Paulus. That's all I need right now."

"Give me an hour."

She gave him an hour. She spent it building the procedural document, organizing everything she had into the form that would survive contact with Hale and the Vatican liaison and the institutional pressure that had been building since the first morning. Prima lectio. Tübingen. The knot. The ink. The Tübingen graduate student four doors from Marco Voss.

At 4:23am Mateo called back.

"Heer was placed there," he said. "By an academic accommodation service that Paulus uses regularly for visiting scholars and graduate students. The apartment is one of six he has standing arrangements with in Rome. My contact confirmed it."

She wrote this down. Her hand was steady. She was aware of it being steady the way she was aware of things that required steadiness.

"Heer was Paulus's eyes," she said.

"And his hands, possibly. He had four doors of access and three days of proximity to establish what needed to be established in that apartment."

She had enough. Not for a conviction. Not even for an arrest. But enough to build from. Enough to protect from the Vatican liaison. Enough to take to Hale and make the case that this investigation needed to look in a different direction than the one it was currently looking in.

"Mateo."

"Yes."

"Get some sleep."

A beat. Something in the quality of the silence that she recognized as a person receiving care from a direction they had not expected it.

"You as well," he said.

She ended the call. She closed her laptop. She looked at the Rome outside the office window — still dark, still ancient, still keeping its counsel. Somewhere in this city or already on a train out of it, a man had labelled his own first lesson and was already planning the curriculum for the second.

She had nine hours.

She had a name, a university, a graduate student, an accommodation service, and three pieces of physical evidence from a crime scene that together pointed at a scholar whose published work had provided the methodology for a murder before the murder existed.

She went back to the hotel. She set an alarm for seven. She lay down in her clothes.

She did not think about 2:47am and a phone that had been answered before the second ring.

She went through the list one more time.

Three connections between Paulus and Tübingen. The ink formulation from the Franciscan binding tradition. The Leonine citation apparatus in his published footnotes. The acknowledgment chain that placed him in documented correspondence with Hardt across four decades. And now Tobias Heer — a graduate student enrolled in Hardt's program, placed four doors from Marco Voss, who had left Rome the morning after the murder on a schedule he had changed by three days.

It was not enough for the warrant. It was enough for the morning briefing.

She opened her laptop and began drafting the briefing document. The professional register came easily at 3am — she had written more briefings in the early hours than she had in working hours, because the early hours had the specific quality of forcing the language into its essential shape. Nothing performative. No institutional hedging. The thing, stated.

She wrote for forty minutes. She was precise. She did not name Paulus in the briefing document — she named the pattern and left the name to follow the evidence, which was how evidence was supposed to work and how it would need to work when this reached a prosecutor. She wrote around the architectural conclusion the same way a structural engineer wrote around a load-bearing wall — acknowledging it, accommodating it, making the rest of the structure legible by reference to it.

She saved the document. She sent it to Hale's deputy for the morning review.

Then she sat for a moment in the quiet of the temporary office and thought about nothing in particular, which was what she did when she had been working very hard for a long time and the work had reached a resting point. The office was empty. Rome outside was doing what Rome did at 3am. The coffee she had made three hours ago was cold.

She thought about the phone call. The specific quality of Mateo's voice at midnight saying the seminary record. The sound of a person who had been awake for the same number of hours she had and had arrived somewhere at the end of them and was calling because calling her was the right thing to do with the arrival.

She had not examined this. She would not examine it now.

She did not think about it for exactly the amount of time it took her to fall asleep, which was less than she expected.

She called Mateo at 3:16am with Tobias Heer's name.

He answered on the first ring for the third consecutive night and she noted this the same way she noted everything she was not examining — carefully, in a file she was not yet reading.

"He ran," she said. "Or he was sent."

"More likely sent." Mateo's voice had the quality of a man who had been awake for this conversation. Not surprised by the call. Prepared for it. "Heer's not the principal. He's junior, he's twenty-six, he's three semesters into a graduate program. He doesn't have the publication record, the standing, or the three decades of accumulated resentment required to stage what was staged in that gallery."

"Then what was he for?"

"Witness. Insurance. Someone who could be recalled later to confirm a specific timeline, or someone who could be used as additional misdirection if the nephew wasn't sufficient." A pause. She heard him moving — the specific sound of a person reaching for something, a notebook, a phone. "Or someone who was simply useful in the city for a purpose we haven't identified yet."

"Such as."

"Delivery. Documentation. A second pair of hands for something that required a second pair of hands at a specific hour." Another pause. This one different — the thoughtful kind. "The parchment was prepared. The knot was tied. The vellum was sourced and aged and inscribed before the murder. All of that was done somewhere — not in the gallery, not in the hotel room. Paulus needed space and time. Heer could have provided cover. Or accommodation. Or both."

She wrote: *Heer — logistics, not staging. Investigate accommodation — any booking in Paulus's name or adjacent.*

"The graduate student's supervisor," she said. "At Tübingen. His name appeared in Paulus's acknowledgments."

"Professor Wilhelm Hardt. Medieval theological studies. I looked him up an hour ago." Mateo had a quality when he was ahead of the conversation — not performed, not strategic, simply the natural result of thinking in parallel tracks. "Hardt and Paulus were at Tübingen simultaneously in the early 1980s. Hardt as an early-career lecturer, Paulus as a graduate student. Forty years of professional proximity. The acknowledgments in Paulus's papers run across three decades — Hardt's name appears in six of the eleven."

"He's not just a former supervisor," she said.

"He's a collaborator. Or the closest thing Paulus has to one."

She thought about this. The specific loneliness of a man who had spent forty years building a private intellectual framework. The acknowledgments — not a list of peers but a list of one sustained relationship. Forty years of a single collaboration, quiet enough to leave only a trace in the footnotes of published papers.

"Hardt knows what Paulus was building," she said.

"Hardt may know everything."

"Can you reach him?"

"Not without going through official channels, which will flag Tübingen before we're ready for Tübingen to be flagged." He paused. "But I have a contact at the university. An academic journalist I worked with in 2018. She has access to the faculty common rooms and a history of people telling her things they've decided in retrospect they shouldn't have told her."

"Is she discreet?"

"She's German. She's discreet until she's published."

"Then don't give her anything she can publish."

"Never do." A brief pause. "Sonya. The Tübingen thread — if Hardt is actively aware of what Paulus was doing, this stops being a lone actor case and starts being something more institutional."

She had thought about this. She had been thinking about it since she wrote the third Tübingen connection in her document and sat with the implications. "Or it starts being the specific kind of intellectual complicity that is never prosecutable," she said. "A mentor who knows his student has built a dangerous architecture and does not act."

"Not the killer. Not innocent."

"No." She looked at the window. Dawn was still three hours away. The Via Margutta outside was quiet in the specific way of Roman streets between 3 and 5am. "Reach your contact. Carefully. And I need the full accommodation records for Heer in Rome — every booking in the conference window. Cross-reference with Paulus's known residence here. I want to know if they were ever in the same building."

"I'll have it by morning."

"I know you will."

A beat. She heard him about to say something and not say it. She did not ask what it was. She ended the call and sat in the dark of the temporary apartment for a moment, not working, simply sitting, which was unusual enough at this hour that she noticed it.

She was tired. Not in the professional sense — she had been tired in the professional sense for eleven days and had managed it. This was the other kind. The kind that was not about sleep.

She thought about Mateo three hours away in his hotel room, also not sleeping, working through the same architecture from a different angle. The journalist's mind finding narrative where she found pattern. Both of them building toward the same center from different directions.

She thought about the center.

She did not think about the quality of his voice at 3am saying *I'll have it by morning.* She did not think about the specific texture of certainty in it — the certainty not of a man who was sure of the evidence but of a man who was sure he would not leave her without the thing she needed.

She did not think about this for exactly the amount of time it took her to fall asleep, which was less than she expected.

Chapter 11

Nineteen Names, Four Scholars, One Satchel

She briefed Hale at eight.

Not the full picture. You never gave Hale the full picture at once — it produced either panic or the specific institutional overcorrection of a man who believed the solution to a complicated problem was a committee. You gave Hale what he needed to authorize the next step. You kept the architecture to yourself until the architecture was solid enough to survive his response to it.

She gave him: physical evidence inconsistencies suggesting the primary suspect was a frame rather than the perpetrator. Academic connections between the crime scene staging and a conference attendee whose published work predated the methodology of the murder. A Tübingen connection across three independent evidence streams. A graduate student placed in proximity to the framed suspect by an accommodation arrangement traceable to the conference attendee.

She did not give him: Paulus's name. Not yet. A name required evidence she could defend. What she had was a pattern she could defend. The name would follow the pattern.

Hale was quiet for forty-two seconds. She counted.

"You have eight hours," he said.

"Twelve."

"Ten. And I need something I can take to the Vatican liaison that explains why we are expanding the investigation rather than closing it against the nephew."

"You'll have it."

She ended the call. She went to find Mateo.

He was already at the café.

Not the one near the Interpol office. A different one, smaller, on a side street she had not been to before. He had found it the way he found everything — by moving through the city with the specific attentiveness of a person who was always looking for the next useful thing. The coffee was better than any she'd had in three days. She did not ask how he knew.

They worked through the morning at a table in the back. Her laptop. His notebook. The conference registry printed in full and divided between them, each working a different section. She had the institutional affiliations. He had the publication records. They were looking for anyone in the four-hundred-and-eleven-name registry whose work intersected with Paulus's in ways that were more than collegial.

The assumption: Paulus had been at this conference specifically. He had chosen this week in Rome for reasons beyond the academic program. He had used the conference as cover — legitimate presence, institutional credential, the specific invisibility of a scholar among scholars. If he had been in contact with anyone at the conference in connection with what happened at the Borghese, there might be a trace.

At ten-forty she found it.

Not in the publication records. In the institutional affiliations. A name she recognized from Mateo's Tübingen documentation — the full professor who supervised Tobias Heer and appeared in the acknowledgments of three Paulus papers. He had attended the conference. He had been registered at the same hotel as Paulus. His check-in and check-out dates overlapped with Paulus's by four days.

She showed Mateo.

He looked at it for a moment. Then he looked at her.

"The supervisor," he said. "Heer's supervisor. Who placed Heer in the Trastevere apartment through Paulus's accommodation service."

"Same hotel. Four days of overlap."

"They were coordinating," Mateo said.

"They were coordinating," she confirmed.

She photographed the registry page. She sent it to the secure document file she had opened for this investigation. She added it to the procedural document under: Paulus — Confirmed Roman Contacts.

The case was building. Slowly, piece by piece, with the specific momentum of an investigation that had found the right thread and was following it with sufficient patience.

She looked at her watch. Eleven-fifteen. Eight hours and forty-five minutes remaining.

Across the table Mateo was writing. He wrote the way he did everything — with full attention, without apparent self-consciousness, the pen moving in the small precise handwriting she could now read upside down as fluently as she read her own. He had ordered more coffee at some point without interrupting the work and there was a cup beside her that she had not asked for and had drunk without noticing she was drinking it. She noticed this now.

She noticed it and did not examine it.

"We need the Paulus itinerary," she said. "His movements in Rome the week before the murder. Hotel records, credit card records, any documented presence at locations relevant to the case."

"I can't get hotel records officially," he said.

"I can." She was already typing the request. "But it'll take four hours to come back through proper channels. I need something faster."

He looked up from the notebook. The expression she was beginning to recognize as the one that preceded a contact she was not going to ask about.

"The Hotel Santa Chiara," he said. "That's where the conference accommodation block was. I know the front desk manager. He's been in Rome since 2009 and he owes me a conversation from 2017 that I've never collected."

"Collect it," she said.

He stood up. He picked up the satchel. He paused at the table.

"The coffee," he said. "Is it all right?"

She looked at the cup. She looked at him.

"It's the best coffee I've had in Rome," she said. She said it as a fact, which it was, not as gratitude, which it also was.

He nodded once. He left.

She watched him go with the specific quality of attention she had been applying to him for three days and had been calling professional assessment.

She was also doing something she had not done in this investigation before: she was noting the way she was working.

Not the method — the method was professional and reliable and she was executing it correctly. She was noting the texture of it. The specific experience of working at a table in a back-corner café with Mateo across from her, the conference registry divided between them, the morning light through the window catching the condensation on the coffee cups. She was noting the ease of it. The absence of friction she had not known she had been carrying.

She had worked with partners before. SIC was not a solitary posting — she had worked cases with the Rome liaison, with Hale's deputies, with the forensics teams, with the various institutional contacts the investigation required. She was good with partners in the professional sense. She managed the shared work clearly, communicated what was necessary, maintained the appropriate professional boundaries that kept the work clean.

This was not that.

She and Mateo were not partners in the institutional sense. He had no Interpol appointment. He had no formal role in the investigation. He was a journalist she had admitted into the working space of an active case because his specific intelligence had been demonstrably useful and because Commander Hale had sanctioned the collaboration with the specific reluctance of a man who had decided useful was useful.

She had been using him the way she used any useful thing. That was the professional version of what was happening.

She was now aware that the professional version was not the only version.

She returned to the registry. She was looking for three things: the remaining conference attendees with Tübingen connections, any institutional overlap between their names and Hardt's publication acknowledgments, and the specific subset of the academic world that would have been familiar with both the Leonine citation apparatus and the Franciscan binding tradition.

It was methodical work. She was good at it. She did it with the complete professional attention she gave to everything that mattered.

She was also, in the portion of her attention that was not the registry, aware of him across the table from her.

She noted this. She filed it. She was working.

She returned to the registry.

She was working.

She was working and she was also aware that she was working in a way she had not been aware of for the previous eleven days.

This was new. This was the third occurrence of something she had been noting without cataloguing — the specific awareness, during the professional task, of herself performing the professional task. The intrusion of the observer into the observed.

She had spent her career inside the investigative mind — not watching it from the outside but occupying it from the inside, which meant there was no gap between the doing and the being. She was not a detective who happened to be doing detective work. She was the work. The distinction between the professional self and the other self had always been, for her, largely theoretical.

The theoretical was becoming practical.

She looked at the conference registry. Four hundred and eleven names. She and Mateo had narrowed them to three. She had narrowed the three to one. She was now building the evidential architecture around the one, and she was doing it well, and she was also, simultaneously, aware of a sensation in the vicinity of her sternum that had nothing to do with the conference registry.

She filed it. She returned to the registry.

Mateo arrived at the café at 9:47am with the Lateran contact's documentation under his arm — printed, not digital, the choice of a man who understood that some sources preferred their contributions to be as deniable as possible. He set it on the table and sat and looked at her across the coffee cups with the specific quality of attention she had now, reluctantly, acknowledged she had been thinking about at 3am.

"The Leonine apparatus," he said without preamble. He opened the documentation to a tabbed page. "Papers one through five — published between 1982 and 1997. Every footnote is in the modern system. No deviation. Clean break from Tübingen from his very first post-doctoral publication."

"And six through eleven."

"Same. Forty years of publications. Zero Leonine citations. Not one." He turned a page. "Until the monograph."

She looked at the page he had turned to. The monograph was the unpublished one — not the two that had appeared in academic press, but a private document, a working manuscript that had been circulating in limited form among a small number of scholars for the past decade. The Lateran contact had obtained a copy through a chain of academic provenance that Mateo had declined to specify and she had declined to ask about.

The title: *The Architecture of Moral Consequence: A Diagnostic Framework for Sin as Self-Knowledge.*

She read the first paragraph. Then she went back and read it again.

The Leonine apparatus was present from the first footnote. Every citation in the monograph was in the Tübingen tradition — the system he had publicly abandoned in 1982 and privately maintained for the entire forty years since. The monograph was written in a different voice than the published papers. Not the careful, institutional voice of peer-reviewed scholarship. Something older. Something that sounded like a man speaking to someone he trusted not to use it against him.

"He wrote this for a reader," she said.

"Not for publication."

"For the work." She looked at the title again. *Diagnostic framework for sin as self-knowledge.* "This isn't an academic paper. This is a methodology. He's describing how to do something."

"How to select a subject," Mateo said quietly. He had read it too. She could see it in the quality of his stillness. "How to identify a person whose sin is their most accurate self-portrait. How to make that portrait visible to them."

She sat with this for a long time.

The conference registry was open beside her. The four hundred and eleven names. The three. The one. And now, in a forty-page private monograph written in a dead footnote system, the intellectual architecture of what he had done in the Borghese Gallery and what he was preparing to do again.

"He's been preparing this for decades," she said.

"The monograph is dated 2009. But there are earlier draft references — he mentions working notes from 1994, from 2001. The thinking has been accumulating for thirty years at least."

She thought about Marco Voss in his Trastevere apartment. About the Cardinal arranged before the Bernini. About the specific patience of a man who had been building toward something for three decades and had waited until every element of the architecture was ready.

"He's not done," she said.

"He was never planning to be done with one." Mateo's voice was careful. "The monograph describes a curriculum. Not a single lesson. A progression."

She looked at him.

"Seven," she said.

He said nothing. He did not need to.

She returned to the registry. She was working. She was also aware, in the specific new way she had been aware of herself for three days now, of the man across the table from her reading the same forty-page document and arriving at the same conclusions from the same evidence and saying nothing that needed to be said because she was already thinking it.

She noted this. She filed it beside the other thing she was not reading.

She returned to the registry.

She was working.

She was working.

She was also, in the portion of her mind that ran below the working, thinking about the methodology.

Not Paulus's methodology. Her own. She had spent fifteen days investigating a crime that was itself an investigation — a man who had applied the tools of academic research to the selection and staging of a murder, who had built the case for his argument with the same patience and rigor that she applied to building cases for prosecution. He had read the literature. He had developed a framework. He had identified his subject. He had constructed an evidentiary record of the subject's sin expression. He had staged the demonstration.

This was her job. Except for the staging. This was, in every other respect, exactly what she did.

She had been aware of this since the first morning. She had been aware of it in the way she was aware of things she was not examining — in the body before the mind, as a physical fact before a considered one. She had been examining it now, in the back corner of a Rome café with Mateo across the table, for approximately three minutes.

She had built her career on the methodology of reading rooms. She had built it on the specific intelligence that understood a scene not just as a collection of evidence but as an argument — as something made by someone for a reason. She had been doing this since she was twenty-three and had stood in her first crime scene and had felt, before she had the vocabulary for it, that the room was speaking.

Paulus had been doing the same thing. In the opposite direction.

She was not alarmed by this similarity. She had worked with dark mirrors before — had encountered perpetrators whose intelligence rhymed with hers, whose methodology was a distorted version of what she did. She had used those rhymes to solve cases. She had used them the way you used all evidence: instrumentally, in service of the investigation.

She was using this one.

But she was also aware — in the new specific way she had been aware of things since Mateo had said *you have built a very efficient machinery* — that the parallel was closer than usual. That the man she was looking for had not just used a similar methodology but had built a framework that described, in its negative space, something about how she saw the world.

The monograph. *The Architecture of Moral Consequence.* She had read it four times. Each time she had found something she recognized. Not in the crimes — in the framework. The argument that sin was always self-revealing, that the specific form a person's sin took was the most accurate portrait of their interior life, that you could read a person's deepest truth through the specific shape of their moral failure.

She believed this. She had believed it for twelve years without naming it.

She noted this. She filed it. She returned to the registry.

She was working.

Chapter 12

The Second Lesson Begins

At two-seventeen in the afternoon, the second lesson began.

It began not in the Borghese Gallery but in the Vatican gardens — a quieter place, a more private place, a place that communicated something about what the second lesson was and was not. The Borghese Gallery had been chosen for its public argument: a Bernini visible to thousands of visitors each year, a staging that would be seen. The Vatican gardens were chosen for the opposite reason.

The Vatican gardens were chosen because they were interior. Because what happened there happened inside the institution itself.

Because the second lesson was not about pride viewed from without. It was about what pride looked like from within its own walls.

Chiara Moretti — twenty-five, archival pass, dark hair, the woman who had pressed a folded note into Sonya's palm at the end of eleven useless interviews — was found on a bench near the Ethiopian College at two-seventeen in the afternoon, unconscious, breathing steadily, no visible injury. She had been there, by the estimation of the grounds staff who found her, for approximately forty minutes.

In her coat pocket: a square of aged vellum.

Not a full parchment. A fragment — torn, deliberately, from a larger piece. A single Greek letter written in iron gall ink in the same small precise hand as the prima lectio annotation on the original parchment.

Alpha.

The beginning. The first.

Sonya was at the Hotel Santa Chiara waiting for Mateo's hotel manager contact when the call came from the Vatican security office. She was there in eleven minutes. The Vatican allowed this with the specific minimal grace of an institution that understood it no longer had the option of not allowing it.

Chiara was awake by the time Sonya arrived. Seated on the bench still, a Vatican medical officer beside her, a glass of water in her hand that she was holding without drinking. She looked at Sonya with the expression of a person who had done something deliberate and was facing the consequences of it with their eyes open.

Sonya sat beside her. She did not produce her identification. She did not produce her notebook. She simply sat, at the distance of a person who was not pressing, and waited.

"I saw him," Chiara said. Her voice was steady. The steadiness of someone who had been afraid and had decided not to be afraid anymore, which was a different kind of steadiness than the kind that had never been tested.

"Where?"

"The gardens. He was near the Ethiopian College. He was not moving quickly. He was not running. He walked through the gardens the way a person walks through a place they know." She paused. "A person who knew the gardens. I thought he was a staff member or a visitor with special access. Then I realized he was leaving."

"Leaving the gardens."

"Leaving through a gate in the northern wall that should require a specific key. He had the key. Or he had something that worked like one." She looked at her hands. "I followed him to the gate. He was already through it. But I saw his face."

Sonya kept her voice exactly level. "Describe him."

"Sixty. Perhaps sixty-five. Silver hair, short. A dark jacket. Academic bearing — the way certain professors carry themselves. As if everything they move through is a seminar room." She paused again. "He saw me see him. He did not run. He looked at me for a moment."

Sonya waited.

"He smiled," Chiara said. "The way you smile at a student who has asked an interesting question. As if I had done something that pleased him. Then he went through the gate and I —" She stopped. "I don't remember anything after that."

The sedative. Forensics would confirm it — a mild compound, fast-acting, administered by contact rather than injection. The pocket of her coat, which she had worn to the garden because the afternoon was cold. Something pressed into the fabric.

He had known she followed him. He had waited for her to get close enough.

He had smiled at her.

Sonya sat with this in the specific way she sat with things that required a moment before they could be processed and moved past. The smile of a teacher at a student who had asked an interesting question. Chiara Moretti had asked the interesting question of following him, and he had found this pleasing, and he had left her with a fragment of vellum in her pocket as if it were a grade.

He was not hiding from the investigation. He was watching it. The briefing room. The gardens. The prima lectio annotation. The alpha fragment.

He was teaching it.

She called Mateo from the Vatican grounds, walking fast toward the northern wall gate.

"He was here," she said when Mateo answered. "In the Vatican gardens. Two hours ago. He has access to the grounds."

A silence. The particular silence of a man for whom something has just shifted. "The alpha fragment."

"You knew about the fragment."

"I guessed about the fragment. Alpha — the beginning. He's labelling the sequence. Prima lectio on the first parchment, alpha on the second. He's not just teaching the sins. He's teaching the course. Numbered. Annotated. Meant to be followed."

She stopped walking. She was at the northern wall. The gate was a heavy wooden door set into old stone, inconspicuous, the kind of thing you did not notice if you were not looking for it. The lock was modern. Recently updated, like Marco Voss's apartment door.

He had access to things that required specific keys. He had been preparing this for longer than the conference week. Longer than the acquisition of the vellum and the ink. He had been preparing the access. The positions. The sight lines. He had been in Rome before, multiple times, learning its institutional geography the way he had learned the Cardinal's personal geography.

Years.

"Mateo."

"Yes."

"He's not in Rome anymore."

A pause. "How do you know?"

"Because the alpha fragment means the first lesson is complete. He labelled it finished. He doesn't stay after the lesson ends." She looked at the gate. The old stone wall. The new lock. "He's already gone. He's been gone since the gardens."

"The hotel records," Mateo said. She heard him moving. The specific sound of a man who had been sitting and was now standing with purpose. "I'll call you from the Santa Chiara."

"Go."

She stood at the gate in the northern wall of the Vatican for a moment. The afternoon was cooling. Rome beyond the wall was conducting its ordinary business with its ordinary indifference. A man had stood at this gate two hours ago and smiled at a young woman who had followed him and then put her to sleep and left her on a bench with an alpha fragment in her pocket as if it were a grade.

The smile of a teacher at a student who has asked an interesting question.

She thought about what it meant that she understood that smile. That she had read it correctly from Chiara's description without a moment of interpretation required.

She did not stay with this thought long enough to finish it.

She had seven hours. She walked.

She walked south along the Via Veneto.

The seven hours were not a gift. Hale had given her ten and taken two for the Vatican liaison briefing and given her what remained, which was operational rather than generous. She walked because walking was the only form of rest she allowed herself during an active case — the body moving while the mind moved differently, the specific quality of Roman streets providing a texture that the interior of an Interpol temporary office could not.

She thought about Chiara Moretti.

Twenty-five. Three years in the Vatican archives. Sedated in the Vatican gardens with a substance that left no lasting trace, which meant the substance had been chosen for exactly that quality by someone who knew what to choose. She had recovered fully, which also meant the substance had been administered in a precise dose by someone who intended her to recover.

The lesson was not about Chiara. Chiara was an interruption.

Or — she stopped at a café, ordered an espresso, stood at the bar the way Romans stood at bars: quickly, with the focus of someone who had somewhere else to be — Chiara was a message. Not the lesson itself. A note in the margin of the lesson. Look here. This is what happens inside the institution when the institution protects itself.

The Cardinal had blocked the Tübingen consortium's access to Vatican archival documents five years ago. Chiara Moretti was a Vatican archivist. The sedation had happened in the Vatican gardens while Chiara was, according to her own account, reviewing a file request that had come in two days prior — a request she had flagged as unusual and had intended to escalate to her supervisor.

She had not yet escalated it when she lost consciousness.

The file request had been for documents relating to a 1972 Vatican council correspondence. The specific correspondence the Tübingen consortium had been blocked from accessing five years ago.

Sonya set down the espresso and left the bar and walked.

Someone had been inside the Vatican archives, inside the institutional machinery, and had removed a file request before Chiara could escalate it. Not Paulus — he was on a plane to

Frankfurt. Someone who was still in Rome. Someone who had access to the Vatican archival system.

She called Mateo.

"Chiara Moretti's file request," she said. "The one she flagged. I need the request number and I need to know what happened to it after she lost consciousness."

"I can reach Father Schäfer's office through the liaison—"

"Don't. Go around Schäfer. He's protecting something — I don't know what yet. Use the archivist channel from the Lateran contact. Someone in the Vatican archival division will know what happened to a flagged file request from three days ago."

"Give me an hour."

"Forty minutes."

She walked. She went through the Pincian Hill gardens, then down into the Piazza del Popolo and across the Tiber on the Ponte della Musica, and she thought about an institution that protected itself across centuries by the simple method of burying what it chose not to know.

The Cardinal had buried the Tübingen consortium's request. He had used the institutional machinery of the Vatican to deny access to documentation that a German academic and his collaborators had considered essential. He had done this because the documentation related to a disputed council decision — which meant the documentation contained something the institution had decided, formally or informally, it preferred to keep private.

And someone — Paulus, she was now near-certain — had taken this as a specific, unforgivable expression of the Cardinal's pride. Not professional opposition. The use of institutional position to suppress inconvenient scholarship. To choose the institution's comfort over the truth of what the records contained.

This was not a crime motivated by academic rivalry. This was a philosophical execution. A man who had spent decades believing that truth was the only moral imperative had watched a powerful man use institutional authority to deny it.

She had seen pride before. In courtrooms, in political chambers, in the specific expression of men who knew they were wrong and chose to be wrong loudly. She had never seen it staged this carefully.

Mateo called at thirty-eight minutes.

"The file request was cancelled," he said. "The timestamp shows the cancellation came from an internal Vatican administrative account at 2:17pm on the day Chiara was sedated. The account belongs to a junior clerical role in the diplomatic secretariat."

"Father Schäfer's office."

"The secretariat, yes. Whether Schäfer authorized it personally or someone in his office acted without his direct instruction, I can't—"

"It doesn't matter right now. What matters is that someone inside the Vatican administration is still cleaning up after the lesson." She stopped walking. She was on the far side of the Tiber, on a street she didn't know the name of, in a city that kept its secrets the way it kept everything — thoroughly, patiently, inside walls that had been standing before the concept of transparency existed. "He has someone inside."

A beat of silence.

"Or someone inside decided, without being instructed, that protecting the institution was worth suppressing a file request," Mateo said. "Institutional loyalty doesn't require coordination."

"No." She started walking again. "But it requires opportunity. Chiara was sedated between 1:17 and 1:30pm. The file request was cancelled at 2:17pm. Forty minutes. That's coordination."

"I know."

"Find me the file," she said. "The 1972 correspondence. Whatever Paulus and the Tübingen consortium were trying to access. That's the origin. That's why the Cardinal was chosen."

"Forty minutes again?"

"Thirty."

She walked faster. She had five hours remaining and the city was warm and old around her and somewhere in the archival machinery of the Catholic Church was the document that explained why a man had spent thirty years building a methodology and then chosen a Roman Cardinal as its first published argument.

She intended to find it before the thirty minutes expired.

She did.

She walked south along the Tiber.

Seven hours before the forty-eight-hour marker. Seven hours to find the thing that made the warrant unambiguous. She had the pattern. She needed the direct connection: something that placed Paulus not just in proximity to the case's intellectual architecture but in documented contact with the specific evidence.

She thought about the vellum. The aging process — authentic, not artificially accelerated. The Franciscan binding knot. The Leonine footnote system. Three techniques that pointed at the same tradition, the same geographical origin, the same period of training.

She thought about a graduate program in theological paleography at the University of Tübingen.

She had three Tübingen connections. She needed to know when Paulus had been in Tübingen, at what point in his training, and what he had studied there. His published CV listed his graduate institution as Cologne. But a man's published CV listed the institution that conferred the degree. It did not always list every institution he had attended for training, for visiting research, for the specific acquisition of skills he would later prefer not to be formally associated with.

She called Mateo.

"Paulus's pre-doctoral research record," she said. "Not the published CV. The actual research history. Any visiting appointments, any training programs, any extended stays in Germany or Austria in the late 1970s or early 1980s. Before the Cologne degree was conferred."

"That's going to be buried in university administration records."

"Yes."

"I'll find it." He said it the way he said things he was confident about. "Two hours."

She continued walking. She had six hours and fifty-eight minutes remaining and a city around her that had been keeping secrets since before the concept of secrets had been formalized and she was not going to let it keep this one.

Chapter 13

What Pride Protects

The archivist's name was Chiara Moretti.

Twenty-six years old. Vatican archival division, junior grade, three years in post. She had been found unconscious on a bench in the Vatican gardens at 1:17pm by a groundskeeper who had initially assumed she was asleep. She was not asleep. She had been administered a sedative — oral, fast-acting, the kind that produced unconsciousness within twenty minutes and left no lasting damage and no reliable way of establishing how it had been introduced. She would recover fully. She was already awake when Sonya arrived at the hospital.

She was also terrified. Not of Sonya. Of the specific thing that had happened to her in the gardens, which she could not fully reconstruct because the sedative had taken the last twenty minutes of her consciousness and left only the twenty minutes before it: walking in the gardens on her lunch break, sitting on the bench, taking out her phone, and then waking in a hospital with a nurse asking her to follow a light with her eyes.

She had not seen who sat beside her on the bench.

She had not seen who put anything in her coffee, which she had brought from the office in a thermos and had left on the bench beside her while she answered a message on her phone.

She had seen one thing. A hand, reaching past her for the thermos, wearing a ring. She described it: a ring with a flat oval face, dark metal, the kind of ring she associated with academic institutions. A signet ring, perhaps. Or something ceremonial.

Sonya wrote this down and looked at what she had written and thought about an iron ring on a right hand that she had not examined closely enough.

She did not say this to Chiara Moretti. She thanked her and told her she had been very helpful and that she should rest and that she should not return to the Vatican until Sonya's team had been in contact with her supervisor. She said this last part in a tone that communicated: your supervisor is not the problem, but something in that building is, and until we understand what it is you are safer here.

Chiara Moretti looked at her with the specific expression of a person who had understood more than had been said.

"The nephew," she said. "Mr. Voss. He didn't do it."

Sonya looked at her.

"He used to come to the archive," Chiara said. "After his uncle cut him from the seminary. He would research his grandmother's estate documents. He was trying to understand what had happened to the inheritance. He was always very polite. He brought the documents back in better condition than he found them." She paused. "I know what someone who is planning a murder looks like. He wasn't planning anything. He was just—" She searched for the word.

"Suffering," Sonya said.

"Yes," Chiara said. "Suffering."

She called Mateo from the hospital corridor.

"A ring," she said. "A dark metal ring with a flat oval face. Academic or ceremonial."

A silence. The silence of a man arriving at something he had known peripherally and was now being asked to name directly.

"Mateo."

"The iron ring." His voice was careful. "Paulus holds the chair of patristic theology at Tübingen. The chair is historically associated with a specific institutional ring — given to the holder of the position at appointment. It's ceremonial. Dark iron. Flat oval face."

She processed this. Paulus had been in the Vatican gardens. He had known Chiara had passed her the note. He had followed her or anticipated her or had sources inside the building she did not yet understand. He had sat beside a young woman on a bench and taken twenty minutes of her life and left a fragment of vellum in her pocket and walked away.

Not to hurt her. To correct the investigation. The archivist's note had introduced a variable Paulus had not controlled for. He had corrected it with precision and without malice and the young woman was awake in a hospital bed and the correction was complete.

This was not rage. This was not panic. This was a man who managed the variables of a curriculum the way an academic managed the variables of a research project. Methodically. Proportionately. Without excess.

"Where is he?" she said.

"Still at the hotel. He checked in for the week and the hotel confirmed he hasn't checked out. His key card was used at 8:14 this morning and again at 2:43pm." A pause. "The Vatican gardens incident was at 1:17pm."

Twenty-six minutes to get from the Vatican gardens to his hotel room. Possible. Easily possible. He had not hurried. He had managed a variable and returned to his schedule.

"Mateo," she said.

"Yes."

"Marco Voss's digital forensics came back on the laptop. The gallery searches." She had been carrying this since that morning. "His browsing history shows the search activity. But the IP address on three of the seven searches is different from the others. It's a mobile IP. Not his building's router. Someone searched from his laptop using a separate mobile connection."

A longer silence.

"From inside his apartment," Mateo said.

"From inside his apartment. Which means someone was in his apartment with a mobile device, using his laptop, planting search history."

"Bauer," Mateo said immediately.

"Is what I think as well. Bauer had the address. Bauer had access. Bauer had a supervisor who needed a frame that would hold." She paused. "I don't believe Bauer knew what he was doing."

"Neither do I," Mateo said. "But Paulus did."

She stood in the hospital corridor and thought about Marco Voss in his apartment in Trastevere with his theological texts and his Bernini book and his grief that was not guilt and his no alibi and his laptop that had been used against him by a person who had spent years studying how to make a frame that would hold.

"I need to talk to Hale," she said.

"Will he listen?"

She thought about the digital forensics. The IP address discrepancy. The ring Chiara had described. The Bauer connection. The four squares of vellum.

"He'll have to," she said.

She was not certain this was true. She said it anyway because the alternative — the alternative was Marco Voss staying where he was while the person who had placed him there managed his next variable in the next European city.

She called Hale.

He listened for twelve minutes without interrupting. Then he said: "I need a signed statement from the digital forensics analyst. I need the IP discrepancy documented. I need the Chiara Moretti ring description in a formal witness statement."

"How long?"

"Forty-eight hours."

"Hale —"

"That's what I need, Sonya. Forty-eight hours and I can take it to the Prosecutor's office. Forty-eight hours and Marco Voss walks out of that cell. But I need the documentation or the Vatican liaison dismantles it before it gets there."

She ended the call. She stood in the hospital corridor for a moment that was longer than it needed to be. Then she walked back to Chiara Moretti's room and asked her to sign a formal witness statement describing the ring on the hand that had reached past her for the thermos.

Chiara signed it without being asked twice.

One document. Forty-eight hours. Marco Voss in a cell he should not be in. Paulus in a hotel room preparing his next lesson.

She had thirty-eight hours of her sixty remaining. She needed to find something in the next thirty-eight hours that made the forty-eight irrelevant.

The file was forty pages.

A 1972 correspondence between a Vatican council committee and three European theologians, relating to a proposed doctrinal clarification on the nature of moral culpability — specifically, the question of whether institutional actors could bear individual moral responsibility for institutional decisions. The correspondence had been initiated by a German theologian whose name appeared, in the first footnote of Paulus's private monograph, as a foundational influence.

The theologian had argued yes. The Vatican committee had argued the question was not within the scope of doctrinal clarification. The correspondence had been closed without resolution.

The theologian's name was Wilhelm Hardt.

Paulus's mentor. Hardt's correspondence with the Vatican committee, thirty years before Paulus published anything, had been the intellectual origin of everything Paulus had built. The argument that institutions could not absolve individuals of moral accountability — that a man who acted under institutional authority was still a man, still accountable — had been made in those forty pages and had been quietly buried by an institution that had found the argument inconvenient.

Paulus had been trying to access the documentation of that burial for five years. The Cardinal had denied it.

She sat in the temporary apartment with the file on her screen and read all forty pages and at the end of them she understood, for the first time, what kind of man she was looking for. Not a nihilist. Not a psychopath. A man who had spent his entire professional life in service of the argument that moral truth was not institutional property — and who had decided, at some point she could not exactly identify, that the most effective way to make the argument was to demonstrate it.

The Cardinal had been the demonstration.

She called Mateo at eleven that night. Not with a question. She told him about the file.

He was quiet for a long time after she finished.

"He's not wrong," Mateo said.

"I know."

"Hardt's argument—"

"Is philosophically coherent. Possibly correct. That doesn't—"

"I know that too." His voice had the quality it had when he was working through something he found genuinely difficult. Not the journalist's careful neutrality. The specific discomfort of a man whose intellectual life had been spent in close proximity to exactly the kind of institutional question Hardt had raised, and who had left the institution partly for exactly this reason. "But you understand what it means that he's not wrong. It means the people who read the crime scene correctly — who follow the argument where it leads — are going to have to sit with the fact that the victim was not innocent."

"The victim is dead."

"Yes."

"The method of making the argument is what I'm investigating."

"Yes." A pause. "I know. I just—" He stopped. "He chose well. Paulus chose a man who embodied the exact institutional pride that Hardt's argument was about. A man who used institutional authority to deny inconvenient truth. A man whose private certainty — his refusal to be known truly — was the engine of everything he did in a position of power."

She thought about the Bernini. The reaching hand. The transformation at the instant of consequence.

"He didn't kill a hypocrite," she said. It was what the crime scene was saying. She was saying it out loud for the first time. "He killed a man who had never once doubted himself."

"Yes." Mateo's voice was very quiet. "That's exactly what he did."

She sat with this for a moment. Then she said: "The forty-eight hours expire tomorrow morning. I need Chiara Moretti's full testimony on record before then. And I need a formal connection between Paulus and the 1972 correspondence — not just the monograph footnote. Something that puts him in documented contact with Hardt's argument before the murder."

"Hardt's publication record at Tübingen will have it. He's been publishing variations of the 1972 argument since the mid-1980s. Paulus's early acknowledgments will reference the specific papers."

"Get me three documented connections between Paulus's published work and Hardt's 1972 argument. Three independent citations. That builds the intellectual motive chain."

"I'll have it before morning."

"I know you will."

She looked at the window. The Via Margutta outside was quiet. She thought about sixty hours and forty-eight of them remaining and everything that needed to happen inside them.

She thought about a man who had never doubted himself, arranged before a sculpture about the precise moment doubt arrives.

She thought: Paulus understood him. That understanding is both the motive and the methodology.

She turned back to the file. She had twenty-three pages left to annotate and the morning coming and the specific knowledge, sitting in her chest like ballast, that the next thirty-eight hours were going to be the most important thirty-eight hours of her professional life.

She was ready for them. She had been ready for something like this since she was old enough to understand what being ready meant.

She annotated the file. She was working. She was also, somewhere below the working, aware of having said the thing out loud — *he didn't kill a hypocrite* — and of the specific quality of Mateo's voice receiving it.

She had been carrying that sentence since the first morning. It was lighter, having been said.

She reviewed the Chiara Moretti testimony one more time.

Twenty-six years old. Vatican archivist. Sedated in the Vatican gardens at a precise dose that produced unconsciousness without lasting harm, which required pharmaceutical knowledge and a careful hand. Not Paulus's hand — he had been at a faculty lunch at the Gregorian at 1:00pm, eleven people who could confirm it. But someone acting with his knowledge, or on his instruction, or in his methodology's shadow.

The file request that Chiara had been processing before the sedation — for the 1972 Hardt correspondence — had been cancelled by someone in Father Schäfer's secretariat twenty-three minutes after Chiara lost consciousness. A forty-minute coordination window between the sedation and the file cancellation. Not improvised. Not institutional loyalty acting alone.

She added to the case map: *Someone inside the Vatican administration is managing the institutional response to the investigation. Not the killer — the killer is elsewhere. An accomplice? Or an institutional actor protecting the institution, independently, without direct coordination?*

She sat with this for a long time.

The answer mattered for the warrant. The warrant was for Paulus. If there was a second actor — inside the Vatican, actively managing evidence — the warrant needed to be broad enough to accommodate the investigation's expansion.

She called Hale's deputy at eight in the evening.

"I need to speak to Hale directly," she said. "Tonight. The warrant request needs a supplemental addendum before it's filed."

He put her through.

She explained, precisely, what she had found. Hale listened without interruption, which was unusual. He was quiet for forty-five seconds after she finished.

"File it at nine," he said. "Include the Vatican secretariat connection as a thread to be developed, not as a named suspect. The Italian prosecutor will be cautious about anything that looks like a Vatican accusation."

"I understand."

"You have until the forty-eight hours," he said. "Find me the direct connection."

"I will."

She ended the call. She had thirty-eight hours. She had work to do.

Chapter 14

Fourteen Names, Four Scholars, One Satchel

She went to the hotel.

Not with a warrant. She didn't have one yet and wouldn't for thirty-eight hours and she was not going to wait thirty-eight hours. She went with her Interpol identification and the specific manner of a woman who was going to speak to the hotel manager about a guest and the hotel manager was going to cooperate because the alternative was a conversation about obstruction that neither of them had the time for.

The manager cooperated. His name was Benedetti and he had been managing this hotel for eleven years and he had hosted diplomats and academics and a significant number of people who required a specific kind of discretion, and he knew the difference between a detective and a bureaucrat, and Sonya was not a bureaucrat.

She asked four questions. The key card records confirmed Paulus had been in his room between 2:43pm and the present. He was in the building now. His checkout was confirmed for Friday, two days away.

She asked if she could speak with him.

She was shown to his floor. She knocked.

He opened the door.

Dr. Heinrich Paulus in person was exactly what the bibliography and the conference registry and the briefing room appearance and eleven days of investigation had prepared her for, which meant he was also nothing she had fully prepared for.

Sixty-one years old. Silver-grey hair, short, precise. Lean in the way of a man who had never particularly remembered to eat. A face composed of planes and patience that had been forming its conclusions for sixty years and was no longer interested in being argued with. He was wearing dark trousers and a good shirt and he had been working — a laptop open on the desk behind him, papers arranged with the specific order of a mind that organized its physical environment the same way it organized its arguments.

He wore a ring on his right hand. Dark iron. Flat oval face.

She noted this without letting it move across her face.

"Commissioner," he said. His Italian was excellent. He used the same title Father Albani had used, which was not quite accurate, and he said it with the same specific courtesy of a man who had decided what register this conversation would occur in and had opened at that register without waiting for her to establish it.

"Dr. Paulus." She produced her identification. He looked at it with the attention of a man who actually read things rather than registering that a document had been presented. "May I come in?"

He stepped back from the door.

She entered. She looked at the room with the part of her mind that looked at rooms: the laptop, the papers, an open volume of Aquinas's Summa on the nightstand, a leather satchel on the chair by the window. Dark brown, worn, worn with years. No visible monogram.

She sat when he indicated the chair. He sat across from her. He did not offer coffee. He simply waited, with the patience she had expected, for her to begin.

"We're speaking with a number of conference attendees," she said. Standard opening. Comfortable. Uninformative about what she knew. "You were at the Symposium on Thomistic Moral Philosophy last week."

"I was."

"And you've been teaching at the Gregorian this week."

"A visiting seminar series, yes. The theology of sin in the Thomistic tradition. I give it periodically when I'm in Rome." He said this with the ease of a man describing something entirely ordinary, which it was. "Is there something specific I can help you with, Commissioner?"

She looked at him. He looked back. His eyes were a specific grey-green that processed everything they rested on with the same quality — the same unhurried, complete attention. She had been looked at by a great many people in twelve years of this work. She had rarely been looked at by someone who appeared to find her genuinely interesting rather than threatening or instrumental.

"The Borghese Gallery," she said. "Have you been recently?"

"Several times this year. The Bernini collection is central to the seminar material." He paused. "I haven't been since the Cardinal's death, if that's what you're asking."

"It wasn't." She let the silence sit. He let it sit with her, which told her he was comfortable with silence in a way that most people weren't. "Do you know Cardinal Voss personally?"

"By reputation. We move in overlapping professional circles. I had not met him directly."

This was almost certainly false. She didn't pursue it. She had not come to confront. She had come to look.

She asked three more questions. He answered all of them accurately as far as she could verify against what she already knew. He confirmed attending the conference. He confirmed the seminar at the Gregorian. He expressed appropriate concern about the Cardinal's death and appropriate uncertainty about whether he could be of any assistance to the investigation.

He was, in every observable particular, a distinguished academic being cooperative with an Interpol inquiry into the death of a prominent Vatican figure. He was also, in every observable particular, the most careful person she had ever sat across from.

She stood to leave.

"Commissioner," he said.

She turned.

"Augustine writes that the proud man's greatest fear is not exposure," he said. He said it the way he said everything — with the precision of someone who had thought about it for a long time before speaking. "His greatest fear is being understood. To be known truly is, for the proud man, a form of annihilation. He can survive exposure. He cannot survive being seen." He paused. "A thought, for your investigation. It might be useful."

She looked at him for a moment.

"Thank you, Dr. Paulus," she said.

She left. She walked down the corridor to the elevator. She pressed the button. She stood with her back against the wall beside the elevator door and breathed.

He had just told her exactly what he was doing and why. The Cardinal's greatest fear had been being known truly. Paulus had made him known. Made him seen. He had told her this directly and she could not use it and he knew she could not use it and he had said it anyway.

Because the curriculum was still in progress.

Because she was, somehow, part of it.

The elevator arrived. She got in. The doors closed.

She called Mateo from the lobby.

"I just sat with him," she said.

A beat. "How?"

"The same way he is. Completely. Without showing what I know."

"Is he going to run?"

She thought about the room. The Aquinas on the nightstand. The papers organized with the precision of a mind that had not finished working. The leather satchel on the chair.

"No," she said. "He's not finished."

"Then we have time."

"We have thirty-seven hours."

"Sonya." His voice had a quality she had learned to pay attention to. The journalist voice giving way to something else. "Go back to the gallery."

She stopped walking. "What?"

"The main room. Tonight. Without the forensics team. Without the case in your head." A pause. "He told you something in that room. Something you documented and catalogued and filed. You need to stand in it again without documenting or cataloguing or filing anything."

She looked at the hotel lobby — the concierge, the tourists, the ordinary business of a Rome afternoon. She thought about the room at 4:53am. The quality of the staging. The patience of it. The thing she had not had a procedural word for.

"I have a contact at the Borghese administration," she said.

"I know." She could hear that he was already moving. "I'll meet you there."

They went in through the lobby together, which was professionally useful and personally significant in a way she decided to address later.

Mateo had the satchel and the notebook and the specific manner of a man who belonged anywhere he presented himself as belonging, which was a quality she had been observing for eleven days and had found professionally admirable and personally — she filed the personally.

The manager, Benedetti, met them in the lobby. He looked at Mateo with the brief assessment of a man who read rooms for a living, made some determination about what Mateo was, and directed his subsequent attention to Sonya.

"Dr. Paulus's room," she said. "And his checkout documentation."

"He settled in cash," Benedetti said. "This is unusual for academic guests, who typically have institutional billing arrangements."

"I know." She had requested the documentation two hours ago. "The checkout time."

"Six-oh-three this morning. The night desk processed it." He handed her the paperwork — a copy of the checkout receipt, the guest registration, the incidental charges. She scanned it. Mineral water. A room service order at 11pm. A scheduled wake call at 5am that had been cancelled at 4:47am.

He had been awake before his own alarm.

She handed the paperwork to Mateo, who had opened his notebook and was already writing something she would read later.

"His room," she said. "I need access."

Benedetti cooperated. He was the kind of hotel manager who understood that cooperation with law enforcement, when documented and conducted correctly, was preferable to the alternative, and he had made his peace with this understanding eleven years ago when he'd found the first guest in circumstances that required official involvement. He was not rattled. He was efficient.

The room was on the third floor. It looked, as hotel rooms in Rome looked, like a hotel room in Rome — the specific anonymous luxury of a space that had been occupied by hundreds of different people and had absorbed none of them. High ceilings. A desk by the window. The Borghese park visible in the distance through the glass.

She stood in the doorway for a moment.

He had stood here. He had looked at that view — the park, the trees, the gallery she could just make out at the far edge — and he had known that what he had done there was done, and that the next thing was already prepared.

She went in.

The forensics team had not been here yet — she had managed to get here first, which was the point, because a forensics team would process the room correctly and she needed to see it first with the specific intelligence she had accumulated and they had not. She looked at the desk. The chair positioned at an angle that suggested he had sat at the window rather than at the desk. The desk itself was clear — no papers, no books, no evidence of work.

He had worked elsewhere. In the gallery. In the Gregorian's visiting faculty offices. Not in his hotel room.

The hotel room was where he rested.

She crossed to the desk. Mateo was at the window, looking at the view she had looked at, not speaking. She appreciated the not speaking. She opened the desk drawer. Empty. She checked the standard hotel stationery slot — two sheets of hotel paper, one pen, both unused. She checked the bedside table. Nothing.

Then she looked at the wastepaper basket.

It had been emptied by housekeeping — the bottom liner was fresh. But the liner had a small imperfection, a slight depression on one side, which meant something had rested in the basket long enough to leave a weight impression. Not trash. Something that had been there and then removed. By Paulus, before he checked out, or by the night desk as part of the checkout process.

She photographed the basket. She looked at the bathroom — cleared, as expected, the complimentary toiletries untouched in the backup drawer, the used ones removed. In the shower, she looked at the drain. Nothing. At the shelf over the sink, where the soap residue showed the placement of items that had been there and moved. Not toiletries — the placement was too far to the left for toiletries. Something square. A book, perhaps. Or a document case.

She came back to the main room. Mateo had turned from the window and was looking at her.

"He didn't leave anything," she said.

"No."

"He didn't leave anything because he takes the methodology with him. Every time." She looked at the desk chair. At the view he had had while sitting here. "He sat there and looked at the park. He could see the gallery from here. He watched the investigation arrive."

"And then left on his own schedule."

"Yes." She looked at the room one more time. The specific emptiness of it — not the emptiness of a room that had never been occupied, but the emptiness of a room that had been occupied and carefully vacated. Nothing left behind. Nothing accidentally revealed. "He's done this before," she said.

Mateo looked at her. "You think Rome isn't the first."

"I think Rome was the first published lesson. I don't think it was the first rehearsal." She picked up her bag from the floor. "Find me his travel records for the past five years. Not conference appearances — actual travel. Every time he left Germany. Every city."

"That's going to take longer than tonight."

"Then start now." She walked toward the door. At the threshold she stopped. "Mateo."

"Yes."

"He watched from the park. He stood at the observer's position in the gallery and watched Bernini's work and chose it and staged it. He stood in the park and watched the investigation arrive." She looked at him. "He has a specific relationship to watching. He observes. He documents. He reads the room. It's not just the methodology — it's the pleasure of it."

She could hear what she was describing. She did not examine the resonance of describing it to this specific person.

"I know," Mateo said.

"I'll meet you at the Borghese administration," she said. "I have a contact at the gallery — they're expecting us."

She walked out. She took the stairs because she needed the two flights to put the room behind her.

Outside, Rome was very loud and the afternoon sun was very bright and she stood on the pavement for a moment in the specific way she stood when she was finishing one thought before beginning the next.

She was thinking about a man who watched.

She was thinking about the gallery.

She started walking.

She stood at the Borghese entrance for a moment after Mateo had gone to find his contact.

The gallery in the afternoon light was different from the gallery at 4:53am. Not transformed — the same stone, the same sculptures, the same institutional architecture of a space that had been containing beautiful things since the seventeenth century. But the light was different and the quality of her attention was different and she was different from the person who had walked through this entrance sixteen days ago with a fresh crime scene ahead of her.

She was not certain yet what she was instead.

She went in. She went to the Bernini. She stood in front of it without the professional framework — not reviewing evidence, not analyzing the staging, simply looking at the sculpture the way the sculptor had intended it to be looked at, which was as a thing in itself, not as evidence of something else.

Apollo reaching. Daphne transforming. The moment of absolute consequence suspended in marble at the instant before everything changed.

She thought about Mateo standing in front of this at twenty-three and thinking *he's never going to catch her* and then standing in front of it thirty years later and thinking something different. She thought about what thirty years of looking at the same thing produced in a person.

She looked at the reaching hand for a long time.

Then she went to find the gallery director.

Chapter 15

The Borghese After Dark

The gallery at night was a different silence than the gallery at 4:53 in the morning.

At 4:53 the silence had been active — the silence of something that had just been made, still warm with the effort of its making. This was different. This was the silence of a room that had been many things across four hundred years and had decided, at this hour, to be nothing in particular. The marble was very white in the emergency lighting. The sculptures were very still. Everything that had happened here had settled into the stone and the stone was keeping it.

Sonya stood in the entrance to the main room.

She did not go in immediately. This was not the twenty-second habit. This was something else. She was aware of the room as a thing that was asking something of her that she did not yet know how to give. The procedural inventory had nothing left to inventory. The evidence had been catalogued and removed and the markers were still on the floor but they were not evidence anymore, they were notation, and notation was not the same as the thing it notated.

She was trying to understand something the evidence could not tell her.

She went in.

The Bernini was extraordinary in the emergency lighting.

She had known this. She had processed it at 4:53am as an aesthetic fact and moved past it because aesthetic facts are not evidence. She had processed it again at noon with Mateo translating the theology of it. She had processed it as argument, as accusation, as grade left by a teacher.

She was not processing it now. She was standing in front of it.

Apollo and Daphne. The god reaching. The woman becoming something else at the instant of being reached for. The moment of transformation that was also the moment of loss — loss for both of them, Sonya understood now, standing in the quiet gallery with no notebook and no procedural category for what she was doing. Daphne lost her human self. Apollo lost the thing he had been reaching for since before the pursuit began. The transformation protected one of them and destroyed what the other wanted. The marble captured the instant before either of them understood this.

She had been standing in rooms like this her entire career. Rooms where something terrible had been done with great care and intelligence. Rooms that asked her to understand something she was not sure she was equipped to understand. She had always been equipped. She had always found the procedural word, the evidential category, the professional framework that held the thing in place while she worked around it.

This room had no procedural word.

This room was about something she had not been looking at directly for thirty-five years.

She did not hear him come in. She knew he was there because the quality of the room's silence changed — became inhabited, became something shared rather than solitary. She did not turn.

He did not speak.

This was the thing she had not expected. She had expected him to translate. To explain. To give her the theological framework she could organize around. She had expected Mateo to do what Mateo did, which was to find the story in the available evidence and tell it.

He did not do any of this. He came to stand beside her and he was quiet.

Not the quiet of a person waiting to speak. The quiet of a person who had decided that speaking was not what this moment required. She was aware of him the way she was aware of things that mattered — completely, without looking at them. The height of him. The specific quality of his stillness, which was different from her stillness: hers was professional, trained, the stillness of a person who had learned to be still in order to see more clearly. His was older than that. His was the stillness of a person who had stood in difficult rooms and waited for the room to be finished with him.

Close enough that she could feel the warmth of him. She filed this under things she was not examining. She was aware that the filing was taking more effort than it usually did.

She looked at the Bernini.

Apollo's reaching hand. The eternally arriving gesture. The thing that would always be about to happen.

She thought: I have been keeping myself unreachable for a very long time.

She did not say this. She did not know, yet, that she had thought it. She was aware of it the way she was aware of things she was not examining — in the body before the mind, as a physical fact before a considered one. A change in the quality of her breathing. The specific awareness of her own hands, which were at her sides and were not holding anything and felt strange for not holding anything.

The room held them both in its four-hundred-year silence.

Mateo did not move. She did not move. Rome outside was doing its late-evening things and the gallery was entirely indifferent to Rome outside and the Bernini above them was entirely indifferent to both of them, which was its nature. It had been indifferent to everyone who had stood before it. It simply continued being what it was.

Apollo reaching. Daphne transforming. The moment that was always about to arrive and never did.

He spoke eventually. Not about the case.

"The first time I stood in front of this sculpture I was twenty-three," he said. His voice was quiet. Not careful — she had heard Mateo careful. This was different. This was the voice of a person speaking without calculation, without the journalist's instinct to frame and assess. "I was in Rome for a theology conference. My first one. I didn't understand yet what the seminaries were actually training me for and I didn't understand what I was, and I stood in front of this for a very long time and I thought: he's not going to catch her. He's never going to catch her. The marble is the end of the story."

She was listening in the way she listened to things that mattered. Completely. Without preparing her response while he spoke.

"And now?" she said.

A pause. The specific pause of a man considering whether to say the thing he had been thinking since he arrived.

"And now I think the marble isn't the end of the story. The marble is the moment before the end of the story. The sculptor stopped there because everything after that moment is less interesting than the moment itself. The pursuit, the transformation, the reaching hand — this is what Bernini found worth four years of his life. Not the resolution. The instant of absolute consequence before the resolution arrives."

She looked at Apollo's hand. The marble fingers eternally almost touching.

She thought: he is talking about the sculpture. She thought: he is not only talking about the sculpture.

She did not say either of these things.

The room was very quiet. The emergency lighting was very low. The Bernini above them was very white and very still and very certain of itself in the way that things which have been what they are for four hundred years become certain. She was aware of him beside her — close enough that she could feel the warmth of him, which was an imprecise observation that she filed under things she was not examining.

She was aware of her own stillness. Not the trained stillness — that one she knew the weight of, had been carrying it since she was eight years old and had learned that stillness was the best available armor against a room organized around someone else's volatility. This was different. This was the stillness of a body that had stopped pretending it was only processing information.

She had not been held in place by a room in a very long time.

She did not examine this. She stood in it.

Something was happening in this room that she did not have a procedural word for and had not had a procedural word for at 4:53am and had still not found one for despite eleven days of trying.

Something that the staging had been about. Something that Paulus had understood about the Cardinal and had made visible in marble and silk and one Latin word.

The refusal to be known truly.

She was aware, for the first time in a very long time, of what that refusal cost.

She turned to look at him.

He was already looking at her. Not at the sculpture. At her. The dark eyes that were warm in a way the rest of his face was not. The mustache. The three-day shadow. The iron ring on his right hand catching the low emergency light. The way he held her gaze without requiring anything from it — without the slight forward lean of someone waiting for something, without the professional calibration of someone assessing. He was simply looking at her the way she looked at things that required her full attention, which was completely, and she understood for the first time that she had been looked at like this across eleven days without recognising it for what it was.

She felt it now. In her sternum. The specific register of being seen by someone who had been paying attention.

She held his gaze.

She was aware of the six feet between them as a measurement she could name exactly. She was aware of her own heartbeat, which was not elevated but was present in a way it usually was not. She was aware of what would happen if either of them moved, and of the specific quality of choosing not to move, which was its own kind of action.

Then her phone rang.

She answered it. The Rome liaison. A development in the Voss case — the Italian prosecutor's office had filed a motion. She listened. She said yes and understood and she would be there in twenty minutes. She ended the call.

She looked at Mateo. He was still looking at her. She could see that he had understood what had been interrupted and had decided something about it — she could see the decision being made in the specific quality of his stillness, the deliberateness of not moving, the patience of a man who had learned that patience was its own kind of answer.

"I have to go," she said.

"I know."

She picked up her bag from the floor where she had set it without remembering setting it down. She walked toward the gallery entrance. At the doorway she stopped without turning.

She did not know what she had been about to say. She said nothing. She stood in the gallery entrance for a moment after the phone call ended.

The Borghese in the emergency lighting. The Bernini above her still white and still certain. The marble floor reflecting the low light back upward, which gave the gallery the quality of a space lit from within rather than from outside, which was not incorrect as a metaphor for what the staging had been doing in this room since 4:53am.

She thought about what had nearly happened.

Not in the way she usually thought about things — systematically, from the evidence outward. She thought about it the way you thought about something that had surprised you, which was without the professional structure, which was simply the direct experience of having been surprised. She had stood in this room and had understood, for the first time in fifteen days of being a detective with this specific professional skin over the other self, that the other self was not as contained as she had believed.

The Bernini was very clear about this. Apollo reaching. Daphne transforming. The moment when the thing you were reaching for changed its nature at the instant of contact. She had not been reaching for anything. She had been standing still. But she had felt the room change around her in the way that rooms changed when something was happening in them, and she had understood that she was not only the observer in this situation.

He had seen this. He had not said what he saw. He had the quality of seeing without announcing the seeing, which was either the journalist's discipline or something older, and she had spent fifteen days deciding it was the journalist's discipline and was now uncertain.

She walked out into the Via Pinciana and Rome received her with its customary ancient indifference and she walked quickly toward the Interpol offices and did not think about the room she had just left.

She thought about the prosecutor's motion. She thought about Marco Voss. She thought about thirty-seven hours and what she still needed to find in them.

She thought about the stillness that was not her trained stillness.

She walked faster.

Behind her, in the gallery, Mateo stood in front of the Bernini for a long time after she left. The sculpture was exactly itself. The god reaching. The woman already somewhere else. The moment of consequence suspended forever in marble at the instant before everything changed.

He stayed until the administration contact locked up at ten.

Then he went back to his hotel and sat at the desk and opened his notebook and did not write anything.

He stayed in the gallery until the administration contact locked up.

He was aware of how long he had been there. He had been there for forty-seven minutes after she left, which was longer than the evidentiary purpose required and shorter than the pull of the room. The Bernini was not something you looked at efficiently. It demanded time. It had demanded time from every person who had stood in front of it since 1625 and it was demanding it from him now, which was either a testament to Bernini's genius or to his own specific susceptibility to this particular argument.

He thought it was probably both.

He looked at the sculpture and thought about what she had almost said at the doorway.

She had stopped. She had not turned. She had stood in the threshold with her bag on her shoulder and the case file in her mind and the phone call that had interrupted the room still active in her hand, and she had almost said something. He had watched her almost say it. He had watched the decision cross her face — not struggle, exactly, but the rapid professional assessment of a person deciding whether a sentence was appropriate to the context.

She had decided it was not appropriate to the context.

He had agreed with her assessment. He was also aware that agreement with her assessment was not the same as not feeling the weight of what had not been said.

He looked at the Bernini.

Apollo reaching. The marble hand extended toward Daphne with the specific ardor of a myth that had been set in motion before the moment captured here. The pursuit was already complete. The reaching hand was the conclusion. What it was reaching for had already decided to become something else.

He had been at twenty-three when he first stood here, and he had thought: *he's not going to catch her.* He had been right. The marble was the proof. The marble was the moment of transformation that was also the moment of loss, and it was permanent, and neither of them was ever going to be anything other than what they were in this exact instant.

He was forty-two now. He had not changed his reading.

What he had changed was his understanding of who, in the myth, he was.

He went back to the hotel. He sat at the desk. He opened the notebook to a blank page. He thought about writing something. He thought about the forty-seven minutes. He thought about the quality of her voice through the corridor wall and the way the room had changed when she walked out of it.

He did not write anything.

He sat at the desk for twenty minutes and then closed the notebook and looked at the window and thought about Venice and what the next two weeks were going to cost him professionally and personally and whether the accounting was going to end up in a place he could live with.

He thought: I have been a journalist for fifteen years. I have been in this situation twice before and both times the correct answer was the same.

He thought: the correct answer and the true answer are not always the same.

He went to bed. He did not sleep immediately. He lay in the dark of the Roman hotel room and thought about the forty-seven minutes and Daphne and the specific quality of transformation that was also loss.

Then he went back to his hotel and sat at the desk and opened his notebook and did not write anything.

Chapter 16

What Mateo Saw

He saw it in the gallery.

Not in the Caravaggio room — that had been something else, something he was still filing in the correct part of his professional understanding and finding the correct part somewhat crowded. This was different. This was the Borghese administration office, where she had asked him to wait while she reviewed the final forensics cross-reference with the gallery director, and he had agreed to wait, and he had then not waited in the way he had agreed to.

He was a journalist. He didn't wait in the way he agreed to.

He had moved along the corridor toward the director's office, not approaching the closed door — not that — but near enough to hear the quality of her voice through it. Not the words. The voice itself. The register she was using. It was the same register she used in the evidence briefings, in the Hale call, in the morning they had stood in the crime scene together at 4:53am. The complete-certainty register. The voice of a person who was not performing authority but was simply operating from it, which was different.

He understood, in the corridor, that this was what she did. Not that she performed competence or professional dominance or the specific authority of a woman in a senior investigative role who had learned to take up her appropriate space — she had moved past all of that twenty years ago. What she did was occupy the position from the inside. She didn't claim the authority. She was it.

He had watched this for fifteen days. He had seen it in crime scenes and briefing rooms and hotel lobbies and the Vatican administration offices where she had made very large institutions cooperate with the specific economy of a person who understood that the request was the concession, not the compliance.

He had found it professionally admirable. He had found it, in the corridor outside the Borghese director's office on the fifteenth day, something other than professionally admirable.

He went back to the waiting area.

He sat down. He opened his notebook. He looked at the page without reading it.

He had spent fifteen years as an investigative journalist and had developed, across those years, the specific discipline of the observer — the ability to look at things without the looking contaminating what he was looking at. You noted and you did not interpret. You recorded and you did not conclude. You held the evidence separate from the feeling the evidence produced and let the distinction between them do its work.

He was not doing any of these things.

He was thinking about the quality of her voice in the corridor and the specific way she moved through a room and the fifteen days of watching both of these things and the accumulating evidence of what that watching had been producing in him, which he had been filing in the part of himself that was not the journalist and was finding less room in that part than he had expected.

She came out of the director's office eleven minutes later. He looked up. She looked at him. She read his face with the speed and accuracy she read everything.

"You didn't stay in the waiting area," she said.

"I moved around."

"You came toward the office."

He did not deny this. It would not have been worth denying. "I heard your voice. Not the words."

"What did you hear?"

He thought about how to answer this accurately.

"I heard someone who doesn't need to try," he said. "Who the room reorganizes around without them asking for it." A pause. "I was trying to understand how you do it and I think the answer is that it's not something you do."

She looked at him for a moment. The specific look she gave things she was not going to examine in the present context but intended to examine later. She had given him this look six times across fifteen days and he had catalogued each occurrence with the care he gave to everything she did.

"The director confirmed the visitor log authentication," she said. "The access record is clean." She picked up her bag. "Come on. We have one more interview this morning."

He stood. He followed her down the corridor. He was a journalist and he knew how to observe without being observed observing, but he was aware, in the way he had become aware of things in her presence, that she knew he was watching and had factored this into how she moved.

He knew that she knew.

She knew that he knew she knew.

Neither of them named this.

They went to the interview. They were professional. They were excellent together in the room — her reading the witness, him reading the text, the specific complementary quality of two very different instruments measuring the same thing from different angles.

He thought: she knows I saw it. She knows what seeing it means.

He thought: she is not doing anything with this knowledge.

He thought: neither am I.

He walked beside her out of the gallery and into the Roman afternoon and the case was still very much in progress and they had three hours before the Hale briefing and he thought about none of the things he was thinking about and focused entirely on the three hours ahead of them.

He was a journalist. He could do this.

He sat in the waiting area of the Borghese administration wing and opened his notebook to a blank page and wrote nothing.

He was a journalist. He wrote things. He had been writing things since he was twenty-three years old and had taken his first notebooks into his first press conference and had discovered that the act of writing was the act of understanding — that the thing became clear in the writing of it in a way it was not clear before. He had notebooks full of fifteen years of clarity. He had notebooks full of cases and sources and arguments and the specific texture of complicated situations that had become navigable in the writing.

He was looking at a blank page.

The situation was not complicated in the journalistic sense. The journalistic sense of complicated meant many moving parts, multiple competing interests, institutional pressures in several directions simultaneously. This situation was, by that measure, clear: they were pursuing a suspect across an evidence trail that was building correctly, he was contributing useful information through his source network, the collaboration was professionally productive.

The situation was complicated in the other sense.

He had been in the profession for fifteen years and had learned, through the specific education of a career spent close to powerful people and dangerous situations, to make precise distinctions. The distinction between the story and the person. The distinction between the information and the relationship that produced it. The distinction between the observer and the observed. He had built his professional practice on these distinctions and had maintained them with the specific discipline that professional integrity required.

He was not maintaining the distinction between the observer and the observed.

He had stopped maintaining it on approximately day six, when she had stood at a crime scene in the specific morning light and read the room with an intelligence that was so structurally similar to his own that he had had the disorienting experience, rare in his professional life, of watching someone do what he did from the inside. He read situations by finding the narrative architecture. She read situations by occupying the room the crime scene had been constructed as. These were not the same thing. They were related things, which was not something he had encountered before in quite this specific form.

He had spent the subsequent nine days managing the recognition.

He had managed it professionally. He had been useful. He had called her at midnight about the seminary record and had not said what he was thinking when he called. He had compiled the footnote documentation and had not said what he was thinking when he delivered it. He had stood beside her in the Borghese emergency lighting and had not moved and had not said the thing he was not going to say.

He was managing it correctly. He intended to continue managing it correctly.

He was not certain how much longer he could do this.

He was not certain how much longer he could do this.

He sat in the waiting area of the Borghese administration wing and thought about a conversation he was not going to have.

The conversation would begin: *I have been watching you work for fifteen days and I have stopped being able to categorize what I am noticing.* This was an accurate sentence. It was also not a sentence he was going to say to the lead investigator of an active homicide investigation in which he was functioning as an unofficial research consultant. The professional situation had clear parameters. He had been inside those parameters for fifteen days. He intended to continue being inside them.

He thought about the parameters.

The parameters had been: he was a journalist with relevant source access who had been granted informal cooperation privileges by Interpol in exchange for documented investigation support. He provided research. She provided case access. The exchange was professional and mutually beneficial and had produced seven distinct evidentiary contributions in fifteen days, each of which had advanced the investigation in a direction it would not have advanced without him.

Those were the parameters.

The parameters did not include the specific experience of watching her occupy a room. The parameters did not include the midnight phone calls that had begun as evidence exchanges and had developed, without either of them deciding this, into something that had the texture of the conversations he had with himself —

the direct kind, without the professional frame. The parameters did not include the forty-seven minutes he had spent in the gallery's administrative office identifying the visitor log entry while being continuously aware that she was thirty meters away in a restricted room doing something that his journalist's instinct would have described as *reading the scene from inside*.

He had not reported the forty-seven minutes to himself accurately at the time. He was reporting them now.

He was also thinking about what he had heard through the corridor wall. Not the words — he had not been close enough for words. The voice. The specific register of it: the authority that was not performed, the certainty that was not constructed, the quality of a person who occupied the position not because they had learned to but because the position was simply where they lived. He had been writing about powerful people for fifteen years. He had encountered this quality exactly three times in that period and had written about all three of them with the specific admiration of a person who recognized something he found genuinely rare.

The third time was her.

He did not know what to do with this. He had, in fifteen years of investigative journalism, developed a fairly complete taxonomy of professional situations and the correct responses to them. He did not have a category for this specific configuration of professional respect and the other thing.

The other thing.

He opened his notebook. He looked at the blank page. He thought: I am a journalist. I write things down. The act of writing is the act of understanding.

He wrote: *She is the most capable person I have worked alongside in fifteen years.*

He read this sentence. He thought: this is accurate and also insufficient.

He wrote: *She does not know I think this.*

He read this sentence. He thought: she probably does know this. She reads everything.

He closed the notebook. He put the pen away. He looked at the ceiling of the Borghese administration wing and thought about the case and the warrant and Venice and the curriculum that had six more cities in it and the specific knowledge that whatever was developing in the professional margins of this investigation was going to have to wait for six more cities to resolve or not resolve.

Six more cities.

He could manage six more cities.

He heard the director's office door open. He heard her footsteps in the corridor — the specific quality of them, which he had learned the way you learned things you were paying attention to without deciding to. He sat up straight. He had the notebook open to a new page. He was a journalist. He was working.

He was not certain how much longer he could do this.

Chapter 17

The Weight of the Eternal City

She did not sleep.

Not in the way of insomnia — not the restless unsuccessful attempt at sleep. She did not try. She returned from the prosecutor's office at eleven-forty and sat at the desk in the temporary apartment with the case files and the Chiara Moretti witness statement and the IP discrepancy documentation and worked until the Via Margutta outside her window began its pre-dawn transformation from the city's private self to its public one.

At 5:15am she put on her jacket and went out.

This Rome — the Rome between 5am and 6am — was the one she had been in on the morning of the murder and had not had time to notice. The streets before the delivery bikes arrived. The specific quality of Roman darkness that was not quite night anymore but had not conceded to morning. A city that was, for this brief hour, entirely itself.

She walked without deciding where she was going. This was unusual. She always decided where she was going. Her routes were chosen for efficiency and sight lines and proximity to whatever the next necessary thing was. She did not take walks. She went places.

She was going nowhere in particular and the city received this with the same indifference it received everything else.

She was not thinking about the gallery. She was thinking about Marco Voss in a cell and Paulus in a hotel room and thirty-six hours and the specific weight of a case that had accumulated more than enough to know and not quite enough to prove. She was thinking about the prosecutor's motion, which was moving with the institutional momentum of something that would close badly if she didn't find the thing that made it irrelevant in time.

She was not thinking about the Borghese after dark.

She was not thinking about a man who had stood beside her without speaking and whose silence had been the most precisely considered thing anyone had done in her proximity in a very long time.

She walked past the church of Sant'Agostino on the Via della Scrofa and stopped.

She was not religious.

She had not been religious at any point in her adult life and had not been particularly religious before that — her family's relationship to faith had been the specific secular-European one of people who found churches aesthetically significant and theologically unnecessary. She had studied enough theology in twelve years of European cases to be functionally literate in it. This was professional. It was not personal.

She went in anyway.

The church of Sant'Agostino was built in the fifteenth century and dedicated to the bishop of Hippo whose definition of pride she had been carrying in her notebook for eleven days. She had not connected these facts when she walked past. She connected them when she was already inside, sitting in a pew halfway down the nave, in the specific quiet of a church in the early morning before anyone else had arrived.

Augustine. The refusal to be known truly. The self constructed so completely that the true self becomes inaccessible even to the person who built it.

She sat with this for a moment.

She had been building something for a long time. She had built it carefully and she had built it well and it had served her. The procedural competence. The professional authority. The specific quality of her stillness that communicated exactly what she wanted it to communicate and nothing she didn't. She had built all of this the way you build something that needs to last — from the inside out, with good materials, with the patience of a person who understood that what she was protecting was worth the effort of protection.

The church was very quiet. The morning light was beginning to find its way through the windows in the specific incremental way of Italian churches, where the light arrived slowly as if it too were being appropriately reverent.

She thought: I have been building a room with no doors.

She did not examine this thought. She sat with it for eleven minutes and then she stood up and she left the church and walked back toward the temporary apartment because she had thirty-five hours and a case to close and the thought would still be there when she was ready for it.

It had been there for thirty-five years. It could wait a little longer.

Hale called at seven-fifteen.

"The Vatican Secretariat filed a formal diplomatic communication with Interpol headquarters at midnight," he said. No preamble. He never used preamble when the information was bad. "They are requesting that the investigation conclude within the existing documented evidence. They are suggesting that the current case against Marco Voss is sufficient."

"It isn't," she said.

"I know it isn't. The Italian prosecutor's office knows it isn't. The Secretariat knows it isn't." A pause with weight in it. "They are making a different argument. They are arguing that the reputational and diplomatic damage of an extended investigation into the murder of a Vatican diplomat outweighs the investigative benefit of pursuing alternative suspects."

She stood at the window of the temporary apartment with her coffee and looked at the Via Margutta below and processed what she had just been told with the specific care of a person processing something that required care.

"They want the nephew to take the frame," she said.

"Sonya."

"Commander. They want the nephew to take the frame."

A longer silence. "I have thirty-two hours before I have to respond formally. Give me something I can put in front of the Director that makes this impossible to close badly."

"Thirty-two hours."

"Thirty-two."

She ended the call. She looked at her phone. She called Mateo. He answered before the second ring and he did not sound like a man who had slept.

"Hale has thirty-two hours," she said.

"I know. I heard from my editor at six. The Vatican Press Office released a statement this morning expressing confidence in the Italian justice system's handling of the Voss case." His voice was flat with the specific flatness of a person who understood exactly what he was describing. "They're building the narrative already."

"Mateo."

"Yes."

"Don't publish anything about the alternative direction yet. Not until I have what I need."

A pause. The pause of a journalist sitting with an instruction he was deciding whether to accept.

"Understood," he said.

Then: "How are you?"

She looked at the Via Margutta. The morning had fully arrived. The city was performing itself. She had not slept. She had sat in a church dedicated to a man whose definition of pride she had been carrying in her notebook and she had thought about a room with no doors and she had left before she understood it.

"I'm working," she said.

A beat. She could hear in the quality of his silence that he knew this was true and also knew it was not the complete answer. She could hear him deciding not to pursue it.

"The Gregorian," he said. "Two hours. Paulus has a seminar at ten."

"We're not going to the seminar," she said.

"No. We're going to his office. He was given a visiting faculty office for the week. His publications are in it. His working notes." A pause. "I know a way in that isn't through the main desk."

Of course he did.

"Two hours," she said.

She put the phone down. She looked at the case files on the desk. The Chiara Moretti statement. The IP discrepancy. The vellum purchase record. The Bauer testimony. The Tübingen connections accumulating across six separate pieces of evidence.

None of it was enough. All of it together was almost enough. She needed the thing that made almost enough into enough.

She thought: it's in his work. It's always in the work. A person that precise, that certain, that long in conversation with a single set of ideas — the thing that revealed them would be in the work. Mateo had said as much. He just hadn't found it yet.

She picked up the case file. She started at the beginning.

She was at page four of the case file when her phone rang.

She looked at the number. She answered.

"You're awake," Mateo said.

"I'm working."

A pause. Not the professional pause. The other kind. She had been cataloguing these pauses for eleven days and had developed a taxonomy: the considering pause, the choosing pause, the finding-the-right-sentence pause, and the pause that was none of these, that was simply him being present across whatever distance separated them and deciding that the presence was enough.

"How are you?" he said.

She looked at the case file on her desk. The Leonine apparatus analysis she had been rereading. The Chiara Moretti testimony. The hotel room photographs. The four hundred and eleven names reduced to three reduced to one.

"I'm working," she said.

"That's not the same as how you are."

She did not answer immediately. She had a list of answers for this question that she moved through with professional efficiency: *fine, managing, progressing well, no concerns at this time.* The list was long and well-practiced and none of the items on it were relevant to what he was asking.

She set down the case file.

"I'm tired," she said. It was not on the list. "Not sleep-tired. The other kind."

"I know." He said it the way he said things he meant — without emphasis, without the reassuring inflection that would have made it easier to hear and less accurate. "I've been watching you work for eleven days. The second kind of tired has been present since day four or five."

"I'm fine."

"You're very good at being fine."

She looked at the window. The Via Margutta outside, pre-dawn, entirely itself. "What does that mean?"

"It means you have built a very efficient machinery for converting exhaustion into continued function, and you have been running the machinery continuously since before I met you, and it works extremely well, and I am also noticing the cost of it."

She was quiet for a moment.

"You're a journalist," she said. "You observe."

"I observe." A pause. "Are you going to tell me that's all it is?"

She thought about this. The specific honesty of 5am, when the professional self was thinner and the other self was more present and the distinction between them was harder to maintain.

"No," she said.

She heard something in his response. Not words. The specific quality of a man who had been offered something he hadn't expected and was choosing to receive it carefully.

"The case file," he said. "What page are you on?"

"Four."

"Go back to page one. Read the opening statement." A pause. "Not for the investigation. For the language. Look at how Hale's deputy structured the initial assessment."

She pulled the opening statement. She read it.

"He buried the anomalies," she said. "The things that didn't fit the Cardinal-as-victim narrative are in subordinate clauses. The framing assumes the nephew before any evidence supports it."

"That's what institutional pressure looks like in document form. Hale's deputy wrote what the institution needed to be true before he knew what was true." A pause. "That's your work, by the way. What you did in the past eleven days — finding the actual truth inside the institutional version of it. That's not small."

She looked at the case file. At eleven days of accumulated paper.

"It's the job," she said.

"It's your specific version of the job," he said. "Which is not the same as the generic version."

She did not answer. She had been told she was good at her work many times and had received this information as professional data and moved on. This was different. This was a man who had watched her do it for eleven days and was describing what he had observed with the specific care of someone who was paying attention to more than the result.

"What are you doing," she said, "at 5am."

"Reading." He said it simply. "The Purgatorio. The canticles on pride — Dante's treatment. I've been trying to understand how he constructs the punishment. The souls in Purgatorio who bore the weight of pride carry great stones on their backs — they're bowed down by the thing that made them stand tall. The posture of pride inverted."

She thought about the Bernini. The reaching hand. The Cardinal arranged before it.

"He used Dante too," she said. "The staging — the Cardinal wasn't bowed down. He was displayed. The pride wasn't inverted, it was presented."

"I know." He paused. "Paulus inverted Dante's logic. Dante punishes pride by making it visible as weight. Paulus made it visible as argument. Externalized rather than internalized."

"The lesson," she said. "He made it a lesson, not a punishment."

"Yes." A pause. "You see it. That's what I mean. You read the room the way he expected someone to read it."

She sat with this for a moment.

Then she said: "I'll have the Chiara testimony on Hale's desk by seven. I need the Tübingen bibliography cross-reference before the briefing."

"I'll have it by six."

"Good night, Mateo."

"Good morning, Sonya."

She ended the call. She sat for a moment with the phone in her hand and the Via Margutta outside and the pre-dawn Rome doing its pre-dawn things and thought about the specific quality of being seen by someone who was paying attention.

She returned to the case file. She started at the beginning.

She was working. She was also, somewhere below the working, aware that the second kind of tired had a different quality now than it had had before the call.

She did not examine this difference.

She worked.

She worked until the light changed outside.

The specific quality of Roman pre-dawn — not dark, not day, the particular suspended illumination of a city between its private self and its public one. She had come to associate this light with the case. She had arrived in Rome at this light, on the first morning, and had been working inside it ever since.

She put down the case file at 5:47am. She looked at what she had. The Chiara connection was now documented — the file request, the sedation timing, the cancellation from Schäfer's secretariat. The

Tübingen connection was across four evidence streams. The bibliography chain was being assembled by Mateo's overnight research and would be ready for the Hale briefing.

She had enough. Not for the warrant — not yet. For the next conversation with Hale, which would authorize the warrant request, which would begin the formal legal process that would follow Paulus to Frankfurt.

She made coffee. She looked at the window. She thought about forty-three years of academic patience building toward a Roman church at dawn.

She thought: I have been at this for sixteen days. He has been at this for forty-three years.

She was not intimidated by this. She had something he did not.

She had the case file. She picked it up. She started at the beginning.

Chapter 18

The Visiting Lecturer

The way in that wasn't through the main desk was a side entrance on the Via della Pilotta used by faculty who found the administrative formality of the main entrance an unnecessary overhead on their time. Mateo knew the code because a colleague at the Gregorian had given it to him in 2019 in exchange for not publishing something the colleague would have preferred unpublished. The code had not been changed.

This was, Sonya reflected, how Mateo operated generally. An accumulation of favors, withheld articles, and institutional relationships that had been cultivated with the specific patience of a man who understood that access was a long-term investment.

The visiting faculty offices were on the third floor. Paulus's had been assigned the smaller of the two available — a room perhaps four meters by four meters with a window overlooking an internal courtyard, a desk, two chairs, and a shelf on which a week's working materials had been arranged with the precision she had by now come to associate with his specific psychology. Everything in its place. Nothing unnecessary. The organization of a mind that found disorder professionally offensive.

The door was unlocked. Academic offices at the Gregorian were unlocked during faculty hours because the institution had determined, across several centuries, that the people who worked here were unlikely to steal from each other. This determination was, in general, correct.

She went in. Mateo followed. He closed the door.

She looked at the shelf.

Seven books. Four journals. A folder of printed materials. A second folder that was thicker and had no label.

She put on gloves. She went to the shelf.

The books were what the bibliography had prepared her for: Augustine, Aquinas, Dante, the Desert Fathers, two volumes of Bernini scholarship, and a slim monograph she did not recognize — a private printing, no ISBN, a title in Latin that Mateo translated without being asked: "On the Taxonomy of the Capital Sins as a Diagnostic Framework for the Human Interior." He looked at the spine. Then at her. The author line was blank.

"His," Mateo said.

"Unpublished."

"Privately printed. It's not in the public bibliography." He was already reading, carefully, without touching more of the pages than necessary. "This is the work he didn't publish. The private theology."

She photographed the spine and the title page and the first three pages while Mateo read. She did not read over his shoulder. She watched his face instead, which told her more than the text would tell her — the specific quality of his expression shifting from professional to something more considered, the journalist processing something the journalist did not have a clean category for.

"Mateo."

"Give me a minute."

She gave him two. He closed the monograph carefully and put it back exactly where it had been.

"He argues," Mateo said, "that each of the seven capital sins is a distorted form of love. That what theology calls sin is not the absence of love but love misdirected — love that has lost its proper object and found an improper one. Pride is the love of self so complete that no other love can exist alongside it. The Cardinal loved his constructed self more than he loved anything the constructed self was supposed to be in service of." He paused. "The argument is genuinely brilliant."

"Don't," she said.

"I'm not defending him. I'm telling you what we're dealing with. A man who has spent forty years developing a theological framework that makes his crimes coherent within a larger system of meaning." He looked at the monograph on the shelf. "He's not going to be stopped by proof. He's going to be stopped by the argument being answered."

She filed this and went to the unlabeled folder.

It contained twelve pages of handwritten notes. Dense. The same small precise handwriting she had seen in the parchment annotation. The Leonine citation apparatus throughout. References to five cities across two pages of what appeared to be a curriculum outline.

Five cities. Rome was first. The others were not yet dated. But they were named.

Venice. Florence. Paris. Barcelona.

She photographed every page. She put the folder back exactly where she had found it.

"Mateo," she said. "The curriculum notes. He has the next four lessons planned."

He looked at the folder. He looked at her.

"That's not evidence that protects Marco Voss," he said. He said it the way he said things he did not want to be true. "That's evidence of intent for future crimes. Hale can use it but it doesn't close the frame on the nephew."

"I know." She was already thinking about the next room. "The published bibliography. The citation style error you identified."

"What about it?"

"You said you found it in his published work. A citation that used the Leonine apparatus from an earlier period of his career. Consistent with how he wrote before 1980."

"Yes."

"If his published work from his post-1980 career consistently uses the modern citation system — if the Leonine apparatus is absent from everything he's published in the last forty years — then the annotation on the parchment, in the Leonine style, can only have been written by someone who used it before 1980 and has deliberately reverted to it." She looked at him. "Which means the annotation was written in a style he abandoned forty years ago and would have no current professional reason to use."

Mateo was very still.

"Unless he wanted it found," he said slowly. "Unless he left it in his old style deliberately. As a —" He stopped.

"As a signature," she said.

The room held this between them.

A man who had published eleven peer-reviewed papers and two monographs without once using the citation style he had learned at Tübingen. A man who had annotated a parchment at a murder scene in exactly that style. Not carelessness. Not habit. A deliberate reversion. A signature written for the person who would be able to read it.

"He was writing for you," she said.

Mateo looked at her.

"Before he knew you existed," she said. "He was writing for the person who would eventually be able to read it. He just didn't know yet who that would be."

A long silence. The small office. The courtyard light through the window. Seven books on a shelf. An unlabeled folder with five cities named in careful handwriting.

"We need his full bibliography," Mateo said. "Every citation in every paper. I need to show that the Leonine apparatus appears nowhere in his post-1980 published work. If it's completely absent — if he scrubbed it entirely and then used it at the crime scene —"

"That's the procedural link," she said. "That puts his specific academic fingerprint on the parchment annotation. Combined with the Tübingen ink, the Franciscan knot, the vellum purchase, the Bauer testimony —"

"It's enough." He was already moving toward the door. "I need four hours and every paper he's published since 1982."

"You have three," she said.

He nodded. He left. She stayed for one more moment in the small office with the seven books and the unlabeled folder and the private monograph with no author name and the window overlooking a courtyard that was entirely ordinary and had no idea what had just been found in the room above it.

Then she left too. She had thirty hours. She had the photographs. She had Mateo working the bibliography.

She had, for the first time since 4:53am eleven days ago, something that felt like it was going to be enough.

The bibliography was everything.

She stood in the visiting faculty corridor of the Gregorian and looked at the spines of the books Paulus had shelved in the small bookcase beside the desk — brought from Germany, returned to Germany, the marks of temporary habitation still on the shelf in the faint rectangular clean-patches where volumes had rested. She photographed the clean-patches. She looked at the desk surface. She looked at the drawers, which Mateo's side-entrance contact had unlocked with the specific resigned competence of a man who had done this kind of thing before and would do it again.

Three drawers. Empty. He had cleared everything before the conference ended. He had been planning the checkout before the lesson was complete.

She looked at the window. The Gregorian's courtyard below, quiet, the specific institutional calm of a space that had been educating people in theology since the sixteenth century and had developed across those centuries a relationship to time that was its own.

"The bibliography," she said.

Mateo was at the desk. He had spread his notebook open and was working through something she couldn't see from where she stood. "Eleven published papers. Two published monographs. And the unpublished working document."

"What connects them to the 1972 Hardt correspondence?"

"Three independent citation chains." He looked up. "Paper two, from 1984. Paper seven, from 2003. The private monograph's opening argument." He turned the notebook toward her. Three columns, each annotated in the cramped but precise hand she had come to recognise as his working handwriting — the handwriting he used when he was thinking fast and accuracy mattered more than legibility. "The 1984 paper cites Hardt's 1976 follow-up publication, which was itself a reformulation of the 1972 Vatican correspondence argument. The 2003 paper cites a 1988 Hardt monograph that made the same argument more formally. And the private document — the unpublished methodology — opens with a direct quotation from the original 1972 correspondence, word for word."

She looked at the three columns.

"He had access to the 1972 document," she said.

"From at least 1984. Before Paulus published his first paper, he had already read what Hardt sent the Vatican committee. Hardt gave it to him — or showed it to him. The mentor and the student, sharing the foundational argument."

"And the Cardinal denied the consortium access to a document that Paulus had been working from for forty years."

"Yes."

She stood in the visiting faculty office of the Gregorian University in Rome and thought about the specific texture of forty years. Forty years of building a methodology from an argument that an institution had buried. Forty years of publishing carefully, of circling the argument without landing on it, of developing the framework in private while maintaining the professional facade of a man who was interested in theology as an academic subject rather than an operational one.

And then the man who had done the burying had been here. In this building. In this city. In proximity.

"It was opportunity," she said. "The conference — Paulus didn't choose the timing to create opportunity. The opportunity existed and he had been ready for it."

"For thirty years at minimum."

"Yes." She photographed the empty shelves again. "I need the Heer connection formalized before I can take this to Hale. The accommodation cross-reference — were they in the same building?"

"Adjacent hotels." Mateo closed the notebook. "Fifty meters apart, on the same street. The booking was made through the conference housing portal, which assigns accommodation by institutional affiliation. Heer's booking was made under Tübingen — his university. Paulus's booking was made under Cologne — his current affiliation. They shouldn't have ended up adjacent."

"But they did."

"The housing algorithm had a processing error on the affiliation coding for the Gregorian conference week. Both bookings were processed in the same batch, two weeks before the conference. The error put Cologne and Tübingen in the same assignment pool."

She looked at him. "That's not coincidence."

"The error has been documented by the conference housing administration as a technical anomaly." He paused. "Whether it was introduced as an anomaly is a different question."

"Someone who knew how the housing algorithm worked."

"Someone with access to the conference administration system."

"Paulus," she said. "Or someone acting for him."

She had what she needed. The bibliography chain. The Hardt correspondence. The accommodation adjacency. The Tübingen connection across three independent evidence streams and now a fourth. She had the intellectual motive and the operational preparation and the specific window of opportunity that the conference had provided.

She did not yet have physical evidence placing Paulus in the gallery on the morning of the murder. That would come through the forensics review of the thread and the impression and the visitor log. It would be enough.

"We go to Hale at eight," she said.

Mateo nodded. He picked up the satchel. He looked at her for a moment with the specific attentiveness she had been cataloguing — the look that was not the journalist's professional attention but the other thing, which she had run out of professional categories for.

"You found it," he said. "The bibliography was yours."

She walked toward the door. She did not know what to say to this, which was unusual. She said: "We found it."

She heard him behind her. She heard the satchel strap settle on his shoulder. She heard the corridor door open.

She had, for the first time since 4:53am eleven days ago, something that felt like it was going to be enough.

She walked down the corridor toward the morning.

She walked back to the Interpol office.

The bibliography was the breakthrough. Not because it was the final piece of evidence — she needed more, she needed the direct connection between Paulus and the Gregorian security rotation, she needed the accommodation cross-reference for Heer — but because the bibliography was the intellectual heart of it. The case's physical evidence was circumstantial. The bibliography was not.

The bibliography said: this man has been building the apparatus for forty years and the apparatus matches the crime scene exactly and the match is not coincidence.

She could defend that in a briefing room. She could defend that in front of the Italian prosecutor's deputy. She could not yet take it to a judge, but she could take it to Hale and Hale could take it forward.

She had what she needed for the next step. The next step was Hale.

She walked faster. She had the bibliography and the Tübingen connection and thirty-eight hours and the specific forward momentum of an investigation that had found its spine.

She was, for the first time since 4:53am sixteen days ago, running toward something rather than behind it.

Chapter 19

What Mateo Knows About Footnotes

He called her at 1:47pm.

She was in the Interpol temporary offices reviewing the curriculum photographs for the fourth time when his number appeared on her phone. She answered immediately.

"Eleven papers," he said. "Two monographs. Combined word count approximately four hundred thousand. I read the footnotes."

"And?"

"The Leonine apparatus does not appear once. In any of it. In forty-three years of published scholarship, Dr. Heinrich Paulus has never used the citation style he was trained in at Tübingen. Not a single footnote. Not a single bibliography entry. He switched to the modern system in 1982 — his first post-doctoral publication — and has not deviated from it once in four decades of prolific academic output."

She sat with this for a moment. Four decades. Hundreds of footnotes. Complete absence of the style that appeared on the parchment beside a dead man in the Borghese Gallery.

"It's a signature," she said.

"It's more than a signature." His voice had the quality it had when he had found the next level of a thing. "It's a paradox. He abandoned the Leonine apparatus in 1982 because it was professionally obsolete. He knew it was obsolete. He has spent forty years demonstrating that he knows it's obsolete by never using it. And then he used it at a crime scene in a two-millimeter annotation that only a scholar who knew his complete bibliography would be able to identify as anomalous."

She understood what he was saying.

"He was writing for a specific reader," she said.

"He was writing for the only reader who would ever exist for whom the Leonine apparatus on that parchment was both recognizable as his specific academic fingerprint and recognizable as something he would never use accidentally." Mateo paused. "That reader was always going to be another theologian. Another scholar in his field. He left a signature that only his intellectual equal could read."

She thought about sitting across from him in the hotel room. The unhurried quality. The complete composure. The man who had told her directly what he was doing and why, knowing she couldn't use it.

He had left a signature. He had written a curriculum. He had placed his graduate student four doors from his frame and bought his vellum eleven days in advance and attended the Interpol briefing as a consultant and sat across from her in the hotel and told her the precise nature of his crime.

He had wanted to be found by someone who could read him.

"Mateo," she said.

"I know."

"Is it enough? The bibliography analysis combined with everything else — is it enough?"

A pause. The pause of a man being precise.

"The bibliography analysis alone isn't. It's circumstantial — the argument that because he never used the style in published work, its appearance at the crime scene is anomalous requires an expert witness who can testify to the history of the citation conventions and his specific deviation from them." Another pause. "But combined with the Tübingen ink, the Franciscan knot, the vellum purchase with the physical description, the Bauer testimony establishing his presence four doors from Voss, the IP discrepancy on the laptop, and the curriculum notes with the five cities —" He stopped. Then: "Yes. I think it's enough."

She exhaled. Not with relief — she did not feel relief. She felt the specific gravity of being right about something that had cost someone else a great deal. Marco Voss in his cell. Chiara Moretti in her hospital bed with twenty minutes missing from her memory. And Paulus, in his hotel room or his seminar or somewhere in this city, preparing the second lesson with the patience of a man who had decided Rome was finished and Venice was next.

"Where are you?" she said.

"Library. Sending you everything now."

The files arrived in four separate messages — the complete citation analysis, paper by paper, footnote by footnote, the absence of the Leonine apparatus documented with the methodical thoroughness of a journalist who understood that evidence needed to be presented as well as found.

She read it. She called Hale.

Hale listened for nineteen minutes.

He asked six questions. She answered all of them. He asked her to send the files and she sent them while he was still on the call and he confirmed receipt and went quiet for a moment that contained his institutional mathematics completing themselves.

"The expert witness for the citation analysis," he said.

"Father Albani at the Gregorian. He identified the Leonine apparatus in the first briefing. He can testify to its historical obsolescence and to Paulus's specific and documented abandonment of it in his published work."

"The Vatican liaison will challenge the Gregorian's independence."

"Not successfully. Father Albani has been at the Gregorian for forty years. His credibility in the field of patristic theology is unimpeachable and entirely independent of anything the Secretariat can call into question."

Another silence. Longer.

"The Director is going to ask me one question," Hale said. "Why would a visiting academic with a distinguished international reputation murder a Vatican Cardinal in a manner specifically designed to leave his own academic fingerprint at the scene?"

She had been waiting for this question since the gallery.

"Because he wanted to be understood," she said. "Not caught. Not stopped. Understood. The entire architecture of this crime — the staging, the theology, the parchment, the annotation in his old style, the curriculum notes, the fact that he attended the Interpol briefing as a consultant — none of this is the behavior of a man trying to evade detection. It's the behavior of a man who has constructed an argument and wants someone to read it." She paused.

"He's been writing for forty years. This is his most ambitious paper. He wanted a reader."

The longest silence of the call.

"Get me Father Albani's signed statement by five o'clock," Hale said. "I'll have a warrant application with the Italian prosecutor by seven. Marco Voss will be released before midnight."

She ended the call. She sat in the temporary office with the case files and the curriculum photographs and twenty-eight hours remaining on a jurisdiction she no longer needed twenty-eight hours of.

She called Mateo.

"Hale has it," she said. "Marco Voss is out before midnight. I need Father Albani's signed statement by five."

A beat. Then something in his exhale that was not quite a laugh and was not quite relief but was the sound of a person who had been working at velocity for a very long time and had just been told the velocity could ease slightly.

"Good," he said.

"Mateo."

"Yes."

"Buy yourself dinner. Something other than café food. You've been working for thirty-six hours."

A pause she had not expected. The pause of a person being looked after in a way they had not anticipated from a particular direction.

"Only if you do the same," he said.

She looked at the case files. She looked at the window. Rome outside was doing its afternoon things — the specific golden quality of October light in a city that knew how to do golden light the way it knew how to do everything: with complete assurance and no interest in being praised for it.

"Near the Pantheon," she said. "Seven o'clock."

A beat. Then: "I'll be there."

She ended the call. She picked up the case file and went to find Father Albani.

She had twenty-eight hours and a warrant coming and Marco Voss going home tonight and a man who had left his academic fingerprint at a crime scene because he wanted to be read by someone who could read him.

She was that someone. She had read him.

And somewhere in Rome, in a hotel room or a library or a seminar or the back of a taxi to a train station, Dr. Heinrich Paulus was closing his curriculum notes and thinking about Venice.

She was at the Interpol office by 4pm with the footnote documentation in her bag and three hours before the Pantheon dinner and a briefing to complete.

Hale had received the morning's evidence summary with the expression he used for things he found professionally credible and personally inconvenient. He had authorized the warrant request. He had authorized the expanded investigation protocol. He had told her she had until the Italian prosecutor's office moved — which would be forty-eight hours at most — before the case became political in a way that would take it out of both their hands.

She had worked through the afternoon with the specific intensity of someone who understood that forty-eight hours was not a deadline but a structure. You didn't work against forty-eight hours. You worked inside them.

At 6pm Mateo had sent a message: *Pantheon. Seven. There's a restaurant on the Via della Rotonda that has been there since 1975 and knows how to be quiet. I'll be at a table outside. Come when you can.*

She had come at seven-fifteen, which was the earliest the briefing allowed. He was at the table he had described, with a carafe of wine and a notebook that was closed for once, and he looked up when she arrived with the specific quality of a person who had been waiting without the anxiety of waiting.

"The warrant," she said.

"I heard." He poured wine. "Hale moves faster than I expected."

"Hale moves when the evidence gives him institutional cover to move." She sat. She looked at the Pantheon. The specific massive confidence of it, lit from below in the October evening, two thousand years of structural certainty against a sky that was doing its darkening. "He'll file the request with the Italian prosecutor tomorrow morning. By tomorrow afternoon we'll have formal extradition authorization for Paulus's current location and a European warrant for apprehension."

"Frankfurt."

"He landed in Frankfurt this morning. German police have him under passive surveillance pending the warrant." She took the wine. "He's not running. He went home."

"He knows we know."

"He's known since we went to the hotel room. Possibly since the briefing at the Gregorian. He's been three steps ahead of the investigation since 4:53am eleven days ago and he's not afraid of us knowing."

Mateo looked at her across the table. The Pantheon was lit. Rome was doing its evening things. He said: "He wants the warrant. He wants the formal recognition that someone followed the argument."

She had thought this. She had been thinking it since she stood in the empty visiting faculty office and looked at the clean rectangular patches where his books had been. "He knows the case is circumstantial. The thread, the impression, the visitor log — none of it places him in the gallery on the morning of the murder. He can contest the physical evidence. He may intend to."

"Which means the trial—"

"Which means the trial becomes the lecture." She set down the wine. "He gets to stand in a court and present the argument in full. The Hardt correspondence, the Cardinal's institutional pride, the forty years of suppressed scholarship. He gets a platform."

A silence. The Pantheon above them in the warm dark.

"And the lesson," Mateo said. "The lesson is unfinished."

"The Avaritia parchment. Venice." She looked at him. "He sent that before we had the warrant. Before he was on the plane. He prepared the sequel announcement before the first lesson was concluded."

"Because the first lesson's conclusion was always going to be the warrant."

"Yes." She thought about this. About a man who had designed his own arrest into the architecture of the argument. About the specific pride of it — the reaching hand. "He thinks we can't stop the curriculum."

"Can we?"

She thought about the seven cities. The monograph. The thirty years of preparation.

"Not the curriculum," she said. "That's inside his head. We can interrupt the lessons. Which is different." She looked at the Pantheon. "He chose Venice next. He knows we know that. He's going to have his subject selected already."

"Then we need to be in Venice first."

"Yes." She picked up the wine again. "I've already booked it."

He looked at her. Something shifted in his expression — not surprise. The other thing.

"When?" he said.

"This afternoon. Between the Hale briefing and the footnote documentation." She looked at the wine in her glass. "I booked you as well. The Gritti Palace. Your preferred conference rate."

A pause. A different pause from the taxonomy.

"You know my preferred conference rate," he said.

"You mentioned it in Venice." She looked at him. "In the first message. When you sent the Paulus file."

He looked at her for a moment. Then he picked up his wine. He looked at the Pantheon. He said, very quietly: "The Pantheon was built under Hadrian. 118 to 125 AD. He dedicated it to all the gods rather than one — the specific political genius of a man who understood that universality was more powerful than specificity."

She waited.

"Paulus made the opposite choice," Mateo said. "He dedicated his argument to one specific instance of pride. One specific man. The universality of the argument — institutional pride, the suppression of truth — but illustrated through a specific case."

"That's what makes it legible," she said. "And what makes it prosecutable. He was specific enough to leave evidence."

"He wanted to be legible."

"Yes." She looked at him. "He wanted the right reader."

She did not examine what she was saying. She was saying it and it was true and she let it be true without the professional framing.

Mateo looked at her. He did not look away. He said: "Thank you. For booking Venice."

"Don't thank me," she said. "I need the bibliography."

He smiled. It was the first time she had seen him smile in eleven days, which she noted and did not examine.

Somewhere across the city, Dr. Heinrich Paulus was closing his curriculum notes and thinking about Venice.

She looked at the Pantheon. She thought about Hadrian and all the gods and the specific genius of universality.

She finished her wine.

She thought about what came next.

She called the Gritti Palace from the taxi.

She booked two rooms in her name, on the same floor, with the invoice going to the Interpol investigation account. This was within her authorization. She had authorization for operational accommodation in any active-case city.

She thought about Mateo's voice when she told him she had already booked it. The quality of surprise that was not quite surprise, which was the quality of a person who had been expecting something and was surprised by how specifically it had arrived.

She had booked them on the same floor because the investigation required proximity.

She looked out the taxi window at Rome passing in the evening. The Pantheon behind her. The case file in her bag. The Gritti Palace booking confirmed on her phone.

She thought about what she was doing. She thought about it precisely, with the honesty she applied to evidence.

She was doing the job. She was also, simultaneously, doing something that was not entirely the job.

She held both things. This was, she was finding, her new mode of operation.

The taxi turned south toward the Piazza Navona and she looked at the city and let the two things sit beside each other and breathe.

Chapter 20

The Pantheon Dinner

Father Albani signed the statement at four-forty.

It was thorough and precise — the work of a man who had spent forty years being an expert witness in his own mind and understood exactly what form the formal version needed to take. He read the citation analysis, confirmed its accuracy, confirmed the historical obsolescence of the Leonine apparatus and Paulus's documented departure from it in 1982, and signed with the unhurried pen of a man who had been waiting for something useful to do with this particular knowledge for a long time.

"The young man in custody," he said as she was leaving. "Mr. Voss. He will be released?"

"Tonight," she said.

He nodded once. The nod of a man who had suspected something for some time and had finally been given the evidence to act on it. She did not ask what he had suspected or for how long. She had what she needed. She left.

The statement went to Hale at five-twelve. The warrant application was filed with the Italian prosecutor's office at six-forty. Marco Voss's release paperwork began processing at seven-oh-three.

At seven-eleven she walked into a small restaurant near the Pantheon that had twelve tables and a kitchen that smelled of garlic and wine and the specific Roman confidence of a place that had been making the same four dishes for thirty years and had never once considered changing them.

Mateo was already there. Of course he was.

He had arrived before her and chosen the table at the back — not the best table for the room but the best table for the conversation, she understood, because it gave her the wall at her back and the sight lines to the door and the specific privacy of a corner in a small restaurant that was filling up around them without pressing in on them.

He had ordered wine. It was already open. He poured hers when she sat without asking and she let him.

They looked at each other across the table. Neither of them reached immediately for the case. This was unusual. She noticed it was unusual and noticed that he had noticed it was unusual and that neither of them was addressing it, which was its own kind of decision.

"Marco Voss is out tonight," she said. Not the case. The human consequence of the case.

"I know." He turned his wine glass slowly. "How does that feel?"

She thought about the question. In twelve years of this work she had been asked by colleagues and commanders and institutional reviewers how cases felt and she had given institutional answers: satisfactory, progressing as expected, consistent with the objectives of the investigation. She had given these answers automatically and they had been accepted and the conversation had moved on and the feeling itself had gone into the place where she kept things she was not examining.

"Insufficient," she said.

He looked at her.

"He spent nine days in a cell for something he didn't do. Hale has a warrant application and a watch list and Paulus will be found eventually in the next city or the one after that and the curriculum will be interrupted." She picked up her wine. "Marco Voss spent nine days in a cell. That doesn't become sufficient because we found the right person eventually."

Mateo was quiet for a moment.

"No," he said. "It doesn't."

He said it without qualifications and without the instinct to resolve what she had said into something more comfortable. She noticed this. The absence of resolution. The willingness to sit with the insufficient thing as an insufficient thing rather than a problem to be converted into an acceptable outcome.

The restaurant filled around them. The waiter came and he ordered for both of them and she let him and the food arrived and was exactly what she would have chosen. This was the third time he had ordered for her and she had let him every time and she was not examining the accumulation of those three times.

They ate. They talked about things that were not the case. She told him about the church of Sant'Agostino that morning — the part about sitting for eleven minutes, not the part about the room with no doors. He told her about his first posting as a journalist in Lisbon, twenty-two years old, covering a banking scandal, filing from a hotel room so small the desk and the bed occupied the same space and he had to choose between working and sleeping. She asked how he had chosen. He said: both. She said: that's not a choice. He said: that's accurate.

She was aware of the specific quality of the evening. The October Rome night outside the restaurant's windows, the temperature having made its decision about autumn and committed to it. The particular light of a restaurant that knew exactly what it was and did not require anything of the people inside it. Two people who had been inside a case together for eleven days finding out that there was something else there when the case stepped back slightly.

She did not name what the something else was. She was not ready to name it. She was aware of it the way she was aware of things she was not examining — in the body before the mind, as a warmth that was not the wine and a quality of attention that went both directions across the table.

He told her about the seminary. Not the ex-communication — she did not ask about that, understanding that it would come when it came and not before. He told her about the theology. About the specific texture of learning Augustine at twenty, the way the Confessions had arrived in him not as a text but as something that had been written for and about a specific kind of interior life that he had recognized as his own before he had words for either the recognition or the interior life. He told her he had loved the Church the way you loved the first place that had ever fully understood you. He told her this was why leaving had cost what it had cost.

She listened without preparing her response.

This was not how she listened during investigations. During investigations she listened for the gap, the discrepancy, the word that was slightly wrong for its context. She listened to evaluate.

She was not evaluating. She was simply receiving what he said and letting it land where it landed.

The restaurant thinned around them. The waiter brought the check without being asked. Mateo took it. She let him take it.

"You're going to let me pay," he said. Not a question. The observation of a man noting a small specific event.

"You ordered," she said.

"I ordered the first time too. And the second."

She looked at him across the small table in the nearly empty restaurant. The dark eyes. The mustache. The iron ring. The way he was looking at her — not with the complete professional attention of the investigation, something else, something that had been present for eleven days in the margins of the professional attention and was present now without the margins.

She said nothing. He paid.

They walked out into the Rome night. The Pantheon was across the small piazza — two thousand years of it, lit softly, completely certain of itself in the dark. They stood looking at it for a moment.

"Paulus is going to be in Venice within the week," she said.

"I know."

"I'm going to need to follow the curriculum."

"I know." A pause. "I'll be in Venice."

She looked at the Pantheon. She thought about the source relationship and its three phases and which phase she was in. She thought about the gallery and the trained stillness and the other kind. She thought about nine days in a cell and the insufficient feeling that did not resolve.

She thought about a man who had said I'll be in Venice with the ease of someone who had already decided it.

"Good night, Mateo," she said.

"Good night."

She walked back toward the Via Margutta. She did not look back. She was aware, with the specific body-before-mind quality of things she was not examining, that he stood watching her go until she turned the corner.

She did not look back.

She thought about this the entire walk home.

She walked home along the river.

Not the direct route — the direct route was twenty minutes and the river route was thirty-five and she chose the river because she had been in enclosed spaces since 4:53am eleven days ago and the Tiber at night, which was not beautiful in the way tourism made it appear but was large and dark and moving and entirely indifferent to the specifics of her professional life, was what the evening required.

She thought about Mateo watching her go until she turned the corner.

She had not looked back. She was precise about not looking back — had been precise about it since the morning on the Via della Lungara when she had established that the best use of a departure was the departure itself, without the ambivalence of the backward glance. Every case had departures. Every case had the moment of leaving the scene, the hotel, the interview room, the restaurant on the Via della Rotonda — and she had learned, across twelve years of investigative work, to make those moments clean.

This one was not clean.

Not because she had looked. She had not. It was not clean because she had been aware, in the specific real-time way that she usually was not aware of these things, of not looking. The decision not to look had required the same cognitive energy that the looking would have required. Which meant the not-looking was its own form of looking.

She walked along the Tiber.

The river was dark. On the far bank, the lights of Trastevere reflected in the water — the same neighborhood she had walked to eleven days ago to find Marco Voss in his doorway with sleep in his clothes and a dead uncle he had been carefully grieving for a year. The loop of the case. She had arrived at the nephew and ended at the Cardinal and was now leaving Rome for Venice to begin again at the next lesson.

She thought about Mateo saying *already booked.* The specific quality of his surprise when she told him — not the professional surprise but the other kind, the one that preceded the shift in his expression that she had been cataloguing for eleven days.

She thought about sitting at the table under the Pantheon and saying *he wanted the right reader* and not examining what she was saying.

She was examining it now.

She was standing on the Ponte Sisto — stopped, which she almost never did on a working walk, but stopped — looking at the river, and she was examining it.

She had said: he wanted the right reader. She had been talking about Paulus. She had also been talking about something else. She had been aware of this and had not said the other thing. She had said only the Paulus version, which was true, and had let the other version sit in the space between the professional sentence and what she meant by it.

Mateo had heard both.

This was the thing she was standing on the bridge examining. Not what she had said. The fact of being heard. The specific experience, which she had not had in the professional context — or not in this form, not with this quality of attentiveness — of being understood past the sentence.

She had built her entire working life on the premise that the detective voice was the sufficient voice. That the precision and authority of the professional self was all that was required in all the rooms she entered. That the other self — the one that needed and wanted and was restless in the way Augustine had described — could be managed, filed, converted into fuel, and kept from the work.

Mateo had been watching her convert it to fuel for eleven days. He had said so, at 5am, on the phone, with the specific care of a man who was paying attention to the cost of the conversion.

She looked at the river.

She had not been seen like this. Not in the professional context. Not by someone whose seeing she had reason to value.

She thought: I am in the middle of an active investigation and I am standing on a bridge thinking about being seen.

She started walking again.

The rest of the walk home she thought about Venice. About the Gritti Palace and the Avaritia parchment and the specific architecture of greed as Aquinas had understood it — the disordered desire for the finite, the mistaking of the partial for the whole. About what kind of man Paulus would have selected for the second lesson and whether they could get to him first.

She thought about these things with the focused professional intelligence that was her most reliable instrument. She thought about them very carefully. She thought about nothing else.

She thought about this the entire walk home.

She thought about not looking back.

Not in the abstract — she had not looked back at the corner, which was consistent with the practice she had been developing since the Via Margutta doorstep, which was the practice of departures made clean. She thought about the specific quality of this particular not-looking, which was that she had been aware, as she turned the corner, of wanting to look back. Not wanting to look back at the investigation — the investigation was not the thing she would have looked at. She was aware of what she would have looked at.

She walked home through the streets between the Pantheon and the Via Margutta. The October evening was warm enough that she had her jacket in her hand rather than on her shoulders and the city was doing its late-evening things and she let them happen around her rather than processing them.

She had spent fifteen years keeping the professional and the personal in their appropriate containers. The skill had been useful. The containers had held. She had built a life that was primarily the work, with the personal in its correct adjacent position, and this had been sufficient and sometimes more than sufficient and occasionally, in the early hours of cities she didn't know, she had looked at the arrangement and found it adequate rather than complete.

She was not going to look at this right now. She was going to walk home and sleep and complete the case and go to Venice and be professional.

She thought about Mateo watching her walk away until she turned the corner.

She thought about the fact that she knew he had been watching without having looked back to confirm it.

She thought about this the entire walk home.

Chapter 21

Sonya Makes the Call

The hotel called her at eight-fourteen the next morning.

Not Benedetti — the duty manager, a younger man whose voice carried the specific register of someone delivering information he had been instructed to deliver and was uncertain about the instruction. Dr. Paulus had checked out. This morning. Early. The checkout had been processed at 6:03am by the night desk. He had settled his account in cash. He had left a message for her.

She was dressed and out of the apartment in four minutes.

The message was a folded piece of hotel stationery left at the front desk with her name on the outside in the same small precise handwriting she had been studying for eleven days. She photographed the envelope before she opened it. She photographed both sides of the folded paper before she read it.

Three sentences.

The investigation has been thorough. I expected nothing less from someone who reads rooms the way you do. The next lesson begins in two weeks.

No signature.

She read it three times. Then she called Mateo.

"He's gone," she said when he answered.

A silence that was not surprise. "Checkout time?"

"Six this morning. Cash. Left me a note."

"What did it say?"

She read it to him. She heard him breathing on the other end of the call and she heard in his breathing the specific quality of a journalist encountering something that was simultaneously evidence, communication, and challenge.

"The next lesson begins in two weeks," he said.

"Yes."

"He wrote to you. Not to the investigation. To you specifically."

She had noticed this. She had noticed it before she called him. She had been sitting with it in the hotel lobby while the duty manager watched her with the expression of a person who was professionally required to be helpful and personally uncertain what was happening.

"The room," she said. "I need to see the room before housekeeping gets to it."

"I'll be there in fifteen minutes."

"You don't need to —"

"Sonya."

She stopped.

"I'll be there in fifteen minutes," he said again. Simply. As if this were the only relevant piece of information.

She told the duty manager she needed access to the room. He processed this with the institutional cooperation of a man who had decided that whatever was happening was above his level of authority and that his most useful contribution was to open the door and step back.

The room was very clean.

This was not unexpected — she had known from the office that Paulus was a person who organized his physical environment with precision. But the specific cleanness of the hotel room went beyond tidiness. It had been deliberately returned to something approaching its pre-occupancy state. The bed made with a care the housekeeping staff was not responsible for. The desk clear. The bathroom dry and arranged.

The shelf above the desk was empty. The laptop, the papers, the unlabeled folder — gone. He had taken everything.

Almost everything.

On the writing desk, positioned in the center with the deliberateness of something placed rather than forgotten: a book. She recognized it before she reached it. Small. Well-worn. The particular fading of a book that had been read many times and carried everywhere.

Augustine's Confessions.

She put on gloves. She opened it carefully. The pages had been read and annotated — pencil, in the margins, the same small handwriting. She photographed every annotated page. There were many of them. He had been reading this particular copy for a very long time.

On the inside back cover, in the same pencil, a single passage had been written out in full. Not a quotation from Augustine — she checked and it wasn't in the text. His own words, in his own hand, written in the back of the book he had left for her:

To be seen by someone who is capable of seeing is not capture. It is the beginning of the only conversation that has ever interested me.

She read this three times. She photographed it. She closed the book.

Mateo arrived six minutes later. She showed him the note from the front desk and the inscription in the Confessions without speaking. He read both. He was quiet for a moment.

"He's been alone with this for a very long time," Mateo said. He said it without sympathy and without judgment and without the journalist's instinct to frame it as a finding. He said it as a simple observation that was also, she understood, a complicated one.

"Yes," she said.

"And he thinks you're capable of seeing."

She looked at the Confessions in the evidence bag. Two thousand years of theology. A man who had written the most honest account of a complicated interior life that the tradition had ever produced. And Paulus, who had spent forty years in intimate conversation with that account, leaving his own copy in a hotel room for the detective who had read his curriculum.

"Hale needs to know he's gone," she said.

"Hale already knows. The watch list flagged his passport at Fiumicino at 7:40am. He flew to Frankfurt." Mateo looked at her. "Frankfurt is a hub. He could be anywhere by now."

She called Hale. He answered before she spoke: "I know. Frankfurt. We're running the connecting flights now. He paid cash for the Rome ticket so the Frankfurt connections are unknown."

"He's going to Venice," she said. "The curriculum. Avaritia is next. Greed. Venice."

"That's an inference, not a location."

"That's where he's going."

A pause. The mathematics of a man deciding whether to act on an inference.

"I'll have Interpol Venice on alert. And Sonya — the warrant is confirmed. Paulus is formally a suspect. The watch list is active across all Schengen borders." He paused. "Maro Voss was released at eleven-forty last night. He's home."

She exhaled.

"Thank you, Commander."

She ended the call. She stood in Paulus's empty hotel room with the evidence bag containing his annotated Confessions and the note from the front desk and the photograph of the inscription and Mateo beside her and Rome outside the window doing its permanent indifferent thing.

He had gone. He had left something for her. He had told her the lesson was not finished.

She picked up the evidence bag.

"When does your Venice assignment start?" she said.

Mateo looked at her with the expression that was not quite the recalibration and not quite the slow arriving warmth and was something between the two that she did not yet have a name for.

"Whenever Venice needs me," he said.

She confirmed the booking at nine-fifteen.

Venice. The Gritti Palace. Two rooms, on the same floor, because the investigation required proximity and she had stopped pretending the investigation was the only reason for anything she had done in the past eleven days. She booked them from the temporary apartment with the carry-on half-packed on the bed beside her and the Avaritia parchment in its evidence bag on the desk.

She looked at the parchment.

A canal sketch below the Latin word. The specific architectural silhouette of a city that had been sinking for five hundred years and had determined that this was simply its condition. He had sketched it precisely — not from memory of a tourist visit but from the knowledge of someone who had been there professionally, who knew which canal, which specific arrangement of Gothic windows, which angle from which the sketch could only have been made from one position.

She had sent the sketch to the Rome forensics team's imaging specialist at three that afternoon. The response had come at six: the perspective and scale were consistent with a sketch made from the Ponte dell'Accademia, looking east toward the Salute. A specific bridge. A specific direction.

He had been there.

She added this to the case file: *Venice — Accademia bridge. Pre-visit confirmed by sketch perspective analysis.* She added it with the specific professional care of someone who understood that each piece of evidence was a stone and the building took the weight of all of them equally. She did not yet know when he had been there. She did not yet know if the second subject had been selected or was still being assessed.

She knew that if she and Mateo arrived in Venice before the lesson began, they had a chance at the thing she had not been able to do in Rome: the intervention. Not after the staging. Before.

Her phone rang at ten.

"Heer," Mateo said. He was moving — she could hear the specific acoustics of a Roman street at night behind him. "His supervisor at Tübingen confirmed it. Hardt personally authorized Heer's conference registration. Not the standard departmental authorization — Hardt signed the research travel request himself."

"Hardt sent him."

"Hardt sent him." A pause. "The specific purpose listed on the travel request is 'archival observation related to the Leonine apparatus documentation project.' Which doesn't exist as a registered project at Tübingen. There is no documentation project."

"He invented a purpose for the travel form."

"Or Hardt did. It's Hardt's signature." Another pause. "Sonya. If Hardt knowingly sent Heer to Rome for a purpose related to what Paulus was doing—"

"Then this is larger than Paulus," she said. "I know." She looked at the parchment on her desk. "Hardt is seventy-three. He's been publishing variations of the same argument since 1976. He watched the Vatican bury the original correspondence. He watched Paulus build the methodology. He may have been involved in building it."

"He may have been the point of origin."

"Yes." She thought about this. "Don't name that in any documentation yet. I don't have enough. And if we move on Hardt before the Venice lesson is resolved—"

"He disappears the evidence."

"Or he warns Paulus. If Paulus doesn't know we're onto the Tübingen connection—"

"He may not. The warrant request went through the standard channel. Nothing in the documentation names Tübingen specifically."

"Good." She stood. She walked to the window. The Via Margutta at ten at night, Rome doing its comfortable things. "What's your flight to Venice?"

"First one tomorrow. You?"

"Same. I'll see you at the Gritti." She paused. "Mateo."

"Yes."

"The sketch. The Accademia bridge, looking east." She looked at the evidence bag on her desk. "He was standing on that bridge looking at what he was going to do. Before he knew who the subject would be."

"He chooses the location first," Mateo said.

"Then he finds the life that fits it." She thought about the Cardinal and the Bernini. About the specific perfection of the match between the location and the subject. "He's patient enough to wait for the right person."

"Or the right person presents themselves."

"Yes." A pause. "Venice has been waiting for someone for a long time."

She heard Mateo's silence. Not the empty kind.

"I know a man," he said, "who has been writing about greed and the specific moral architecture of mercantile civilization for most of his professional life. He'll be at the Venetian conference."

She looked at the parchment.

"His name," she said.

Mateo told her.

She wrote it down. She looked at it. She thought about the Accademia bridge and the canal sketch and the patience of a man who had been waiting for the right configuration of subject and location.

She thought: we have to be there first.

"I'll see you at the Gritti," she said. She ended the call. She looked at the parchment one more time — the careful Latin word, the precise canal sketch, the knowledge of a second lesson already prepared.

Then she finished packing.

She had a plane to catch in the morning. She did not have time to be anything other than the detective.

She also did not have time to pretend that the detective was all she was.

She packed. She went to bed. She thought about a man standing on the Accademia bridge with the patience of someone for whom thirty years was not a long time to wait.

She thought about the warmth of Mateo's voice at ten at night saying *whenever Venice needs me.*

She thought about what that warmth meant.

She slept.

She confirmed the Frankfurt intelligence from the Rome liaison at nine-fifteen.

Paulus had boarded a Lufthansa flight at 6:47am. The passenger manifest was confirmed. He was in Frankfurt, which was where German scholars went when they were done with Rome and needed to be somewhere that felt like home.

He had not run. He had not disappeared. He had gone home with the methodical regularity of a man who had done what he had come to do and had no reason to be anywhere other than where he was supposed to be.

She thought about this. About the specific confidence it took to go home. About the warrant that was coming and the European arrest protocol and the German authorities' cooperation requirement and the thirty to ninety days that the institutional machinery typically needed to process an extradition.

He knew all of this. He had built the timing into the architecture. He had known from the beginning that he had thirty to ninety days after Rome before the institution caught up with him.

He intended to use them.

She looked at the Avaritia parchment in its evidence bag. The canal sketch. The east-facing perspective from the Accademia bridge.

She called the Gritti Palace in Venice.

She booked two rooms.

She stood in the hotel lobby for a moment after the manager had given her the checkout documentation.

6:03am. A five-hour head start. Cash checkout. A 5am wake call cancelled at 4:47am, which meant he had been awake and preparing for at least an hour before the call would have rung. He had been ready to leave before the institutional machinery had registered that he was leaving.

This was not improvisation. You did not cash-settle a hotel in the pre-dawn hours of a working day and cancel your own wake call as an improvisation. This was a planned departure with a planned timing.

She thought about what the timing meant.

The forensics team had confirmed their work at 11pm the previous night. The formal case transfer to the Italian prosecutor had been filed at 8pm. The warrant request had been initiated at 9am that morning — after he had already left. He had departed Rome in the window between the prosecutor's formal involvement and the warrant's initiation. He had known the window. He had planned around it.

He had been watching the investigation's timeline.

She thought about the visitor log. The two-hour seventeen-minute access to the Bernini collection four days before the murder. He had studied the space. He had studied the security rotation. She now understood that he had also been studying the institutional machinery — the pace at which Interpol investigations moved, the specific timeline from crime scene documentation to suspect identification to warrant request. He had built the departure window into the architecture the same way he had built everything else into it.

He had designed this to conclude with his exit intact.

She returned to the temporary office. She put the hotel documentation with the case file. She sat at the desk and thought about a man who had been three steps ahead of the investigation from the moment he had planned it.

She thought: the only way to stop being three steps behind is to stop following and start anticipating.

She looked at the evidence bag with the Avaritia parchment.

He had sent it before he left Rome. He had prepared it before Rome was concluded. He had been in Venice — or had arranged the Venice reconnaissance — while he was still here. He was three steps ahead because he had started planning the second lesson before the first one was complete.

She needed to start planning the second lesson before she arrived in Venice.

She called Mateo.

She opened her laptop.

She booked two rooms.

Chapter 22

The Architecture of Closing

The case closed in layers.

The outermost layer — the formal transfer of jurisdiction — happened at 8am on the twelfth day. She met the Italian prosecutor's deputy at a conference room near the Campo de' Fiori and transferred the physical evidence, the witness statements, the forensics documentation, and the chain-of-custody record with the specific efficiency of a handoff she had practiced in fourteen previous investigations across nine countries. The deputy — a careful, mid-level official named Vitale who had been working financial crimes for a decade before this and was clearly uncertain what to do with a theological homicide — received each folder in order and signed the transfer receipt with the unhurried care of a man who understood that his signature was a boundary.

She shook his hand. She left.

The second layer — the internal Interpol report — she completed at the temporary office, alone, from ten until two. It was the longest report she had written in four years, not because the case was complex — she had worked more complex cases — but because the complexity that existed was of a kind that the standard reporting structure was not built to accommodate. The standard structure had boxes for physical evidence and witness testimony and suspect identification and chain of custody. It did not have a box for *the staging was a philosophical argument addressed to a specific reader.* It did not have a box for *the subject was selected according to a methodology the suspect has been developing for thirty years and intends to continue developing across six additional European cities.*

She wrote around the boxes. She used the supplemental notes section for the architecture that didn't fit the form.

She was precise. She was thorough. She used language that would allow Hale to understand what had happened and the prosecutor to work with it and any future investigator — in Venice, in Florence, in cities she had not yet been to — to understand the methodology they were dealing with.

She did not use the word *curriculum* in the formal report. She used the word *methodology* twenty-three times.

At two-fifteen she sent the report to Hale's deputy and sat in the empty temporary office for a moment. The accumulated paper of fifteen days had been filed or transferred or photographed and the desk was clear for the first time since she had arrived and the office had the specific quality of a space that had been used for something and had resumed being simply a space.

She thought about the case the way she thought about closed cases — from the outside, now, looking at the shape of it. The Cardinal. The Borghese Gallery. The parchment. Fourteen days of architecture-building that had ended in a European warrant and a confirmed suspect and an unresolved question she had not included in the formal report.

The unresolved question was: what was he selecting for in Venice.

She had the Ferrini hypothesis. She had the 2017 provenance questions and the Hardt acknowledgment and the conference registration adjacency. She did not yet have the specific quality of Ferrini's institutional pride — the thing that made him the second page of the argument, the Avaritia to the Cardinal's Superbia. She needed to understand it before she arrived in Venice, because understanding the selection criteria was the only way to intervene before the lesson.

She had carried the front desk note from Rome to Brussels in her jacket pocket and had then placed it in the desk drawer when she unpacked, which was more deliberate than the jacket pocket, which was something she did not examine.

On the third day she took it out of the drawer and read it again.

To be seen by someone who is capable of seeing is not capture. It is the beginning of the only conversation that has ever interested me.

She sat with it at the Brussels desk with the coffee cooling beside her and thought about the specific problem of a man who had left her a note about conversation and whose conversation she was professionally required to interrupt.

There was something she had not yet named to herself about the case. She had been precise about the evidence and the methodology and the institutional motive and the intellectual architecture. She had been less precise about the thing that had been sitting in her chest since the briefing room on the first morning when she had processed the room and processed him simultaneously and had filed the second processing under things she was not reading.

She was reading it now.

She was, at some level she was not going to articulate in a case file or a Hale briefing or a transfer document, interested in him. Not in the way she was interested in perpetrators as problems to be solved — she had that interest, it was professional, it was the engine of the investigation. In a different way. The specific interest of a person who has encountered another person of comparable intelligence operating in an incompatible direction and finds the incompatibility generative rather than simply obstructive.

She found this troubling. She found it accurate.

She put the note back in the drawer. She made more coffee. She sat at the desk and thought about Venice and what she was going to find there and whether finding it first would be enough.

She thought: it has to be enough. It is the job.

She thought: the job has never required this specific calibration before.

She thought about Mateo. About the bar near the Pantheon and the specific quality of his attention at ten at night and the seven days she had spent in Brussels thinking about calling him and not calling him. She thought about the fact that he was going to Venice, and that the case was going to continue, and that she had fifteen days of very specific evidence about what it was like to work alongside someone whose intelligence complemented rather than duplicated her own.

She thought: I have been alone inside this work for a very long time.

She did not answer this observation. She made the coffee and put it beside the laptop.

She opened her laptop. She began.

At four she heard a knock at the temporary office door. She looked up.

Mateo.

He had the satchel and the notebook and two coffees in cardboard cups and the specific expression of a man who had been in the city doing what he did — accumulating information through the network of relationships and withheld articles and professional obligations he had built across fifteen years — and had arrived at something he needed to tell her.

"Come in," she said.

He came in. He set a coffee on the desk without asking if she wanted it. She did want it.

"Hardt," he said. He sat in the chair across from her. "He called Ferrini this morning. I have a contact who monitors Hardt's institutional phone — legitimate journalistic purpose, longstanding authorization, I won't explain the details." He opened the notebook. "The call was seven minutes. The content was not recorded. But the call happened, and the timing—"

"The timing is the day after Paulus flew to Frankfurt."

"Yes." He looked at her. "Hardt called Ferrini. The day after his student left Rome."

She processed this. "He's telling Ferrini the Rome lesson is concluded."

"Or warning him. Or checking that Ferrini is ready for whatever comes next." Mateo closed the notebook. "I don't know which. But the call happened."

She looked at the laptop. At the research she had been building since 2pm. "Ferrini knows," she said. "He's not the innocent subject. He knows about the curriculum."

"Or he knows about Hardt's work. The argument. The thirty-year intellectual project." A pause. "Which is different from knowing that the argument is being made in the way it's being made."

"Is it?"

He was quiet for a moment. This was the considering pause — the one she had learned to read as a man reaching for the accurate thing rather than the convenient one. "Hardt has been publishing variations of the same argument for forty years. Every person who has engaged seriously with his work has understood the philosophical position. Ferrini cited him. Ferrini knows the argument."

"But knowing the argument is not the same as knowing that someone has decided to demonstrate it."

"No." He looked at her steadily. "But it might mean that Ferrini knows what he represents in the argument. That he knows his own relevance to it."

She thought about this for a long time. The coffee was getting cold. She drank it.

"Then the selection is mutual," she said. "Paulus selects the subject. But the subject — on some level — presents themselves. The Cardinal didn't know he was being selected. But the quality that made him the subject was visible. Readable. In his public record, his institutional decisions, his published positions."

"His specific form of pride."

"Yes. It was documented. It was in the record." She looked at the laptop. "If Ferrini's greed is also in the record — if what he did in 2017, whatever was withdrawn—"

"It's documented somewhere," Mateo said. "The journalist who withdrew the story didn't destroy her notes. I know her. I've been thinking about calling her for three days."

"Call her."

"In Venice, or now?"

She thought about this. "Now. Before we arrive. If Ferrini knows we're coming — if Hardt warned him — we need to arrive knowing more than he expects us to know."

Mateo nodded. He picked up his coffee. He looked at her across the desk — the same desk she had been sitting at for fifteen days, the desk that was now clear of the case files and held only her laptop and two cups of coffee.

"The report," he said. "Is it filed?"

"Filed and transferred. Formally closed on the Rome end."

"Then you're done for the day."

"I'm working."

"You're always working." He said it without reproach. "The case is closed in Rome. The next one opens in Venice." He paused. "There are a few hours between those two facts."

She looked at him. He was not suggesting anything specific. He was simply — as he had been doing for fifteen days — seeing something she was not attending to.

She saved the document. She closed the laptop. She picked up the coffee.

"One hour," she said.

He smiled. It was the second time in fifteen days she had seen him smile. She was noting the frequency.

"One hour," he said.

They walked out into Rome. The afternoon light was very specific. She had one hour between a closed case and an open one, and Rome was very good at receiving a person who had an hour and no particular plan for it.

They walked south along the Via del Corso and then west through the small streets toward the Piazza Navona, which was not on the way to anywhere in particular but which was Rome at its most deliberately, confidently beautiful, and she had an hour and nowhere to be and Rome was offering this.

She had never walked through a city without a case purpose before. Not in twelve years of investigative travel. She had walked through cities with destinations: crime scenes, interview locations, the offices of people she needed to speak to. She had walked through cities in transit between those destinations. She had walked through cities with the specific urgency of a person whose mind was processing the case and whose body was providing the processing time.

She was walking without destination or urgency. This was unusual enough that she noticed it for the first four minutes and then stopped noticing it and simply walked.

Mateo walked beside her. He was quiet in the way he was quiet when he was paying attention to something other than the investigation — when he was in the city rather than in the case. She had noticed this distinction across fifteen days: his journalist's attentiveness shifted when the investigative context dropped away, became less directed and more open, more like someone receiving the world rather than reading it.

She was receiving the world. This was also unusual.

At the Piazza Navona she stopped. Not for any reason. The fountain — the Bernini again, the Four Rivers, the specific muscular confidence of stone that had been commissioned to outlast everything around it and had succeeded. She looked at it.

"He liked Bernini," she said.

"He chose well," Mateo said. He was looking at the fountain too. "Bernini understood that the most interesting moment is always the one before the consequence arrives."

"The instant of transformation."

"Yes." He looked at her sideways. The look she had catalogued. "You've been standing in a lot of those instants."

She thought about this. About the gallery, and the Pantheon dinner, and the Via Margutta doorstep, and this piazza now, in the last hour before the case transferred and became someone else's structure to maintain.

"So have you," she said.

He looked at the fountain. "Yes."

They stood in the Roman afternoon in front of the Four Rivers fountain and she let the hour be what it was, which was the specific suspended quality of time between one thing and the next, which was Rome receiving them both, which was something she had not expected to be in at any point in this investigation and was in now.

She was aware of him beside her. She was aware of the case behind them. She was aware that in approximately forty-five minutes she was going to pick up the carry-on bag from the temporary apartment and go to the airport and this particular configuration of things was going to end.

She did not say any of this.

He did not say any of this.

They stood in front of the Bernini and the afternoon light was very specific on the stone.

She let it receive her.

Chapter 23

The Frame Holds

She went to see Marco Voss.

Not because the case required it — the case required nothing from him now. His release had been processed. The Italian prosecutor's office had the warrant documentation. The watch list was active. Everything that needed to be in motion was in motion and Marco Voss was no longer part of the procedural architecture.

She went because she had signed a report nine days ago that had not prevented his arrest. She had known he was innocent and she had signed a report that was accurate and inadequate simultaneously and she had not been able to live with the signing and she had found the thing that made it irrelevant and he had gone home at eleven-forty and she had not been asleep at eleven-forty.

She knocked on the door of the apartment on the Via della Lungara at ten in the morning. He answered more quickly this time — the sleep-worn dishevelment of the first visit was gone. He had showered. He was dressed. He looked at her with an expression that was not yet the expression of a person who had fully understood that the danger had passed.

"Commissioner," he said.

"Mr. Voss. May I come in?"

He stepped back.

The apartment was the same: the theological texts, the desk, the mismatched kitchen chairs. She sat in hers — the older one. He sat across from her and looked at his hands in the way he had looked at them during the first interview, which she understood now as a habit rather than guilt, the gesture of a person who processed difficult things by attending to something immediate and physical.

"They told me the warrant was for someone else," he said. "They didn't tell me who."

"I can't discuss the details of the ongoing investigation," she said. She said it carefully, which was not how she usually said things she couldn't discuss. "What I can tell you is that the evidence against you was fabricated and that the person who fabricated it has been identified and is being pursued."

He was quiet for a moment.

"Why me?" he said. Not with anger. With genuine inquiry. The specific question of a person who has had nine days in a cell to think about what they represent to someone they have never met.

She thought about the answer. The curriculum. The lesson. The Cardinal's specific form of pride and the nephew who had been collateral to it for eight years before being repurposed as its consequence. She thought about what she could say and what she could not and what the truth was and whether they overlapped sufficiently.

"Your uncle's life made you a convenient narrative," she said. "The person who did this is very good at understanding how institutions read stories. Your history with your uncle was a story institutions could read."

He looked at his hands. "He's been making me a convenient narrative for eight years."

"I know," she said.

She did not stay long. She told him she might need a formal statement at some point in the prosecution process. She told him to contact her directly if anything unusual happened — any unfamiliar contacts, any unexpected correspondence. She gave him her card. He took it. He looked at it for a moment.

"Did you know?" he said. "During the investigation. Did you know it wasn't me?"

She met his eyes. "Yes."

"From when?"

"From the beginning."

He nodded slowly. The nod of a person integrating something difficult.

"Then why —"

"Because knowing and proving are different things," she said. "And the system moves at its own speed. I'm sorry for the nine days."

She said it simply and without the institutional language that would have made it easier to say and less worth saying. He looked at her for a moment. Then he said: "Thank you for not letting it be longer."

She stood. She shook his hand. She left.

In the stairwell she stopped for thirty seconds. Not because she needed to. Because the specific weight of what she had just done required a moment before the next thing.

Then she walked down to the Via della Lungara and into the Roman morning and began the procedural work of closing Rome: the final evidence reports, the transfer of jurisdiction to the Italian prosecutor's office, the formal communication to Commander Hale, the documentation for Interpol's central registry that would flag the Paulus case across all member states.

She worked through the afternoon. At four-thirty she returned to the temporary apartment and packed. The carry-on bag she had arrived with. The case file, which was complete and would be handed to Hale's deputy at the airport. The Augustine Confessions in its evidence bag, which would go to the Rome laboratory before she left and which she had read the inscription from seventeen times since finding it.

She did not take the Confessions. She was aware that she wanted to. She did not take it.

She did take the note from the front desk. This was not procedurally correct. She put it in her jacket pocket and did not examine why.

She was sitting at the desk reviewing the final documentation when her phone showed a message from the Rome liaison. A package had been left at the Interpol temporary office address. No sender. She had been named on the exterior.

She went.

The package was a small envelope. The outside: her name in the now-familiar small precise handwriting. She photographed it before she opened it. She photographed the interior before she removed the contents.

A square of vellum. Fifteen by fifteen centimeters. The color of old teeth. Iron gall ink.

One word in Latin. Center of the square. Surrounded by so much empty space it looked almost modest. Almost humble.

Avaritia. Greed.

Beneath the word, barely visible, a pencil sketch. Not the main hand — the finer annotation hand. She brought the overhead light closer. A canal. Gothic windows reflected in still water. Rain on the surface. The specific architectural silhouette of a city that had been sinking for five hundred years and had decided this was simply its condition.

Venice.

She photographed it. She placed it in an evidence bag. She sat for a moment at the desk in the temporary Interpol office where she had sat for eleven days with this case, with her coffee, with the accumulation of evidence that had been enough and then more than enough, looking at a piece of vellum that was the beginning of the next lesson.

He had left Rome before she had the warrant. He had packed his curriculum notes and his unpublished monograph and left the Confessions and the note and been on a plane to Frankfurt before most of Rome had finished its morning coffee. He had sent this from somewhere — from the airport or a Roman post office or a contact he had established before the lesson began — because the lesson included its own sequel announcement and he had always known where the sequel would be set.

She called Mateo.

"It arrived," she said when he answered.

A beat. "What does it say?"

"Avaritia." She looked at the evidence bag. "And a canal sketch."

A longer beat. She heard something in the quality of his silence that was not surprise and was not resignation and was, she understood, the specific response of a man who had already known this was coming and had already decided something about it.

"So," he said. "Venice."

"So." She put the evidence bag in her carry-on beside the note from the front desk that she had not examined why she had kept. "Venice."

She photographed the parchment three times and put it in the evidence bag and sat at the desk in the temporary Interpol office and looked at it through the plastic.

He had prepared this before Rome was concluded. He had drawn the canal sketch — that specific east-facing perspective from the Accademia bridge — while he was still in the city, or before he arrived, which meant Venice had been selected before Rome was staged. The curriculum was not improvised. The curriculum was written in full before the first page was turned.

She thought about what it meant to be inside a book that had already been finished.

She called Mateo. She told him about the parchment. She heard him process it with the specific quality of a man who had also been awake too long and had arrived, in the exhaustion, at the same place she had.

"Already booked," he said. "See you there."

She ended the call. She sat for a moment with the evidence bag and the fifteen days of accumulated paper and the knowledge, sitting in her chest like something that had been placed there carefully and was waiting, that the first lesson was over and the second had already begun.

Venice. Avaritia. Greed.

She looked at the canal sketch through the plastic of the evidence bag. The specific view from a specific bridge in a city that had been built on the premise that beauty and commerce were the same word.

She heard something in the quality of his silence that was not surprise and was not resignation and was, she understood, the specific response of a man who had already known this was coming and had already decided something about it.

She sat at the desk in the temporary Interpol office for twelve minutes after ending the call.

Not working. The desk was covered in the accumulated documentation of fifteen days and she was looking at it the way you looked at the end of something — with the specific recognition that the shape of it was now complete and readable as a shape, which it had not been while you were inside it.

The shape was: a Cardinal arranged before a Bernini to demonstrate the theology of pride. A German academic who had spent forty years building a methodology and had applied it, once, in Rome. An Avaritia parchment that proved the methodology was not finished. Six more cities waiting.

She looked at the parchment in its evidence bag.

The canal sketch was precise. Not the sketch of a man who had looked at photographs — the sketch of a man who had stood there. She had confirmed the perspective: the Ponte dell'Accademia looking east, with the Santa Maria della Salute in the middle distance and the specific angle of the Gothic palazzo facades on the right bank. He had stood on that bridge. He had looked at what Venice was going to mean.

She thought about what Venice meant.

She knew the theological architecture of greed — she had been reading since the third day in Rome, when she had understood that reading the theology was reading the methodology, that the sin framework was both the intellectual content of the argument and the selection criteria. Avaritia in Aquinas: the disordered desire for finite goods treated as though they were infinite. The mistaking of the partial for the whole. The corruption of legitimate desire through illegitimate means.

Venice had been built by merchants who had understood that the world's wealth moved through water and had positioned themselves accordingly. A city whose entire aesthetic — the palazzo facades, the gilded ceilings, the six centuries of accumulated beauty — had been financed by commerce conducted with the specific ruthlessness of people who had decided that the beautiful and the profitable were the same category. Venice did not apologize for this. Venice had decided this was simply its nature.

Paulus had chosen Venice the way he had chosen the Borghese Gallery: not arbitrarily, but with the specific intelligence of someone who understood that the location was also an argument. The crime scene was always the argument.

She was going to find his subject before he staged the lesson.

She had Ferrini as a hypothesis. She had the Hardt connection and the 2017 provenance questions and the conference registration. She had Mateo's contact at Ca' Foscari who was going to know what the journalist who withdrew the 2017 story had known and why she had withdrawn it.

She had one week.

She picked up the Avaritia parchment one more time. She looked at the canal sketch through the plastic. She thought about a man standing on a Venetian bridge looking east, with a pencil in his hand, drawing what he saw, knowing what it was going to mean.

She thought: he prepared Venice before Rome was staged. He was already there when we were here.

She had called Mateo. She had told him about the parchment. She had heard something in the quality of his silence that was not surprise and was not resignation and was, she understood, the specific response of a man who had already known this was coming and had already decided something about it.

She had heard, in that silence, that he had already decided he was going to Venice.

She put the parchment back in the evidence bag. She put the evidence bag in the carry-on beside the front desk note. She filed the formal notification. She did everything the procedure required.

Then she locked the temporary office for the last time and walked out into Rome and began the sequence of things that would end, in twelve hours, at Marco Polo airport.

She had a curriculum to interrupt.

Chapter 24

What Augustine Said About Rest

Her last evening in Rome.

She had filed the final documentation by six. She had transferred formal jurisdiction to the Italian prosecutor's office by seven. She had packed at seven-thirty. The carry-on bag stood by the door of the temporary apartment with the case file and the front desk note and the evidence bags and the absence of the Confessions she had not taken.

She called Mateo at eight.

"One drink," she said. "Before I leave."

He said yes before she finished the sentence.

They met at a bar near the Pantheon — not the restaurant from the night before, a different place, smaller, the kind of Roman establishment that didn't bother with ambiance because it had been there since 1947 and had decided that was ambiance enough. Two stools at the end of the bar. Wine. The barman who did not ask what they wanted but brought what was appropriate for the hour and the appearance of the two people sitting down, which was the particular gift of a barman who had been reading customers for forty years.

They sat for a moment without speaking. Not the silence of the investigation — that silence had been purposeful, working, two people processing information in the same direction. This was different. This was the silence of people who had been inside something together and were now, briefly, on the other side of it and were finding out what remained.

"The Confessions," she said.

"You left it."

"I left it." She turned her wine glass. "The inscription. What he wrote."

"To be seen by someone who is capable of seeing is not capture," Mateo said. He said it from memory. She had read it to him once. "It is the beginning of the only conversation that has ever interested me."

She looked at her wine.

"He thinks I can see him," she said.

"You can." Mateo said it without qualification or hedging. "That's not a comfortable thing, but it's true."

"Seeing someone isn't understanding them."

"No. But it's the beginning of it. Which is what he said." A pause. "He's been alone with his curriculum for a very long time. He's found one person who he believes is equipped to be his reader. Whether that's accurate — whether you actually see what he thinks you see — is a separate question."

She thought about this. She thought about sitting across from him in the hotel room and the specific discomfort of being looked at by someone who processed everything they looked at with the same complete attention. She had felt, in that room, the particular exposure of a person being read by someone who was very good at reading.

She thought about whether she was frightened by this or by something else.

"The Confessions," she said. "The passage he left underlined. The one in the text." She had photographed it. She had not asked Mateo to translate it because she had not been ready to ask. "Translate it for me."

He was quiet for a moment. She understood from the quality of his quiet that he had already read it and had been waiting for her to ask.

"Thou awakest us to delight in Thy praise," he said slowly, "for Thou madest us for Thyself, and our heart is restless until it repose in Thee." He paused. "It's the most famous passage in the Confessions. Augustine's argument that the human soul is constituted by a longing that nothing in the world can satisfy — that the restlessness people try to resolve through sin, through appetite, through the construction of a self no one can reach, is actually the mark of a creature made for something that the world cannot provide."

She sat with this.

"Our heart is restless until it repose in Thee," she said. "And he left it for me."

"Yes."

"What do you think it means?"

Mateo looked at her directly. Not with the professional attention of the investigation. Something else. The attention that had been in the margins of the professional attention for eleven days and was present now without the margins.

"I think," he said carefully, "that he recognized something in you that he recognized in himself. The specific quality of a restlessness that has been very thoroughly managed. He left you Augustine's argument that the management is not the solution." A pause. "I think he's not entirely wrong."

She held his gaze for a moment.

Then she picked up her wine and looked at the bar and they sat in a companionable quiet that was different from all the other quiet they had shared and was, she thought, the most honest thing that had happened between them in eleven days.

She left at ten. He walked her to the Via Margutta — not to the door of the apartment, to the street. They stood on the cobblestones in the October dark.

"Venice," she said.

"Venice," he said.

She went inside. She did not look back. She was becoming very practiced at not looking back and this was not the same as not wanting to.

She went upstairs. She showered. She put on the clothes she slept in and she sat on the edge of the bed in the temporary apartment and she looked at the wall.

The wall was the wall of a furnished apartment rented by Interpol for investigators on assignment. It had no particular quality. It was a wall.

She sat on the edge of the bed and she let Rome happen to her.

This was the unusual thing. She was not, in this moment, managing Rome — filing it, processing it, converting it into procedural currency. She was letting it come in through the window: the October sounds, the particular quality of the city's nighttime hum, the smell of stone and motor exhaust and somewhere distant the specific sweetness of something being cooked that she couldn't name. She was letting the exhaustion sit in her body instead of converting it to fuel. She was letting the room be a room.

She thought about the doorstep. She did not manage the thought. She let it sit.

She had been in charge of things since she was eight years old. In charge of her own presentation, her own armor, the specific management of being a person who required nothing from anyone in a way that was always legible, always controlled, always held. She had built this capacity because the alternative — the unmanaged self, the one that needed and wanted and allowed itself to be affected — was not safe. She had learned this early. She had learned it from watching what happened to people who were not in charge of themselves in rooms organized around someone else's needs.

She sat on the edge of the bed.

She thought about Mateo standing on the cobblestones. The specific quality of him not saying the thing. The way he stood in a doorway the same way he stood in a gallery — without requiring the room to accommodate him, taking up exactly the space he occupied and not performing around its edges. She thought about eleven days of this quality and the specific feeling of being in its proximity, which was something like rest, which was something she had very little practised vocabulary for.

She thought about Augustine's line. Our heart is restless until it repose in Thee. She thought about what it meant that she had been looking for the rest of that sentence without knowing it was a sentence, without knowing there was a word for the specific fatigue of a person who had been managing their own restlessness for thirty years and had become so good at the management that the restlessness itself had become invisible.

It was not invisible tonight.

She lay back on the bed. She looked at the ceiling of the temporary apartment. She allowed herself, for sixty seconds, to stop being in charge of the question. Not to answer it. Not to resolve it. Simply to stop holding it at arm's length and let it be the size it actually was.

It was large.

She had known this. She had been managing the knowledge of this for — she thought about when it had started, the specific beginning, and arrived at the gallery with the Bernini and understood that it had not started there. It had started before. She had been managing it since the first morning, since the crime scene, since the moment Mateo had walked into the room with his Vatican press credential and his brown satchel and his particular quality of paying attention and she had looked at him and something in her had looked back.

She did not do anything with this understanding. She held it.

Then she let it go the way she let everything go before sleep — filed, not resolved, put away carefully in the part of herself that was not the detective and not the professional and was simply the thirty-five-year-old woman who had grown up inside pride's architecture and had been investigating it, she understood now, her entire career.

She lay in the dark for a long time.

Not not-sleeping. Not the active wakefulness of a mind still running the case. This was different — a specific quality of presence in the dark, the body at rest and the mind at rest differently, not working but not empty. Present. She was aware of the sound of Rome through the window, which she had been aware of for fifteen nights and had processed as background until now. Now it was specific. The particular traffic. The specific church bell three streets east. The way the city breathed at this hour, which was nothing like the way a city breathed in the day.

She thought about the doorstep.

She thought about what she had said in the bar, without planning to say it: *Our heart is restless until it repose in Thee.* She had said it back to him as though she were quoting it, but she had been doing something other than quoting it. She had been receiving it. She had let it come in through the professional membrane and sit somewhere that was not the case file.

She had spent fifteen years becoming very precise about what she let in. The cases came in because the cases were the work and the work was what she had built herself to do. The rest she had managed — the personal history, the relationships that had not survived the quality of attention the work required, the specific loneliness that was not loneliness exactly but was the particular result of being a person whose primary relationship was with the truth of a situation rather than with any individual human being in it.

She had managed this for fifteen years. She had gotten good at the management.

She was lying in the dark of a furnished apartment in Rome and she was aware that the management was currently requiring more effort than usual, and she was not, for this particular hour, applying that effort.

She was letting the restlessness be the size it was.

It was larger than she had calculated.

She thought: I have been building this fortress for thirty-five years and I have not once seriously considered what I would do if someone built a door in it.

She thought: he didn't build a door. He found the one that was already there.

She did not examine this further. She had learned, across the fifteen days, when to examine and when to hold. This was a holding moment. She held it.

She did not answer this question. She slept.

She lay in the dark and thought about the fortress.

Not the word — she did not use the word, had not ever used it, would not use it now. The concept. The specific architecture of a self that had been built for protection and had been built well and had been maintained across thirty-five years with the diligence of someone who understood that what you maintained was what held.

She had been building since she was eight years old. The construction had been necessary. The construction had been successful. The fortress was solid and reliable and had served exactly the purpose it had been built for — the protection of the interior from the specific forms of damage that the exterior world, in her particular experience of it, tended to produce.

She had not, in thirty-five years of construction and maintenance, seriously considered the possibility that something would come at the fortress from inside.

She was considering it now.

Not Mateo. Mateo was outside the fortress, in the appropriate position — close enough to be professional, distant enough to be manageable. He had not come at the fortress from inside. He had simply been present, with the quality of presence he had, and the interior of the fortress had begun to notice.

The interior had been very quiet for a very long time.

She thought about the first morning. The crime scene. The gallery. The way she had stood in front of the Bernini and had felt, before she could name it, the specific recognition of a person who had grown up inside the architecture being demonstrated. She had known what pride looked like from inside. She had been managing her own version of it for thirty-five years — not the Cardinal's version, not the grandiose institutional version, but the quieter, more controlled version, the version that said: *I will not need anything from anyone, and this will protect me.*

Augustine had said it differently. *Our heart is restless until it repose in Thee.* He had meant God. She was not certain what she meant. She was certain that the restlessness was accurate.

She thought about Mateo's voice at 5am saying: *You have built a very efficient machinery for converting exhaustion into continued function.* She thought about the specific accuracy of this — not as a criticism, which he had not intended, but as a description, which she had received correctly. He had seen the machinery. He had described it without judgment. He had then said: *the management is not the solution.*

She held this in the dark.

The management was what she had. The management was what had made her career. The management was what had kept the interior safe for thirty-five years while the exterior work got done — the cases, the arrests, the evidence, the twelve years of building something professionally significant from the materials available.

The materials available had been: considerable intelligence, considerable physical capability, considerable institutional will, and the specific quality she had developed at age eight when she had understood that being the most capable person in the room was the only reliable form of protection.

She had been the most capable person in most rooms since she was eight years old.

She had met Mateo Padilla in a Roman gallery and had been in the same room as someone who did not require her to be the most capable person in it.

She was aware of what this meant.

She was not, in the dark of the Brussels apartment, going to do anything about what it meant. She was going to hold it the way she held the front desk note — in the personal pocket, not the professional pocket, filed as material that required the right moment.

The right moment was not the middle of an active investigation with six more cities in the curriculum.

The right moment was not now.

She held it. She filed it. She let the restlessness be the size it was.

She did not answer this question.

She slept.

Chapter 25

The Last Morning

￼

She was at the desk at 5am.

Not working. The laptop was closed. The case file had been transferred and the report had been filed and there was nothing on the desk except the carry-on bag she had packed at midnight and the front desk note she had been carrying for fifteen days in her jacket pocket and had now placed on the desk because the jacket pocket was no longer appropriate and she had not yet found the right container for the note.

She was looking at the note.

To be seen by someone who is capable of seeing is not capture. It is the beginning of the only conversation that has ever interested me.

She had been carrying this for fifteen days. She had read it the morning she found it, filed it as evidence, photographed it, and then — without examining the decision — kept the original in her jacket instead of submitting it with the physical evidence transfer. This was procedurally incorrect. She was aware that it was procedurally incorrect. She had been aware of this for fifteen days and had continued to carry it.

She picked it up. She read it again.

She thought about the man who had written it. Who had seen what he said he saw. Who had left Rome before the warrant, on his own schedule, with his curriculum notes and his unpublished monograph and the Avaritia parchment prepared before the Superbia lesson was concluded.

She thought: he underestimated me. Or he estimated me correctly and the estimation is, in itself, the point.

She thought about the difference between these two things and decided she did not yet know which was true and that the not-knowing was, for the moment, the appropriate position.

She put the note in her bag. Not in the evidence bag, which was in the transferred case files. In her bag. She was aware of this decision and did not reverse it.

At six-fifteen, Mateo knocked.

She had not told him she was leaving at seven. He knew anyway — this was a quality she had stopped cataloguing because the catalogue was full.

She opened the door. He was in the field jacket and the boots and the satchel and the look she had come to associate with him at early hours — alert but not performing alertness, simply present in the way of someone who had been awake long enough to have settled into the wakefulness.

"Coffee?" he said. He had two cups. Again.

She let him in.

They sat at the desk, side by side, because there was one desk and two chairs positioned for it and because sitting side by side rather than across from each other was different in a way she was choosing to acknowledge and not name. The coffee was good. She looked at the Via Margutta through the window. The specific pre-departure quality of a morning.

"The Hardt connection," she said.

"I spoke to my contact last night. Ferrini had a private collection of fifteenth-century Venetian commercial contracts. Three of them — the provenance of the acquisition was never established. In 2017 a journalist suspected they had been acquired from an estate sale that was itself irregular — documents that should have been donated to public archives were instead sold through a private channel that benefited the estate's legal representative."

"And the legal representative."

"Was also Ferrini's accountant." A pause. "The journalist withdrew the story because she received documentation establishing that the acquisition had been disclosed to the appropriate archival authorities and approved. The documentation was a letter from a minor official in the cultural ministry."

"Forged," she said.

"Or procured." He was quiet for a moment. "Ferrini knew the acquisition was irregular. He covered it. He used an institutional relationship to generate a document that made the irregular look regular."

She processed this. Aquinas on avaritia. The disordered desire for the finite goods. Not just accumulation — the use of institutional position to acquire what should have been public, to keep what should have been shared, to arrange the language of legitimacy around the thing that was not legitimate.

"It fits the framework," she said.

"Exactly." He turned the coffee cup in his hands. "He's not a villain in the way that word is usually used. He's a man of significant intelligence and accomplishment who has spent thirty years in the company of questions about moral accountability in commercial practice — studying it, publishing on it — while maintaining a private arrangement that embodied the problem he was studying."

"He knows the argument," she said. "He uses the framework professionally and violates it privately."

"Yes." A pause. "The Cardinal blocked Hardt's archival access to maintain an institutional fiction. Ferrini acquired documents that should have been public to maintain a private collection. Different mechanisms. Same architecture."

"Pride that uses the institution as a shield," she said. "Greed that uses the institution as an instrument." She looked at the window. "He selects for the specific failure mode. Not just the sin — the sin as expressed through institutional power."

"The sin the institution enables."

"Yes." She looked at the coffee. "He's not punishing these people for being sinners. He's demonstrating what the institution permits. What it looks away from. What it actively enables."

"Hardt's 1972 argument," Mateo said. "The institution cannot dissolve individual moral accountability."

"He's proving the argument by demonstration." She looked at Mateo. He was looking at her. The same quality of attention she had been cataloguing for fifteen days, which she had stopped cataloguing because the catalogue was full. "He's very good," she said.

"Yes."

"And he knows we're going to Venice."

"Yes."

"And he's going anyway."

"Yes." A pause. "Sonya."

She waited.

"I've been thinking about something you said. The last morning. About whether he underestimated you or estimated you correctly." He looked at the window. "I think the answer is that it doesn't matter to him which is true. Because either way, he's interested in what you're going to do with it."

She thought about the Confessions inscription. *The beginning of the only conversation that has ever interested me.*

"He wants the conversation," she said.

"He wants a worthy opponent. He's been making the argument alone for thirty years and he wants someone to argue back."

She looked at him. "And you?"

He met her eyes. "I want to stop the second lesson."

"So do I."

"I know." He looked at the coffee. "But stopping the second lesson is not the same as finishing the conversation."

She did not answer this. She was aware of what he was saying beneath it and was not ready to respond to what was beneath it. She was also aware that she would be ready in Venice, or in Florence, or in Paris, or in whichever city the conversation between herself and the evidence and the man who had left her a note finally arrived at the right moment for the words.

She finished the coffee. She stood. She picked up the carry-on bag.

"The transfer meeting is at eight," she said.

"I know." He stood. He picked up the satchel. "I'll walk you."

"You don't have to."

"I know," he said.

They walked. The Via Margutta in the October morning — the cobblestones damp, the light beginning, the bougainvillea still holding. They walked without speaking for most of it, which was not the silence of people with nothing to say but the silence of people who had enough to say that the silence was the appropriate form for it.

At the Campo de' Fiori he stopped.

"Thank you," she said. Not for the walk. He knew what she meant.

"Same," he said. He also did not mean the walk.

She continued to the transfer meeting. She did not look back at the corner.

She thought about this — the not-looking, which was now a practiced thing, which had been practiced at the Via Margutta and on the Ponte Sisto and at the door of the Borghese Gallery on the night of the almost-moment — and for the first time she thought about it as a practice with a cost.

She was keeping very careful track of what she was not looking at.

She went to the transfer meeting. She shook Vitale's hand. She transferred the final documentation. She was professional. She was done.

She called Mateo from the taxi to the airport.

"Thank you," she said. "Again. For the bibliography. The Hardt connection. Everything."

"Whenever Venice needs me," he said.

The taxi moved through Rome toward the airport with the specific efficiency of a driver who had done this run many times and had stopped finding the city interesting. She sat in the back with the carry-on on the seat beside her and her phone in her hand and looked at the city going past the windows.

She had been in Rome for fifteen days. She had arrived with a crime scene and a dead Cardinal and a case that Hale had expected her to close in ten. She was leaving with a European warrant, a confirmed suspect, four independent evidence chains, the intellectual architecture of the most sophisticated crime she had investigated in twelve years, and the specific knowledge — which she had not included in the formal case file — that there were six more cities and six more parchments and she was going to be in all of them before the lessons were complete.

She was also leaving with something she had not arrived with and had not been expecting to acquire.

She looked at her phone. Mateo's contact. She looked at it for a moment and then put the phone in her bag.

She thought about the note in the Confessions. She thought about the specific quality of being told you were capable of seeing and understanding, for the first time, that the capability had a cost. That the person who could read the room was also the person the room was partially constructed for. That being the right reader meant being inside the argument.

She had always been inside the arguments she investigated. This was what made her good — the ability to not just process the evidence from the outside but to occupy the interior of the thing that had been made and understand it from there. She had been doing this for twelve years.

She had not previously had the experience of being in an argument where the person who made it had chosen her specifically as the reader.

The taxi joined the motorway. Rome fell away behind them. She looked at the receding city in the side mirror — the specific skyline, the domes, the particular color of Roman stone in afternoon light — and thought about fifteen days inside that city and what they had made of her.

She thought: I arrived here professional and I am leaving professional. Everything that happened between those two states is material for the next city.

She thought: that is the accurate version of what happened.

She thought: it is not the complete version.

She did not say either of these things to the taxi driver, who was listening to a football commentary at low volume and was entirely uninterested in the internal landscape of the passenger in his back seat. She did not say them to Hale, who had sent a one-line message at 11am: *Good work. See you at the Venice briefing.* She did not say them to the Rome liaison, who had shaken her hand at the transfer meeting with the specific relief of a man who was glad the fifteen days were concluded.

She said them, silently, to herself, in the back of a taxi on the motorway to Fiumicino, in the way she sometimes worked through things that were not quite finished — by naming them honestly to herself first and then deciding what to do with the honesty.

She did not yet know what to do with it.

She was working on it.

She ended the call before she said the other thing.

She was working on it.

She was working on it.

She had been working on it since the first morning in Rome when she had looked at Mateo Padilla across a crime scene and had noted, in the professional way she noted things, that something was happening that she did not yet have the correct category for. She had been working on the category for fifteen days. She had filed it under: *the specific experience of working alongside someone whose intelligence complements rather than duplicates your own.* She had filed it under: *professional respect of an unusual intensity.* She had filed it under: *the particular case of a person who does not require me to manage them.*

She was aware that none of these categories were accurate.

She was also aware that the taxi was moving and Rome was receding and she had a plane to catch and Venice was twelve days away and she did not have the specific interior space, at this moment, to examine the category question with the attention it required.

She put her phone in her bag. She looked out the taxi window at Rome going past.

Rome in the afternoon: the specific gold of the light on terracotta, the specific quality of the city's relationship to time, which was to have so much of it layered in every surface that the present moment felt thin by comparison. She had been here for fifteen days and had not been a tourist and had not had time to simply receive the city. She had processed it — as evidence, as context, as backdrop for the work. She had not simply been in it.

She was being in it now. For the twenty minutes between the case and the airport.

She thought about the Pantheon. She thought about standing in front of the Four Rivers fountain with Mateo in the afternoon light, both of them looking at the Bernini rather than at each other. She thought about what he had said: *You see it. That's what I mean.* She had not asked what he meant by this, which was unusual for her — she asked clarifying questions as a professional habit. She had not asked because she had understood what he meant. She had understood it in the specific way you understood things that were close enough to be seen clearly and close enough to be dangerous simultaneously.

He meant that she could read the argument.

He also meant, in the specific way he said things that meant more than one thing, that she could read him.

She had spent fifteen years building a career on reading rooms. She had never been read in return — not in this specific way, not by someone whose reading she weighted. She had been evaluated. She had been assessed. She had been found capable and occasionally found exceptional. She had not been seen.

She had let him see. She was working on what that meant.

The taxi pulled onto the motorway. Rome fell away behind them. She looked at the side mirror for a moment — the receding city, the receding fifteen days, the receding configuration of things she was going to carry into Venice and was not yet sure what to do with.

She thought about the note in her carry-on. The front desk note.

She was going to Venice. She was going to find Ferrini. She was going to interrupt the second lesson if she arrived before it was staged. She was going to be professional and excellent and completely in command of every room she entered.

She was also going to be in the same city as Mateo Padilla.

She was working on it.

She ended the call before she said the other thing.

She was working on it.

Chapter 26

The Second Parchment

She was at the airport by seven.

Fiumicino in the early morning had the specific quality of all large airports — the suspension of ordinary time, the population of people between places, the institutional neutrality of an environment designed to process rather than welcome. She moved through it with the carry-on bag and the case file and the focused emptiness she brought to the beginning of every new thing.

The Interpol Rome liaison had met her at the terminal entrance to collect the formal case transfer documentation. He was young and precise and slightly relieved, she thought, that the investigation was concluding in a manner that was professionally tidy even if the primary suspect was currently somewhere in Europe on a train or a plane heading toward a canal. He took the files and shook her hand and she went through security and found her gate.

She sat at the gate with a coffee that was airport-quality, which was a specific category of inadequate she had learned to accept, and looked at her phone.

Two messages. The first from Hale, timed at 6:47am: warrant confirmed, watch list active across all Schengen states, Interpol Venice notified, formal briefing of the Venice unit scheduled for Monday. The second from Mateo, timed at 6:52am.

Five words: Already booked. See you there.

She looked at this for a moment. She put her phone in her jacket pocket beside the front desk note she had not been examining why she kept. She picked up the airport coffee. She drank it.

She thought about Venice.

She had been to Venice once, four years ago, for a conference that had been procedurally necessary and personally forgettable. She remembered the specific quality of the November light on the canals — grey-green, cold, the kind of light that arrived late and left early and spent the hours in between making everything it touched look slightly underwater. She remembered the smell of the city, which was salt and age and the particular damp of a place that had made its peace with slow dissolution. She remembered thinking that Venice was the most beautiful city she had ever seen and the most honest, because it did not pretend that beauty was permanent.

Greed. Avaritia. The replacement of the infinite with the finite. The love of what can be counted.

She thought about Dante's Purgatorio, which Mateo had mentioned once in the gallery — the souls of the avaricious lying face down in the dirt, unable to lift their eyes from the earth. The specifically earthward quality of greed. The eyes that could not look up.

She thought about a man who had been studying avaritia for decades and had chosen Venice as its city and had already, she was certain, chosen his victim.

Her flight was called. She boarded.

She found her seat. She put the carry-on in the overhead. She sat and looked out the small oval window at the Fiumicino tarmac — the ground crews, the baggage vehicles, the flat grey morning of a Roman airport on an October Tuesday. Rome beyond the perimeter fence, invisible from here but present, the weight of it still in her bones from eleven days of its stones and light and the accumulated theological history of a city that had been arguing about sin since before the argument had a name.

She put her hand in her jacket pocket. She felt the folded note from the hotel front desk. She did not take it out. She did not need to read it again. She had read it enough times to know it without looking.

The investigation has been thorough. I expected nothing less from someone who reads rooms the way you do. The next lesson begins in two weeks.

She had one week before Venice. One week in Brussels in the apartment on the Rue du Commerce with the excellent coffee maker and the worse view and the careful smallness of a life arranged to contain exactly as much as she had wanted it to contain.

She thought: I might want it to contain something different now.

She did not examine this thought. She filed it in the place where she kept things she was not ready to examine, which was becoming crowded.

She had filed the Avaritia notification at 6:22am, twenty minutes before boarding. She had written it in the airport café with one hand and a coffee in the other, the standard Interpol notification format that her fingers could execute now without occupying the conscious part of her attention. She had CC'd Hale's deputy and the Venice liaison office and the general registry that maintained the open-investigation flags across all member countries.

Then she had photographed the parchment one more time from the overhead angle and added it to the case file and sat with the coffee and thought about what it meant that he had sent it before she had the warrant.

He had sent the Venice announcement before the Rome case was formally closed. This was not a mistake — he did not make mistakes of that kind. It was a statement. The curriculum did not pause for institutional timelines. The curriculum proceeded according to its own schedule, which was not the schedule of the investigation pursuing it.

She thought about what it meant to be inside something that was proceeding on its own schedule.

She had always been the one who set the schedule. In every investigation she had run, she had been the organizing intelligence — the one who determined the pace, who decided when evidence was sufficient for the next step, who managed the institutional machinery to move at the speed the investigation required rather than the speed the institution preferred. She was very good at this. It was one of the things she was best at.

She was not setting the schedule here. She was reading the schedule he had set and moving as quickly as she could inside it.

She had never been in this position before. She was finding it, with the specific honesty she applied to herself in the early hours of airports, genuinely interesting.

She also found it, with the same honesty, somewhat alarming.

She finished the coffee. She boarded. She found her seat. She looked at the seat-back in front of her for a moment without seeing it and thought about a man who was somewhere in Europe right now, on his own schedule, with his curriculum notes and his vellum and his pen and the patience of someone for whom thirty years had been a reasonable preparation time.

She put Mateo's number in her contacts under *Venice — Case.*

She deleted the label and left it as his name.

The plane began to move.

She read the case file transfer documentation for forty minutes and then stopped reading it.

She had read it six times. The documentation did not change between readings. The Rome case was as closed as it was going to be before the trial, which would happen in Germany after the extradition, which would happen after the European warrant was processed, which was someone else's forty-eight hours. She had done her portion of the thing.

She looked at the Avaritia parchment photograph on her phone. The canal sketch. The specific East-facing perspective from the Accademia bridge that the Rome imaging team had confirmed. He had stood on that bridge. He had looked at what Venice was offering him.

What had Venice been offering?

She thought about greed as Aquinas had defined it — not mere accumulation but the disordered desire for finite goods as though they were infinite. The city built on water, founded by merchants who had understood that the world's wealth flowed through their hands and had structured their entire civilization around managing that flow. A city where the aesthetic and the mercantile had been interchangeable for six hundred years. Where beauty had always been a form of commerce and commerce had always been a form of art.

Where pride became greed by another name.

She opened her laptop. She had requested the conference registry for the Venice Symposium on Medieval Commercial Ethics — a three-day academic conference scheduled at the Ca' Foscari University in two weeks. The registry had arrived in her inbox at three in the morning and she had not yet read it.

She read it now.

Four hundred and twelve names. She did not have Mateo's particular gift for the cross-reference — she had the detective's gift, which was different, which was the ability to read a list as a room and feel which names were cold and which were not. She read the four hundred and twelve names with this feeling active and stopped at two.

The first: Professor Luca Ferrini, Ca' Foscari University, Venice. Chair of the symposium organizing committee. Emeritus professor of economic history. Published works including a 2009 monograph on the moral theology of Venetian mercantile practice. She looked up the monograph. In the acknowledgments: *I am grateful to Dr. Wilhelm Hardt of the University of Tübingen, whose correspondence first drew my attention to the theological dimensions of this question.*

She wrote: *Ferrini — Hardt connection. Symposium chair.*

The second name was harder to read. Not because it was obscure — it was perfectly legible. Because it was familiar in the specific way that names became familiar after you had been building a case around them for eleven days.

Professor Wilhelm Hardt. University of Tübingen. Presenting a paper at the Venice symposium on moral accountability in institutional commercial practice.

He was going to Venice.

She sat with this for a long time. The plane was still moving below her — the Alps visible through the window on the right side, white and indifferent. She looked at them and then looked back at the registry.

Hardt was going to Venice. For an academic conference where the chair was a man who had acknowledged Hardt in a 2009 monograph. A conference organized around the moral theology of greed.

Paulus was going to Venice. Had been there already.

She wrote: *Hardt at Ca' Foscari conference. Ferrini — Hardt connection. Cross-reference with Paulus's Venice visit timeline.*

She wrote one more thing: *Is Ferrini the subject?*

She stared at this sentence. She was speculating. She did not speculate professionally. She had learned, across twelve years, the cost of moving from pattern to assumption without sufficient evidence connecting them.

But the pattern was strong.

She called Mateo. He answered on the second ring.

"I'm looking at the Venice conference registry," she said.

"So am I." His voice was clear — no plane noise behind him. He had an earlier flight. "Hardt."

"Hardt."

"And Ferrini," Mateo said. "I know him. We've met twice. He was a subject in an article I wrote in 2019 about the Vatican's historical investment practices. He was careful. Very careful. The kind of careful that suggests he has things to be careful about."

She processed this. Mateo's source network — the accumulated relational geography of a journalist who had been covering institutional wrongdoing for fifteen years — was a different instrument from her investigative methodology. Both instruments were useful. Sometimes they pointed at the same thing from different distances.

"What kind of things," she said.

"He managed a private archival collection in Venice for a family foundation. The collection included documentation of historical commercial contracts from the fifteenth and sixteenth centuries.

There were questions, in 2017, about the provenance of certain documents — whether the foundation had acquired them through legitimate channels or had purchased them from sources the market preferred not to examine too closely."

"The questions were resolved?"

"The questions were withdrawn. By the journalist who had raised them. I've always wanted to know why."

She looked at the Alps. "Ferrini has something in his past that someone knows about."

"Something that a man who has spent forty years studying the moral architecture of institutional pride might find significant."

"Something that the Avaritia framework fits."

"Yes." A pause. "Sonya. If Ferrini is the second subject — if Paulus has already selected him—"

"We have to reach him first." She closed her laptop. "I need everything on Ferrini. The 2017 provenance questions. The foundation. The archival collection. Whatever was withdrawn and why."

"I have sources in Venice. A journalist who covers Ca' Foscari. She'll know."

"Tonight."

"Tonight." Another pause. She heard him moving. "Already booked. See you there."

She ended the call. She looked out the window. Rome was well behind her now. The Alps were passing. Below them, on the other side of the mountains, the Po valley was flat and agricultural and entirely uninterested in the curriculum of a German academic.

Venice was two hundred kilometers to the east.

She had one week.

The plane began to move faster, which was not possible because it was already at altitude, but she felt it anyway — the forward pull of a case that had not finished with her.

She was not finished with it either.

She looked at Mateo's contact entry on her phone.

She had added him on day two as *Padilla M. — Vatican Press* with the institutional note that indicated a professional source. She had not changed the entry in fifteen days. She was looking at it now because the plane was moving and she had his number and the case was open and she had a legitimate professional reason to call.

She called.

He answered on the second ring. Rome still audible behind him — she could hear the specific quality of a Roman street at mid-morning, the particular acoustic of old stone amplifying and containing the sound of the city simultaneously.

"I'm at the airport," she said.

"I know. Your flight is at 10:35."

She had not told him her flight time. She noted this without commenting on it. "The conference registry for Venice. I found two names."

"Hardt and Ferrini," he said.

She held the phone. "You're already there."

"I was going to call you." He said it simply. "I pulled the registry this morning. Hardt presenting a paper. Ferrini as symposium chair. The connection is direct."

"Hardt called Ferrini the day after Paulus flew to Frankfurt."

A pause. She heard him processing this. "You have the call log."

"I have the timestamp. Not the content."

"Hardt told Ferrini Rome was concluded." He said it with the specific flatness of a man stating a fact he found distasteful. "He told him the first lesson was complete."

"Or he warned him," she said. "If Ferrini is the subject—"

"He's not afraid," Mateo said. "That's the thing. If Ferrini knew Paulus's methodology — which he does, through Hardt's published work — and if he understood that the methodology had been applied in Rome — which the warrant announcement would have made clear — he would know he was a potential subject."

"And he's still attending the conference."

"He's chairing it." A pause. "Either he doesn't believe he's been selected. Or he believes the selection doesn't apply to him. Or he believes he can manage the situation."

She thought about this. About a man who had spent thirty years managing situations. About the specific confidence of someone who had been the most intelligent person in most rooms for a very long time and had concluded this was a permanent condition.

"He's not afraid," she said.

"No."

"He should be."

"Yes." Mateo's voice had the quality it had when he was thinking and talking simultaneously. "I have a call in to the journalist who withdrew the 2017 story. She's in Milan. She's going to call me back this afternoon."

"Get me everything she has. Whatever was in the story before she pulled it. The documentation that made her pull it."

"If it was forged—"

"If it was forged, it was forged by someone with access to the cultural ministry's correspondence format and letterhead. That's not a skill set Ferrini has personally. Someone provided it."

"Hardt's network," Mateo said. "Forty years of academic correspondence across European institutions. Someone in that network had the access."

"Find out who." She looked out the terminal window at the planes on the tarmac. "I land in Brussels at noon. I have one week before the conference."

"I'll have the journalist's materials by tonight."

"Good." A pause. The professional pause had always been the pause before she ended calls. She did not end this call. "Mateo."

"Yes."

"The Avaritia sketch. The canal perspective. He was on the Accademia bridge looking east."

"I know the spot."

"He chose it before Rome was staged." She looked at the parchment photograph on her phone. "He was already thinking about what Venice would mean while he was still in preparation for Rome."

"He thinks very far ahead."

"Yes." She picked up the carry-on from the floor. "So do we."

She heard something in his response. Not words. The specific quality of warmth he directed at things he found genuinely satisfying — the journalist's pleasure in the correct sentence.

She was not finished with it either.

Chapter 27

The Flight North

She read on the plane.

Not the case file — she had transferred the formal case file to the Rome liaison at the terminal. She read the photographs she had taken in Paulus's Gregorian office. The curriculum notes. The five cities in careful handwriting. Venice, Florence, Paris, Barcelona, and a fifth she had not named to Hale because she was not certain enough to name it to Hale.

The fifth was not written as a city. It was written as a question in the margin of the curriculum page, in a hand slightly less controlled than the rest — as if the question had been added after the rest, as if it had arrived later or been resisted longer before being committed to paper.

The question was in Latin. She photographed it at the time and had not yet asked Mateo to translate because she had not been ready to ask. She looked at it now in the photograph on her phone screen at cruising altitude above the Italian countryside.

She called Mateo.

"You're on a plane," he said.

"Yes. The curriculum notes. The fifth city isn't a city. There's a question in Latin in the margin. I need you to translate it." She read it out slowly. The phonetics of a language she had absorbed procedurally rather than studied.

A silence. Not the pause of recollection. The pause of a man sitting with a translation he had arrived at immediately and was deciding what to do with it.

"Mateo."

"It says," he said, "Is she capable of what I think she is capable of."

The plane moved through clear air above Italy. The seat belt sign was off. The person beside her was asleep. The window showed a sky that was very blue and very indifferent.

"She," she said.

"Yes."

She looked at the photograph of the curriculum notes. The five cities. The question in the margin in a hand slightly less controlled than the rest.

He had been asking this question about her since before he knew her name. He had been asking it, she understood, since the briefing room. Since the gallery photographs that had been taken before she arrived. Since the specific way she had stood in his crime scene for eleven minutes without speaking, which Lukas Bauer had documented in the attendance notes as a remarkable quality of attention.

He had been selecting her as carefully as he selected his victims.

Not as a victim.

As a reader.

"Mateo," she said. "Don't tell Hale about the question yet."

A beat. "Understood."

"I'll tell him when I understand what it means."

"Sonya." His voice had a quality she had learned to attend to. "Do you understand what it means?"

She looked at the sky through the oval window. Forty thousand feet over Italy. Rome already invisible behind her. Brussels ahead, then Venice.

"I'm working on it," she said.

She ended the call. She put the phone in her pocket beside the note from the hotel front desk. She looked at the seat-back in front of her for a long time.

The curriculum had a question in it about her. Written in a hand slightly less controlled than the rest. As if the question had been harder to commit to paper than the cities.

She thought: he is not certain. After forty years of certainty about everything, this is the one thing he has not resolved.

She thought: I am not certain either.

She thought about what it meant to be readable.

Not in the abstract — she had been thinking about Paulus's inscription for fifteen days and had developed a thorough abstract understanding of what it meant to be seen by someone of his specific intelligence. She thought about it in the particular: what it felt like in her body to have been looked at carefully by someone who was looking for something specific and to have given them what they were looking for.

She was not accustomed to being found. Not because she was uninteresting — she had a sufficiently accurate self-assessment to know that was not the issue. Because she had been building the structure of her professional life for fifteen years on the premise that the things worth finding about her were the things you could see from the outside: the investigative competence, the authority in a room, the specific gift for reading situations that had made her career.

He had read something else.

The specific quality of a restlessness that has been very thoroughly managed. Mateo had said this at 5am in a darkened apartment and she had not answered him. She had held it. She had been holding it for three days while the case finished around her and she packed and filed and transferred and said goodbye on a Roman cobblestone street without looking back.

She was holding it at thirty-eight thousand feet over the Alps and she was aware that holding it indefinitely was not a strategy. It was a practice. And practices, she had learned across thirty-five years of various forms of practice, had consequences when continued past the point of usefulness.

She had been managing the restlessness for thirty years. Mateo had said so. He was not wrong.

She thought about Edinburgh. The seventh lesson. The final page. The city she had been to twice and found severe and magnificent and correct in the way of places that had decided permanence was the only appropriate architectural value.

She thought: if there are seven lessons and the seventh is Edinburgh and Edinburgh is the end of the argument, then I am inside an argument that has not concluded yet. I am a figure in an argument that will not be finished until Edinburgh.

She thought: I am going to finish it on my own terms.

She did not know yet what her own terms were. This was, she recognized, the most honest thing she had thought in fifteen days.

She put in her earphones. She closed her eyes. Rome receded.

She read the curriculum notes for the third time.

Not the photographs — she had the photographs memorized. She read the handwritten transcription she had made in Rome, four days before the lesson concluded, when she had looked at Paulus's Gregorian office and seen the five city names in careful ink and had understood, without yet having the evidence to confirm, that she was looking at a reading list.

Venice. Florence. Paris. Barcelona. The fifth, in the margin in a slightly different hand — slightly less controlled, the ink weight suggesting a pen held with more pressure, the letter formation of something committed later, after resistance had been overcome.

She had not yet told Hale about the fifth city. She had not yet told Mateo. She had barely allowed herself to think it clearly, because thinking it clearly required accepting what it meant about the scope of what Paulus had been preparing, and accepting that scope required a significant reorientation of how she understood the case she was in.

She looked at it now.

It was not a city name. It was a place name — a proper noun she had recognized when she first photographed it, had recognized with the specific recognition of a thing you know in your bones before you know it in your mind. She had filed it in the part of herself she was not reading. She was going to read it now.

Edinburgh.

She wrote it in her transcription notebook. She stared at it.

Six cities. Seven sins. The curriculum notes had five named and one written in the margin and she understood, looking at it with the altitude and the Alps behind her and the case conclusion in Rome still fresh, that the curriculum was not five cities and a question.

It was seven. The marginal question was not uncertainty about whether. It was uncertainty about when.

She called Mateo.

"Edinburgh," she said when he answered.

A silence.

"Show me," he said.

She photographed the transcription and sent it. She waited while he looked at it.

"The margin hand," he said. "It's different."

"Added later. After the core five were committed to the notes."

"Which means Edinburgh was not the original plan. Or not the original order." He was quiet for a moment. She heard him thinking. "Or it was always the plan but he resisted naming it. Because naming it made it real."

"Edinburgh is the end," she said.

"The Ultima Scriptura."

"The final lesson." She looked at the window. The Po valley below, flat and green. "Seven cities. Seven sins. He's not building a curriculum. He's building a book. Each lesson is a chapter."

"And Edinburgh is the last chapter."

"Yes."

She sat with this. The full weight of it — not the operational weight, which she would manage, but the other weight: the weight of understanding that the man she was chasing had planned not one murder and not five but seven, and had been planning them for thirty years, and had made a reading list with the specific patience of a man who was not in a hurry because he understood that patience was the prerequisite for what he was building.

"Venice," she said. "We stop it in Venice. And Florence. And each one after that."

"By finding the subjects before he does."

"By finding the subjects and understanding the selection criteria." She opened her notebook. "He selects for a specific sin expression. Pride — the Cardinal. Greed — Ferrini, probably. The sin has to be the defining characteristic, not just a quality. It has to be the engine of the person's relationship to their institutional power."

"And it has to be suppressible," Mateo said. "The subject has to be someone whose sin is being actively concealed within an institutional framework."

"Yes." She looked at the transcription. "Edinburgh is the final lesson. Which means it's the culmination. The sin that contains all the others. Or the subject whose sin is — exemplary."

"The most perfect example."

"Yes." She looked out the window. She thought about Edinburgh — a city she knew, had been to twice, had found cold and severe and architecturally magnificent in the way of places that have decided stone is the only appropriate material for anything permanent. "We have time."

"Five cities between here and there."

"Five cities." She closed the notebook. "Mateo."

"Yes."

"He's been watching us. Since Rome. He knows who we are."

A pause. The considering kind.

"I know," Mateo said.

"Does that concern you?"

"Yes." He said it simply. "It also—" He stopped.

"Also what?"

"It also means he's interested in us. Specifically. A man who stages crimes for a specific reader has now identified the reader. We're inside the curriculum."

She had thought this. She had been thinking it since the inscription in the Confessions. *To be seen by someone who is capable of seeing is not capture.* "He thinks I can read him."

"Can you?"

She looked at the final city name in the margin of her transcription.

"Yes," she said.

"Then the question—" Mateo paused. "The question is what being readable by him costs you."

She did not answer immediately. This was the question she had been not-asking for eleven days and was now being asked directly, from the other end of a phone call, by a man who was asking it carefully. With the specific care of someone who had an interest in the answer that was not only professional.

"I don't know yet," she said.

She heard him receive this. She heard the quality of his silence receiving it.

"I'll have the Ferrini documentation ready when you land," he said.

"Thank you."

"Sonya."

"Yes."

"Edinburgh is a long way from here."

"I know."

She put her earphones in. She closed her eyes. The plane held its altitude and the Alps receded and Italy spread itself flat below her toward the Adriatic.

She thought: I am not certain either.

Rome receded. Venice approached.

She put in her earphones.

Not music. She put in the earphones and turned off the sound and simply wore them as the specific signal she had developed over twelve years of investigative travel — the signal that meant: I am processing and I am not available for conversation, which on an aircraft meant I am not available for conversation with the people in the adjacent seats, who were two Belgian businessmen discussing quarterly projections in the manner of people who found quarterly projections genuinely compelling.

She looked at the seat-back in front of her. She thought.

Edinburgh.

She had been carrying the word since she had written it in her transcription notebook over the Alps. She had been carrying it with the specific care she applied to evidence that was not yet actionable — held separately from the institutional case, in the personal file, awaiting the moment when it became something she could take to Hale.

She could not take it to Hale yet. *There is a seventh city in the curriculum and I believe it is Edinburgh* was not a sentence that produced useful institutional response. What produced useful institutional response was: *there is a second lesson in Venice and here is the subject and here is the evidence connecting the subject to the methodology.* That was the next twelve days.

Edinburgh was after the next twelve days.

She thought about Edinburgh as a city. She had been there twice — once for a conference, once for an extradition that had required three days of institutional navigation and had concluded with the correct outcome and had given her very little time to see the city itself. What she had seen: old stone and grey sky and the specific architectural confidence of a place that had decided centuries ago that permanence was the only aesthetic worth pursuing. The castle on the rock. The Royal Mile. The specific quality of cold that was not Rome's cold or Brussels's cold but its own cold, older and more certain.

She thought about what sin expression a man of Lucas's framework would find in Edinburgh.

Not pride — she had pride. Not greed — she had Venice. Not envy — Florence. Not lust, gluttony, wrath, sloth — the remaining four were Paris, Barcelona, Seville, Prague.

Edinburgh was the seventh. The last.

She thought about what the seven sins looked like in sequence. The academic tradition — Evagrius, Cassian, Gregory the Great — had argued for a hierarchy among them, with pride at the root of all the others. She had read this in the secondary literature. Paulus had structured the curriculum with Pride first for a reason: not just because Rome was geographically convenient, but because pride was, in the theological framework he was working from, the origin. The sin from which all others derived.

Which meant Edinburgh was not the seventh sin in an arbitrary sequence. Edinburgh was the culmination — the sin that gathered the others, or the subject whose sin was the most complete expression of the full argument.

She thought: he has been planning Edinburgh for thirty years. He has known who the seventh subject is for longer than he has known who the first one was.

She thought: who is the seventh subject?

She did not yet know. She was going to find out. Not in Venice — she had enough for Venice. In the cities after Venice, as the curriculum progressed and the argument developed, the seventh subject would become visible the way all subjects became visible: through the specific quality of their sin's expression, the specific way it used institutional power to make itself invisible.

She thought: he is already in Edinburgh.

She thought: no. He will not be in Edinburgh yet. Edinburgh is the end. He will not go to Edinburgh until the seventh lesson is prepared.

She thought: the seventh lesson has been prepared for thirty years.

She closed her eyes. She let the aircraft noise be what it was. She thought about Venice and Ferrini and the Avaritia parchment and the twelve days she had.

The Alps were behind her.

Rome receded. Venice approached.

Chapter 28

The Voss File

Brussels landed at noon.

The apartment on the Rue du Commerce was exactly as she had left it three weeks ago. The excellent coffee maker. The worse view. The specific stillness of a space that had been waiting without urgency for its inhabitant to return. She set down the carry-on and stood in the doorway for a moment and let the apartment re-establish itself around her.

She did not unpack immediately.

She made coffee — good coffee, the first good coffee since the Via Margutta apartment, which had been adequate and nothing more — and she sat at the desk by the window and opened the carry-on and removed what she had brought back from Rome.

The front desk note. The Avaritia parchment in its evidence bag, which she had transferred to herself with the proper documentation before leaving the Rome office. The curriculum photographs on her phone. The translation of the margin question.

And at the bottom of the carry-on, beneath the case file she had transferred to Rome, a file that was not part of the formal case.

The Voss file. Marco Voss. Her personal documentation of everything she had assembled about the nephew who had spent nine days in a cell: the seminary dismissal record, the inheritance dispute, the IP discrepancy analysis, the note from Chiara Moretti that had started everything. Not the official file — that was in Rome, transferred and processed. This was her file, assembled separately, the one she had built the way she built the things she did not yet have names for.

She had not left it in Rome. She had brought it home in her carry-on because she was not finished with it, which was not a professional assessment, it was a personal one, and she was aware of the difference.

She opened the Voss file. She looked at the photograph she had taken of Marco's apartment on the first visit — the theological texts, the Bernini book, the laptop, the mismatched kitchen chairs. The face of a person who was suffering without being guilty.

The Italian prosecutor's office would pursue the case against Paulus. The watch list was active. Interpol Venice was briefed. The formal machinery was in motion and it did not require her anymore, specifically, to keep moving.

She would go to Venice anyway.

Not because Hale had assigned her. He had not yet. The formal jurisdiction ended with the Rome case. Venice would be a new case with a new assignment, which would come when Paulus acted and not before.

She would go to Venice because the curriculum was not finished and because she was the person who could read it and because Marco Voss had said thank you for not letting it be longer and because the question in the margin of the curriculum notes had been written in a hand slightly less controlled than the rest.

She closed the file. She put it in the desk drawer that contained the things she kept that were not quite professional and not quite personal and occupied the specific territory between those two categories that she had never managed to satisfactorily define.

She finished her coffee. She opened her laptop. She began to read everything ever published about Dante's conception of greed.

She had one week.

She read for seven days.

Not the case file — the case file was filed, closed on its operational side, open on its investigative side, pending the European warrant's formal processing and Paulus's location confirmation in Frankfurt. She had left those threads to the German liaison and the Italian prosecutor's office and the Interpol administrative machinery that existed precisely to handle the weeks between the identification of a suspect and the formal legal action.

She read Dante.

The Inferno first, because that was the order, and she was someone who followed orders even when they were her own. The second canticle. The eighth circle. Malebolge — the evil pouches. She read the Bolgia of the Sowers of Discord, the Bolgia of the Falsifiers, the Bolgia of the Usurers. She read with the specific attention she gave to evidence — looking for structure, for what the text was organizing.

She found it in Canto XI, where Dante categorizes sin into three types: incontinence, malice, and bestiality. Greed fell under incontinence — the failure of will against the appetites. Not evil in itself but disordered. The sin not of bad desire but of good desire misdirected. The finite mistaken for the infinite.

She wrote in her notebook: *Aquinas and Dante agree. Greed is not about wanting too much. It is about wanting the wrong thing with the intensity appropriate only to the right thing.*

She read the secondary literature. She read a 2019 analysis of greed's theological history. She read Ferrini's 2009 monograph on Venetian mercantile moral theology. She read it carefully — not as evidence but as text, looking for the quality of mind behind it, the specific way Ferrini thought about the intersection of commerce and conscience.

He was brilliant. He was also, she noted, very careful about what he claimed to know and what he claimed merely to consider. The monograph was full of the careful hedges of a scholar who had spent his career in proximity to questions he preferred not to answer directly.

That was interesting.

She took notes. She cross-referenced the monograph's bibliography against Hardt's publication record and found four shared citations — texts both men had engaged with across their careers, conversations across decades in the specific medium of academic footnotes.

She sat in the Brussels apartment and did this work for seven days. She ran in the mornings. She made good coffee. She did not call Mateo except for two professional exchanges — one to confirm the Ferrini documentation he had compiled, one to review the Venice conference logistics.

She thought about calling him for other reasons and did not.

She thought about the Via Margutta and the October dark and the specific quality of standing on a doorstep and not going through it. She thought about this the way she thought about cases — thoroughly, systematically, from multiple angles. She arrived at no conclusions. She filed what she had and waited for the next piece of evidence.

On the fifth day, she received the formal notification from Interpol Brussels that the European warrant for Dr. Heinrich Paulus had been processed and issued. He was to be held for extradition pending the German authorities' formal cooperation request. He was, as of the notification, at his apartment in Cologne. He had made no attempt to leave Germany.

She sat with the notification for a long time.

He had gone home. He had packed his curriculum notes and taken them to Cologne and sat in his apartment and waited for the warrant. He knew it was coming. He had designed it to come. The first lesson was concluded not with the crime scene but with the warrant — the institutional recognition that the argument had been made and received.

The lesson was complete when someone capable of reading it had read it.

She looked at her notebook. Seven days of reading. She understood Venetian greed better than she had understood it a week ago. She understood Ferrini's intellectual terrain and where the fault lines in it were. She understood what a man with Paulus's specific methodology would look for in a second subject and where he would find it.

She was going to Venice because the curriculum was not finished. Because five cities remained after Venice and she was going to be in each one first. Because a man she had been in a room with for eleven days in Rome had told her she could read the argument, and she had said yes, and she intended to prove it.

She was also going to Venice because Mateo was going to Venice and she had spent seven days in Brussels not calling him and was aware that this restraint was costing something she could not yet name.

She closed her notebook. She opened her laptop. She booked the water taxi from Marco Polo airport to the Gritti Palace.

She had one week.

She began to pack.

She packed with the efficiency of someone who had been packing for investigations since she was twenty-three.

The carry-on. The case file — not the formal transfer, which had gone to the prosecutor, but the working copy she maintained in parallel. Her own notes, which she kept separate from the institutional documentation. The front desk note in the desk drawer, which she took out and held for a moment and then placed in the inside pocket of the carry-on, not the document pocket, the personal pocket, which she did not examine.

She packed Dante's Purgatorio, which she had bought at a Brussels bookshop on the second day and had read in the evenings while Rome processed the warrant. She packed the secondary literature on Venetian commercial ethics. She packed the Ferrini monograph, which she had read twice and annotated in the margins with the specific tight handwriting she used when she was building a case around a text.

She looked at the annotations.

The moral theology of greed as Ferrini describes it is not a theology of wanting too much. It is a theology of wanting the correct thing through the incorrect means. She had written this on page twelve and had not yet understood what she meant by it until the fourth day of Brussels, when she read it again at 3am and understood: Ferrini was not writing about greed in the popular sense. He was writing about the specific disordering of desire that occurred when the legitimate pursuit of beautiful things — art, scholarship, the preservation of history — was conducted through illegitimate channels.

He was writing about himself. He had been writing about himself for thirty years and had presumably found this sufficiently distancing that he had never stopped.

She added to her annotation: *He knew. He always knew. The scholarship was the alibi.*

She packed the laptop. She packed her running shoes — Brussels to Venice was a change of city and a change of case phase, not a change of routine. She ran in the mornings. She had run in Rome, in every city she had investigated in for twelve years, the volleyball player's body still requiring the specific investment of physical effort that kept the mental investment sustainable.

She thought about running along the Zattere in Venice. Along the fondamente with the lagoon visible. She had not been to Venice in four years but she remembered the quality of the light on the water — the water-doubled light that painters had been chasing for six hundred years and had never fully captured because the doubling was temporal as much as visual, the same moment arriving twice.

She zipped the carry-on.

She stood in the Brussels apartment and looked at it for a moment. The excellent coffee maker. The worse view. The specific stillness of a space that had been waiting without urgency for her to finish what she needed to finish in it.

She had finished what she needed to finish.

She thought about Mateo. She thought about the call where she told him she had booked the Gritti Palace and the specific quality of his response — the warmth in it, the ease, the way he had said *already booked* about his own flight as though it had been obvious that he would be there, as though Venice was simply the next place they were both going and the logistics were merely administrative.

She had spent seven days in Brussels not calling him for personal reasons. She had spent seven days being professional and working and reading and preparing.

She had also spent seven days being aware, in the specific new way she had been aware of things since Rome, that the professional and the personal were occupying the same space and were becoming harder to hold in separate containers.

She picked up the carry-on. She picked up her bag. She looked at the apartment one final time.

She booked the water taxi from Marco Polo airport to the Gritti Palace.

She had one week.

She began to pack.

Chapter 29

The Eternal City Keeps Its Secrets

Rome would not remember her.

This was not a failure. This was simply the nature of a city that had been containing the important things that happened inside it since before the calendar that tracked those things had been invented. Rome absorbed. It received and held and continued. The Bernini was still in the gallery. The cardinal's name was in the records now, in the archive of things that had happened here, in the long Roman accounting of violence and faith and the specific human capacity to dress both of them in beauty and call the result civilization.

It had seen all of this before. It would see all of it again.

And still the stones endured. And still the light came.

Six days into her week in Brussels she received the formal assignment.

Hale called at eleven in the morning on a Thursday. His voice had the specific weight of a man who had spent the intervening days managing the diplomatic aftermath of a case that had concluded correctly but not cleanly. The Vatican Secretariat's communication had been addressed. The Italian prosecutor's office had acknowledged the watch list. The Gregorian University had quietly accepted that one of its visiting lecturers was wanted for questioning in a homicide investigation and had expressed appropriate institutional regret.

"Venice," Hale said. Not a question.

"Venice," she confirmed.

"We've had a report from Interpol Venice. A body was found this morning in a deconsecrated church near the Rialto. Staging consistent with the Rome profile. The Venice unit found a parchment."

She was already standing. She did not remember standing up. Her hand was on the carry-on bag she had not fully unpacked.

"What word?"

"Avaritia."

She thought: two weeks. He had said two weeks. It had been six days.

She thought: he accelerated. The watch list. The warrant. He understood that the investigation had arrived at him faster than he'd planned and he had adjusted his schedule.

She thought: he is not rattled. He adjusted precisely, without panic, and proceeded.

"I'll be on the next train," she said.

"The journalist," Hale said. The specific weight of the word.

"Will be useful in Venice as he was in Rome," she said.

A pause. The mathematics. Then: "Don't let it become a problem."

"I won't," she said.

She ended the call. She called Mateo.

He answered before the second ring. She could hear, from the quality of the sound behind him, that he was already not in Brussels. She could hear canal acoustics. The specific echo of water in narrow stone passages.

"You're already there," she said.

"The story moved," he said. "Six days. He's faster than he said."

"I know." She was already pulling clothes from the wardrobe one-handed. "The deconsecrated church near the Rialto."

"I'm four minutes away from it." A pause. "Don't tell me not to go in."

She considered this for exactly the amount of time it took her to decide that telling him not to go in would be both professionally correct and entirely useless.

"Don't touch anything," she said.

"Of course."

She ended the call. She packed in eleven minutes. She was out the door of the Rue du Commerce apartment at eleven-forty-three.

On a train moving north through the Italian countryside, a man in a dark jacket sat at a window seat with a leather satchel on the overhead shelf and a volume of Dante's Purgatorio open across his knee.

He was reading Canto Nineteen.

The souls of the avaricious. Face down in the dirt. Unable to lift their eyes from the earth. Dante's argument that what we love with disordered intensity becomes the thing we cannot stop looking at —

the thing that pulls the gaze downward even when there are better things above.

He found this, as he always found the best theology, accurate.

The train moved through the landscape without urgency. The Italian countryside received its passage with the same indifference it had always received passages — the Romans, the Lombards, the armies of various nations who had decided that northern Italy was worth crossing and had discovered, as everyone who crossed it eventually discovered, that the land kept its own counsel regardless.

In the satchel: a notebook. The curriculum, revised. A new timeline, adjusted for the acceleration that the investigation had made necessary. Three unused squares of vellum, fifteen by fifteen centimeters, cut by hand from the sheet he had prepared in Brussels six weeks ago. A steel-nibbed pen. A small glass bottle of iron gall ink in the formulation from the 1962 Tübingen treatise.

And beneath all of these, in a folder he had sealed before leaving Rome: the first draft of what he had privately titled, in the precise Latin of his formation years, Ultima Scriptura.

He was not finished. He was not close to finished. The curriculum required patience and precision and the specific unhurried attention of a man who had decided long ago that the important arguments deserved the time they required and no less.

He turned a page of the Purgatorio. The train continued north. Venice approached through the flat Venetian plain the way Venice always approached — gradually, reluctantly, the city appearing from the water as if it were rising from it rather than built upon it, as if it had always been there and was only now permitting itself to be seen.

He had been here before. He had been everywhere before.

He closed the Purgatorio. He looked at the window. He watched Venice arrive.

He was looking forward to the lesson.

He closed the Purgatorio. He looked at the window. He watched Venice arrive.

He was looking forward to the lesson. He had been looking forward to it for a long time — not in the way of anticipation, which required a gap between desire and satisfaction that he had spent forty years narrowing. In the way of a man who has prepared something carefully and is now in the final stages of preparation, which is its own specific pleasure. The pleasure of a craftsman looking at the work before it is complete.

The water taxi moved through the lagoon. He watched the city assemble itself from the distance — campanile first, then the domes of Santa Maria della Salute, then the specific compressed verticality of buildings that had decided, centuries ago, that their relationship to space would be managed differently than anywhere else on earth. A city built on water by merchants who understood that the real estate under their feet was temporary and had built accordingly: beautifully, expensively, temporarily.

He had the vellum in his bag. The pen. The ink. The monograph he would not show anyone here, because this was not a scholarly conference for him — it was a research visit, and the research was of a kind that required a different kind of access than academic credentials typically provided.

He had the access.

Professor Ferrini had responded to his conference registration with the warm surprise of a man who was genuinely pleased that a scholar of Hardt's caliber had submitted an abstract. They had corresponded twice — brief, collegial, the professional warmth of men who had been citing each other for years without meeting. Ferrini had offered him dinner on the second evening of the conference.

He had accepted.

He was looking forward to dinner.

He had read Ferrini carefully over the past eight months — not the published work, which he had known for a decade, but the unpublished materials: the private correspondence that had been made available to him through channels he preferred not to specify, the conference presentations that had been recorded but not transcribed, the specific texture of a man's thinking when he believed he was speaking only to colleagues.

Ferrini was a man who had spent thirty years studying the moral architecture of greed and had spent those same thirty years maintaining, with careful precision, a private arrangement that embodied it. The provenance questions of 2017 — the ones that had been withdrawn — had been withdrawn because someone had shown the journalist in question a document. He did not know if the journalist still had the document or what she had done with it. He did not need to know. He had his own copy.

He had his own copies of most things.

The water taxi turned into the Grand Canal. He watched the palazzo facades pass on either side — the light on the water in the October afternoon, the specific quality of Venetian light that painters had been chasing for six hundred years, which was the light of reflection, of water-doubled illumination, of the same beam of sun arriving twice.

He thought about the woman.

She was good. Better than he had expected, which was a qualified statement because he had expected someone good — the case had required it, had in fact depended on it, since there was no point in making an argument to an audience that couldn't follow it. He had read her career before selecting Rome. He had read the commission reports and the Interpol files and two published papers she had written on the methodology of staged crime scenes and had concluded she was equipped.

She had exceeded his assessment. This was satisfying.

She was coming to Venice. He knew this. He had known it since she booked the water taxi, which he knew she had booked because he had a contact in the booking system, because he had contacts in many systems, because forty years of academic correspondence built a different kind of network than most people understood was possible.

She was coming to Venice to find Ferrini before he did.

She would not succeed. Not because she lacked the capability — she had more than the capability — but because she didn't yet know what she was looking for. She knew Ferrini was a subject. She didn't know what she needed to know to see exactly what had made him the subject.

He had arranged for her to find out.

He had left something for her in the Gritti Palace.

The water taxi docked at the Gritti's private landing. He stepped out onto the fondamenta with the leather briefcase and the bag and the Purgatorio and looked up at the facade of the palace — the fifteenth-century Ca' Foscari, which had been a private palace for a Doge who had understood better than most that greed and beauty were not opposites but synonyms.

He checked in. He unpacked, precisely, in the order he always unpacked — which was the order of what he would need first.

He opened the vellum to the blank page that followed the SUPERBIA page, which had been the first lesson and was complete.

He took out the pen.

He was not in a hurry. He had never been in a hurry. He wrote carefully, in the tradition he had learned from Hardt and had maintained for forty years through every circumstance that had suggested a different tradition might be more convenient. Patience was not a virtue he had cultivated. It was a quality he had been born with and had chosen, each time a choice was required, to honor.

He wrote the word. He read it. He set the pen down.

He looked at the Grand Canal through his window. The water-doubled light. The city that had been built on the premise that beauty and commerce were the same word.

He thought about the woman who was coming.

He thought: she is almost ready.

He looked at the Swiss landscape outside the train window and thought about the monograph.

He had been thinking about the monograph for twenty-three years, which was not unusual — he thought about it the way he thought about all work in progress, which was continuously, which was the specific quality of a mind that did not easily separate from its objects of attention. The monograph was the foundational text. Everything else — the published papers, the conference presentations, the careful academic career built in the spaces around the core project — had been produced in relation to the monograph. The monograph was the thing.

He had written forty-six drafts. He had the first forty-five in a locked drawer in his Cologne apartment. He had the forty-sixth in his briefcase. The forty-sixth was the one he had been certain of for eight months, since the conference invitation had arrived and the configuration of circumstances had arranged itself into the shape he had been patient enough to wait for.

He was not going to publish the monograph. Not in any conventional sense. Publication implied an audience of colleagues, a peer review, a citation chain, the institutional apparatus through which academic knowledge moved. He was not interested in that apparatus. He had participated in it for forty years and had found it to be, at its best, a slow and imperfect mechanism for the movement of useful ideas, and at its worst, a mechanism for the suppression of inconvenient ones.

He had watched the Vatican suppress Hardt's 1972 argument. He had spent forty years watching institutions suppress inconvenient arguments. He had written the monograph as a different kind of publication — a demonstration rather than an argument, a proof of concept that operated not in the space of academic discourse but in the space of actual consequence.

The forty-six years since Hardt had showed him the original correspondence had produced in him a very specific patience. Not the patience of a man who was waiting for things to change. The patience of a man who understood that the correct moment required waiting for, and that the waiting was not passive but active — a sustained attention to the configuration of circumstances that would eventually produce the moment.

The moment had arrived. The first lesson was complete.

He opened the briefcase. He removed the vellum case and set it on the table beside his coffee. He opened it and looked at the first page. SUPERBIA. The word in his careful hand, the ink dried to the specific darkness of iron gall on aged vellum that he had prepared with the attention he applied to everything.

He turned to the second page. AVARITIA. He had written it in Brussels, before Rome, in the small apartment he had rented for the week in a city that was appropriately anonymous for the preparation of a second lesson.

He read both words. He closed the vellum case.

He thought about the woman reading the Avaritia parchment in Rome. He thought about what she had understood and what she had not yet understood and the specific pleasure of a curriculum that was designed so that understanding arrived incrementally, each lesson adding a dimension that the previous lesson had prepared the ground for.

By Edinburgh she would understand everything.

He was looking forward to finding out.

Chapter 30

The Next Lesson

He was in Frankfurt when the warrant was issued.

Not at his apartment — he had packed what he needed before the conference ended and had no reason to return to Cologne immediately, and Frankfurt's main train station offered excellent connections to destinations that would, in time, require his attention. He sat in the first-class lounge of Frankfurt Hauptbahnhof with the leather briefcase across his knees and the Purgatorio open to the canticle on avarice and read carefully.

He had been reading carefully for forty years. It was perhaps his most reliable quality.

The warrant notification arrived through a channel he monitored — not official, not illegal, simply the specific product of forty years of academic correspondence that had produced, among other things, relationships with people who knew things and had decided he was worth knowing them. He read the notification twice. He put his phone in his breast pocket.

He was not surprised. He had not intended to be unsurprised — surprise was not something he engineered. He was simply a man who had been thinking about the structure of a situation for long enough that the structure's behavior had ceased to be unpredictable. The warrant was the correct next step. He had designed a situation in which the warrant was the correct next step. The warrant arriving was therefore confirmation that the situation was developing correctly.

He returned to the Purgatorio.

He thought about the woman.

He had thought about her, with increasing specificity and increasing interest, since the morning in the Gregorian briefing room when she had sat across from him and processed the room and him and the dead Cardinal and the investigation and the institutional machinery with the specific speed and completeness of a person who was doing several very different things simultaneously and keeping all of them clean. He had been interested in her analytically before he saw her. He had become interested in her in a different way after.

The analyst and the other thing were not, for him, easily separable. He was aware of this. It was a quality he had examined many times over many years and had concluded was simply constitutive — the way some people tasted colors or heard mathematics, he experienced persons as arguments. What a person was, was also what a person meant. The Cardinal had meant one thing. This woman meant something considerably more interesting.

She had read the crime scene. He had known she would. He had designed the scene to be readable by exactly the kind of mind she had — not general intelligence, not investigative competence, but the specific intelligence of a person who understood that a room could be an argument and that the argument could be read the same way a text was read, which was from the inside out, which was by occupying the position of the person who had made it.

She had occupied his position. She had stood in his spot — the dust impression four meters from the primary marker — and read the scene from there. He knew this from the forensics report, which he had read through his channel, which had noted the specific angle of her examination at the observer's position.

She had been where he had been. She had seen what he had seen.

This was what the inscription was about. Not a provocation. Not a challenge. A recognition. *To be seen by someone who is capable of seeing is not capture.* He meant it exactly. He had spent thirty years making an argument in complete private, which was the most rigorous form of argument because there was no resistance, no counterpoint, no genuine dialogue — only the echo of his own thinking. She was the first person whose seeing constituted a genuine reading.

He did not find this alarming. He found it, in the specific way he found most things interesting, extremely interesting.

He closed the Purgatorio. He looked at the station concourse.

She was going to Venice. He knew this. She had the Avaritia sketch and the Ferrini hypothesis and the Hardt connection, and she was very good, and she was going to arrive in Venice believing she was ahead of the lesson.

She was not behind the lesson. But she was not ahead of it either. She was inside it.

This was the thing she did not yet understand. The curriculum was not a series of crimes she could interrupt by arriving before the staging. The curriculum was a series of demonstrations of an argument she was, herself, in the process of demonstrating. Every choice she made — to follow the evidence, to read the room, to call Mateo Padilla at midnight and trust his judgment and file his discoveries as evidence — was part of the demonstration.

He was not demonstrating what pride looked like and what greed looked like and what envy looked like. He was demonstrating what it looked like when a person capable of seeing saw those things and was changed by the seeing.

She was the demonstration.

She would understand this, eventually. He was in no hurry. The curriculum had seven lessons and she would read all of them and by the time she reached Edinburgh she would understand completely what she had been reading.

He opened the briefcase. He removed the vellum case. He set it on the table beside the Purgatorio and looked at it.

Inside: the pages. Seven sections, each awaiting its word. Superbia was written. Avaritia was sketched, the word ready to be inscribed after Venice. Five more. Five more cities. Five more subjects whose sin was the engine of their institutional power and whose power was the engine of their sin's invisibility. He had selected them carefully. He had been selecting them, with the patience of a man who understood that the right subject could not be rushed, for many years.

Edinburgh was the last page. He had not written the word for Edinburgh yet. He was not certain yet what the word would be. Not which sin — he knew which sin. He was not certain yet which word, in which language, at which hour of which Edinburgh morning.

He would know when the time came. He had always known, at the moment of knowing.

He closed the vellum case. He closed the briefcase. He picked up the Purgatorio and his coffee and walked to the departure board and looked at the trains.

One was leaving for Basel in nineteen minutes. From Basel, connections south. He did not need to be in Venice before she arrived. He needed to be in Venice before the lesson was over.

He had considerable time.

He bought a sandwich from the station bakery because he would need to eat at some point and efficiency was a virtue he applied to everything, including the body's requirements. He sat with the sandwich and the coffee and the Purgatorio and thought about the woman reading the Avaritia parchment in her Interpol office in Brussels.

He thought: she is reading Dante. Or Aquinas. Or both. She is preparing for Venice the way she prepares for everything — with the complete attention of someone who has decided the work is worth doing properly.

He thought: she is going to be excellent.

He looked at the departure board. Nineteen minutes.

He finished the sandwich. He finished the coffee. He picked up the briefcase.

He walked to platform eight.

The train to Basel was on time. It was always on time. He approved of this.

He boarded. He found his seat. He set the briefcase beside him and took out the Purgatorio and opened it to the page he had been reading and read for a long time while Germany passed outside the window and then Switzerland began.

In his briefcase, beside the vellum case and the monograph and the curriculum notes and the specifically German pen he had used for forty years and the reading glasses he had not needed when he was forty and needed now, was a single sheet of hotel stationery.

He had written on it in Frankfurt, at the desk in the hotel room, at 4am, in the same small precise handwriting he used for everything.

The sheet was addressed to the Rome hotel's front desk. He had not sent it. He had been carrying it for twenty-four hours while he decided whether the right moment to send it had arrived.

He looked at it now. He read it.

She will be in Venice by the end of the month. Tell the Gritti Palace concierge there is a package in my name to be held for her arrival. She will know to ask.

He sealed the envelope. He wrote the Rome hotel's address on the outside.

He would post it in Basel.

He had considerable things left to teach her. He was looking forward to the curriculum.

The train moved south through Switzerland. He read the Purgatorio. The mountains arrived and passed. He thought about greed and what it looked like in a specific Venetian man of sixty-three who had spent thirty years studying the moral architecture of the thing he was practicing.

He thought about the woman who was going to find him first.

He thought: she is almost ready.

He was looking forward to finding out.

The train reached Basel at 9:47pm.

He changed platforms with the efficiency of someone who had been changing platforms in European train stations for thirty years and had long since stopped finding the process interesting. Frankfurt to Basel. Basel to Milan. From Milan, the connection east. He had done this route before, for different reasons, at different points in the years of preparation.

He thought about preparation.

The preparation had begun, in the most honest account of it, when he was twenty-four years old and Wilhelm Hardt had shown him the carbon copy of the 1972 Vatican correspondence. They had been sitting in Hardt's office at Tübingen — the small office with the inadequate heating that the university had provided for junior lecturers and had not improved in thirty years — and Hardt had slid the document across the desk and said: *Read this. Then tell me what you think about the relationship between institutional authority and moral truth.*

He had read it. He had read it three times in the following week. He had thought about it for forty years.

The document was forty pages of carefully reasoned argument. Hardt had written it in 1972 as a position paper for a Vatican committee convening to review doctrinal language around moral culpability. He had argued, with the specific rigorous patience of a German academic in his middle period, that institutional actors could not dissolve individual moral accountability — that a man who ordered a wrong thing through institutional channels was still a man who ordered a wrong thing. The committee had reviewed the argument. The committee had determined that the question was not within the scope of doctrinal clarification. The correspondence had been closed. The document had been filed.

The Vatican had been filing inconvenient arguments for two thousand years. It was very good at it.

Hardt had never published the argument formally. He had published variations of it for forty years in the academy's cautious manner, never quite landing on the original claim, always circling it from a distance that preserved his institutional standing. He was a careful man. He had always been a careful man.

He had given a copy of the original to his most promising graduate student in 1983 and had said: *Keep this. Think about it. Don't do anything with it that I would need to explain to the faculty board.*

He had kept it. He had thought about it. He had spent forty years doing something with it that Hardt would definitely need to explain to the faculty board, though by now the faculty board's opinion was not a consideration he found relevant.

The Basel connection departed at 10:14pm. He settled into his seat. He opened the Purgatorio to the canticle on avarice and read while Switzerland became Italy in the dark outside the window.

He thought about Ferrini.

He had known Luca Ferrini for eight years, in the way academic correspondents knew each other — through the paper trail of citations and conference acquaintances and the occasional collegial email. He had known for five years that Ferrini's 2009 monograph on Venetian mercantile moral theology was also, in its careful way, a description of a private arrangement. He had known this the way he knew most things about people he was considering: by reading them closely and cross-referencing what they published against what they did.

Ferrini was intelligent. He was also the specific kind of intelligent that produced blind spots — the intelligence that had spent so long being the smartest person in the room that it had stopped accounting for the possibility of a room where this was not true.

He was not the smartest person in every room. He was aware of this. It was one of the few things he was genuinely modest about.

The woman was very good.

He had been thinking about this since the briefing room on the first morning, and had thought about it with increasing specificity as the fifteen days progressed. She had read the crime scene with an accuracy that required not just intelligence but a specific kind of interior familiarity — the familiarity of someone who had grown up inside a version of the thing being staged, who recognized the architecture from the inside rather than analyzing it from the outside.

He had selected Rome for many reasons. One of them was that the investigation would inevitably produce this reader.

He had not known her name. He had known the profile: the investigator who could read the argument, who had the specific psychological architecture to understand what the staging was saying rather than merely cataloguing what it was doing. He had read the Interpol assignment pool for the Rome jurisdiction and had found three candidates and had evaluated the three with the care he applied to all selections.

She was the correct one.

He was looking forward to Venice.

He thought about the monograph in his briefcase. The private document, the working framework of forty years. He had been considering, since Frankfurt, whether to leave her another note in Venice. Not the same kind of note — the Confessions inscription had been an opening, a recognition, a first word of a conversation. The Venice note would be different. The Venice note would be the second word.

He had not decided yet what the second word was.

He looked out the window at the dark Italian countryside. The Alps were behind them. The Po valley ahead. Venice two hours to the east.

He thought: she is already reading about Ferrini. She is already building the case from the evidence she has. She is going to arrive in Venice knowing more than she arrived in Rome knowing, which was the correct progression.

He thought: she is almost ready.

He was looking forward to finding out.

— END OF BOOK ONE —

Pride · Rome

THE SERIES CONTINUES IN

Between Heaven and Hell · Book Two

GREED — Venice Mateo Padilla POV

Marco Ferrante, founder of the Ferrante Foundation for the Preservation of Venetian Cultural Heritage, is found face-down on the floor of a deconsecrated church on the Fondamenta del Soccorso. A circle of seven Byzantine coins surrounds the body. A Latin word is written on vellum beside his right hand.

Avaritia.

The second lesson has been delivered.

Sonya Logan arrives in Venice on the morning train. Mateo Padilla was already there.

Available from Lewis Publishing House and Amazon Kindle in 2026.

ALSO BY DR. MATTHEW LEWIS

Between Heaven and Hell — A theological thriller series in eight books

Book One Pride · Rome (this volume) Book Two Greed · Venice Book Three Envy · Florence Book Four Lust · Paris Book Five Gluttony · Barcelona Book Six Wrath · Seville Book Seven Sloth · Prague Book Eight Ultima Scriptura · Edinburgh

The Confession — A prequel novella to the Between Heaven and Hell series. The night before Mateo left the Church. Free to ARC program members.

ABOUT THE AUTHOR

Dr. Matthew Lewis, PsyD, is a sport psychologist, educator, and Story Architect. He believes the modern publishing model treats writers like content factories and readers like data, and is building a small imprint that does neither.

ABOUT LEWIS PUBLISHING HOUSE

Lewis Publishing House is an independent literary imprint owned and operated by Dr. Matthew Lewis.

Web · lewis-publishing-house.com Editorial · dr.lewis@lewis-publishing-house.com Rights & translation · rights@lewis-publishing-house.com Press & review copies · press@lewis-publishing-house.com

---

JOIN THE ARC PROGRAM

Members of the Lewis Publishing House Advance Reader Copy program receive each new Between Heaven and Hell release four to six weeks before public launch, in exchange for an honest review posted on launch day.

We send only when there is a book to send. No newsletter spam. No sequence funnels. One email per release.

Join at lewis-publishing-house.com

If PRIDE moved you, the single most useful thing you can do for the next reader is leave a review on the platform you bought it from. Two sentences are enough. Reviews are how independent imprints survive.

Thank you for reading.

— Dr. Matthew Lewis Lewis Publishing House 2026

---

lewis-publishing-house.com

Don't miss out!

Visit the website below and you can sign up to receive emails whenever Dr.Matthew Lewis publishes a new book. There's no charge and no obligation.

https://books2read.com/r/B-A-DFSNF-TAYHJ

www.ingramcontent.com/pod-product-compliance
Lightning Source LLC
LaVergne TN
LVHW100515110826
845146LV00002B/649

9798995706601